NADINE LITTLE

Captivity

The Faction War Chronicles 1

LITTLE PUBLISHING

First published by Little Publishing 2020

This novel is entirely a work of fiction. The names, characters, and incidents portrayed in it are the work of the author's imagination. Any resemblance to actual persons, living or dead, events, or localities is entirely coincidental.

Nadine Little asserts the moral right to be identified as the author of this work.

Nadine Little has no responsibility for the persistence or accuracy of URLs for external or third-party Internet Websites referred to in this publication and does not guarantee that any content on such Websites is, or will remain, accurate or appropriate.

Designations used by companies to distinguish their products are often claimed as trademarks. All brand names and product names used in this book and on its cover are trade names, service marks, trademarks, and registered trademarks of their respective owners. The publishers and the book are not associated with any product or vendor mentioned in this book. None of the companies referenced within the book have endorsed the book.

Cover design by Serifim.com

This book is written in British English.

First edition

ISBN: 978-1-8380884-0-8

This book was professionally typeset on Reedsy.
Find out more at reedsy.com

Sign up for my mailing list to get a free and exclusive prequel to *The Faction War Chronicles*. Discover the explosive origins of the Faction War ten years before the events of *Captivity*. Members of my mailing list get other bonus stuff and behind-the-scenes material.

Members are also the first to hear about my new books and discounts.

Join at nadinelittle.com

'Do not go gently into that good night.
Rage, rage against the dying of the light.'
Dylan Thomas, *In Country Sleep, And Other Poems*

'The enemy is anybody who's going to get you killed,
no matter which side he's on.'
Joseph Heller, *Catch 22*

1

Rarely a day goes by where I don't think of my sister and wonder how different it could have been. How normal.

Okay, maybe not normal. Just not this.

Hannah sighs from the driver's seat beside me. "I hate no man's land."

She twists the key and the rumble of the biodiesel engine fades under my butt. Fat blobs of rain splat on the reinforced windscreen.

"I'm surprised you volunteered," I say, my voice neutral.

She slides me a look anyway, her helmet cocked on her perfect chestnut hair. "I'm a soldier, too, Anita. Not as active as you but that shouldn't be a fault."

"That's not what I meant, though there's no shame in a non-combat role."

She wrinkles her nose. "What, give up my dog-tags and work in a factory? You'd love that."

We both know Marshall won't make her work in a factory.

A gust of wind shakes our armoured Reaver and shivers through a mangled branch caught on the front-mounted blade. I ease a breath in and out.

Tempting as it is to punch Hannah's crabbit face, she's the closest thing I have to a sister now.

"Whatever makes you happy," I say instead. "I'll support you."

Her hazel eyes flash. "This will make me *very* happy so are we going to sit here or do what we came for?"

"Ladies," a voice oozes from the rear passenger compartment, "why don't we all kiss and make up?"

A hand squeezes my shoulder but I shrug it off.

"Fuck off, Reece."

How are his palms always moist? It's April and cold as balls.

"Such language, Carmichael," he says. "It's really unbecoming."

He laughs at my glare, his platinum hair flopping over his right eye, the left side of his head shaved short. My door clunks, the wind spearing icy bursts through my combat jacket. Hannah, Reece and the three other soldiers in my vehicle join me outside, Reece still chuckling.

I hope he gets eaten by an abomination.

The boxy Reaver sits at the end of a mangled path between the trees. A second vehicle parks beside ours, a belch of fumes fogging in the chilly air. I check my SA80 A3 rifle, the Glock in my waist holster, my flick-knife.

I wish I had more weapons—a rocket launcher, a portable machine gun.

Like Rambo.

We creep through the dripping forest, our gun barrels sweeping the undergrowth. The second team set up a defensive perimeter at our backs.

The gloom brightens, the trees ending in a hacked area sloping downward to a rusted barbed wire fence a couple of metres tall. A cracked road winds towards a rickety metal gate. Shoots of green speck the field of massacred wood. We spread out on our bellies. A bitter-smelling elder leaf slaps me in the cheek with every gust of wind. I pull out my binoculars and scan the encampment beyond the fence. Bullet-pocked buildings, scorched stone, crumpled brick.

"Look at them," Reece sneers, flopping next to me. "They have no defences. We could storm their shitty boundary and wipe them out. Goodbye, Embra."

I inch away from the press of his hip. "This is recon only, Reece. We watch. Nothing else."

"But it's *boring.*"

"Would you rather be with the team watching Rebel State?" I say, still searching for movement, dampness seeping into my uniform.

His silence tells me he's quite happy surveying the once-fine capital of Scotland instead of the wasteland surrounding Glasgow.

I roll my eyes at Hannah. Her hair trails in the dirt.

"I *am* glad you're here," I whisper. "Usually, it's just me trying to herd these assholes and not die."

Her lips twitch.

Maybe she's past her huff. I should probably talk to her when we're safe back in Calders but I hate all that girly shit.

We shift position twice, sticking to the tree line, Hannah my permanent shadow. Nothing moves in the shattered sprawl of Edinburgh.

Are they all dead? Maybe there was a disease or they starved or a pack of abominations slipped through their drooping fence and slaughtered them. How disappointing. I need someone alive to answer the question that's been burning in my gut since this whole mess started.

"We have sounds of pursuit on our six," says a voice from

the comms system attached to my collar. "Stand by."

I roll to my knees, my rifle pointed into the murky woods. My heart thumps five painful beats before the voice returns.

"Fecking deer," he says. "Stand down."

Reece grins and wiggles his eyebrows. "Fresh venison, lads."

He disappears into the foliage, leaving me and Hannah alone. I tap the shiny screen of my transmitter.

"Knives only," I say, and jerk my head at Hannah. "Come on. Two hours in no man's land is enough for me."

Hannah glances at the encampment, something flickering over her face too fast for me to read. Her fingers tighten on her rifle. Gunfire clatters deeper in the trees.

I jab the comms system and bruise my collarbone. "Are we under attack?"

The gunfire stops, replaced by the rush of wind and the patter of rain.

"Reece," I say through gritted teeth, "did you shoot the motherfucking deer?"

"It was getting away."

An alarm wails from the depths of Embra.

"Huh," Reece says. "I guess there is someone in there."

"Everyone back to the Reavers."

Voices and squealing metal drag my gaze to the encampment. Soldiers in grey and brown shove the rusted gate open, leaping into a line of jeeps. Tyres bounce on cracked concrete and lopped trunks.

Can't fault their response time. Perhaps they wanted us to think they'd be easy to topple.

Hannah's boots thump in tandem to mine, her breath puffing white. Brambles rip my camouflage-patterned combats. We sprint around a fallen pine in a bloom of rhododendron,

Hannah lagging behind my stride.

She may be curvy but she's short. And she's more used to lying on her back than running for her life.

I crash through a snarl of elder bushes, my blonde hair tugged from its ponytail. My boots skid on moss and wet mud.

"Hannah," I say on a whoop of air, wobbling on the edge, "careful, there's a—"

A weight slams into the small of my back.

I fall into the crevasse, slamming my chest on the opposite edge, my fingers scrabbling on slick rock. The momentum bounces me off and my boots hit the ground, the force crumpling my legs. I lie and blink at a slice of grey sky. Dirt peppers my face. A figure peers over the edge, chestnut hair spiralling free and fringed with moss.

"Hole," I groan, struggling to my feet, "was going to be the end of that sentence."

I pat myself down. Bruises but no broken ribs, my rifle secure on its sling.

An oak cants across one end of the crevasse, roots snaking over the stone. I grab one, test its strength, and wedge my boot in a crack. I hoist myself up, wood creaking under my fingers.

"Hannah, don't just stand there, give me a hand."

"Why couldn't you have died in battle like everyone else?" she says.

My mouth flaps for a full minute but no words drop out.

I must have misheard her.

"You have *everything*," she says. "Perfect Anita Carmichael, riding on her sister's memory and the people love you for it. Well, there's one thing you can't have."

I lick my lips and say very calmly, "Hannah, what the fuck are you talking about?"

Her silhouette disappears. I yank on the root, pulling myself higher. It snaps and I land on my ass, my teeth clicking together. The walls of the crevasse muffle a burst of gunfire. I tap my comms system but it stays dark beneath a crack spiderwebbed across the screen. Hannah thrusts her head back over the space.

"I know about you and him," she says, twisting to look behind her.

Oh shit.

"It's not what you—"

"You might want to shoot yourself. Who knows what these soldiers will do to you. Our faction is the only civilised one left." She sticks her arm over the gap and wiggles her fingers in a cheery wave. "Goodbye, old friend. Tell Ailsa I miss her."

She leaves me with my slice of stormy sky.

"Hannah! I said no!"

I lunge for the roots, claim a couple of inches then drop down, my palms stinging.

"Hannah?"

She's been moody for *weeks*. I'd understand some hair-pulling, maybe a bitch slap. A normal, outraged response.

She can't abandon me to die.

Rain mists my upturned face. I swallow the urge to keep yelling her name. Voices echo above the lip of the crevasse. I tuck myself beneath a bulge of rock and suck in a breath of mulch and spiders. Branches crack. Excited cries swell and fade. My fingers cramp on my rifle.

She left me to die.

How the hell did she find out?

I shiver in my nook of stone but give myself a shake.

Survive first. Freak out later.

Hannah better be pretty damn contrite when I set the record straight.

Wind sighs through the trees. I stare upwards but the sky offers no advice. I slide my rifle on its sling and start to climb, scraping my boots, my hands, my knees. Roots hiss free from seams of soil. My fingers curl on the crevasse edge and I peer over. Wet trees, no soldiers. I haul myself up, stalking through the forest to where we parked the Reavers. A crumpled path stretches away, pale bark flashing in the gloom.

The bitch must have told them I was dead.

"I thought The People's Republic was all about the people," a man drawls behind me. "Seems they forgot about you."

I freeze trying to decide whether to go for my gun or reason with the guy.

He didn't shoot me in the back so he's not a total savage.

I turn slowly, hands spread but not too far from my weapons. The man's gun points away from me, his army fatigues and tan boots splattered with mud. The beaded metal chain of his dog-tags angles beneath his collar.

"We are about the people," I say. "Protecting the people."

The man shakes his head. "Oh, yeah, I feel very protected."

You're not on my side, dipshit.

"We're not the ones who struck first," I say out loud. "We didn't start this."

Vivid, cornflower-blue eyes meet mine. "Are you sure?"

I frown at him. My hands droop. His gun swings and I dive, my shoulder thumping into the dirt. My bullets strafe the guy from stomach to chest. Shouts bounce beneath the canopy. I scamper to the body and take the guy's rifle—a battered but serviceable SA80 plus a spare clip. My searching hands avoid his shredded torso and transfer a five-inch knife from his pocket to mine. I sprint down the chewed path between thick trunks.

"Over here!" a voice cries.

Gunfire mangles the vegetation to my right. I lurch in the opposite direction and tumble down a valley slope. I re-join the crumpled route of the Reaver and gallop up the far side, the stolen rifle banging my hip. Ivy-choked trees end past a rotten fence, its wires rusted to flecks of bronze. Abandoned agricultural fields stretch to the distant hills, flattened tracks in the wavering grass marking where the Reavers have been, Calders beyond.

Home.

I bound along the woodland edge, knee-high grass whipping my legs and tangling my boots. Shattered bricks form ankle-breaking mounds.

There was a village here, once.

A ragged group of soldiers spills from the woods, their shouts rolling over the meadow. I throw myself into a band of trees. A river meanders towards the hills, a corpse bobbing in the shallows, one scalded foot anchored in sludge. An eel-like form writhes next to it, taking dainty bites.

That's not going to be me. I haven't fought this long to become a meal for an aquatic monster.

Or any other kind of monster.

I battle the undergrowth and follow the river downstream. It'll eventually curve south, emptying into a reservoir at the base of the hills. Better cover than a sprint through open grassland.

But slow.

Feet thunder in the fields and draw level.

Not long before they cut me off. Not long before I die.

Shut up.

My darting gaze passes over it twice before registration sparks like a meteor—a boat, half-hidden in yellow iris. I jump inside and the hull jerks out of the vegetation. Reactive camo-skin morphs from gold and green to dull brown. The vessel rocks and I fall, gasping as my hands and knees hit water.

No burning. Just rainwater.

I scramble to the controls and pump the manual intake. Liquid sloshes into the outboard. My finger hovers over the water splitter.

A dusty solar panel on the bow will power the electrolysis. If the electrodes haven't degraded. The boat could have sat out here since before the war. The fuel cell should be fine—no moving parts, no combustion.

"No problem," I say, and push the button.

A green light flashes and I sag against the controls.

Saved by clean technology.

Pity it's about fifteen years too late for the rest of the planet.

A wave of soldiers pours through the trees, rushing parallel to my boat drifting on the lazy current. I hip-fire the rest of my rifle ammo into them. Their bodies splash into the watercourse, comrades for the nibbled corpse.

The light on the instrument panel blinks at me.

"Come on, come on."

Bullets pepper the river, the water raising angry red blotches on my exposed skin. Shots clang into the starboard side and liquid slurps into the boat. I yank the stolen rifle on its sling, aiming for the shine of eyes and bared teeth. More bodies tumble but other soldiers replace them, darting behind trees. The gun clicks empty.

The light on the control panel strobes. Sweat drips into my eyes, nipping like the river water. A bullet whines past me. I go for my Glock.

The light changes to solid green.

I slap the switch and the engine judders. The boat leaps forward when I shove the throttle, catapulting me into the bottom. Furious voices echo over the water. Shots ring against metal and I curl in the recess beneath the control panel, guiding the boat by feel and sound.

Scraping equals bad.

The yelling and gunfire fade to the ripple of water and the sigh of wind. My free hand grips the dog-tags beneath my shirt, my thumb rubbing the embossed metal.

The People's Republic. The good guys.

Okay, the dog-tags don't say that but they should.

The man didn't know what he was talking about. Just a tactic to distract me. It's one of the few things I *am* sure of.

We're the only faction who didn't start with blood on our hands.

3

The thick door crashes against the wall and slices through the chatter. Sprawled bodies tense and swivel in their seats, the weak light from bare bulbs jaundicing their faces. The recon team are still in their camouflage uniforms, their SA80 rifles hanging from the chair backs. The scent of fried venison and boiled cabbage turns my stomach.

"Carmichael, you're alive!"

"Excellent powers of observation, Reece," I growl. "Now, where the fuck is Hannah?"

"Marshall's office."

Reece slinks towards me but I spin on my heel and stomp out of the canteen. My boots slosh through the muddy roads to the church surrounded by a line of withered trees. I climb the concrete steps and heave open the door. The pews are gone, the building stripped of all symbolism.

It's a creepy place for an office.

Not that I'd tell Marshall that.

He sits behind his battered desk in a black recliner, Hannah curled in his lap. She's taken the time to change her outfit to a boob-hugging shirt, and fix her hair. Her mouth drops open. Marshall leaps to his feet, nearly tossing her to the floor. She grabs onto one of the filing cabinets lining the room as he brushes past her.

"Anita, I worried we'd lost you," he says, folding me in a hug though I'm soaked with rain and sweat.

Hannah curls her lip. I try to ease away from Marshall but my arms are pinned. I meet Hannah's hostile gaze over his shoulder.

"You're my best friend," I say quietly, "how could you leave—"

"I'm not your best friend! *Ailsa* was my best friend. You didn't even care what she stood for." Her lip curls higher, twisting her face. "But look at you now—perfect soldier, perfect role model, Ailsa's perfect little sister. You have everything else, why did you take what's mine?"

"I haven't taken anything from you."

She raises an eyebrow at the man clinging to me. I wriggle and break his hold.

"Marshall, what did you say to her?"

He tugs on the cuffs of his eggshell-blue shirt and gives me a bland smile. "Nothing."

"He's obsessed with you," Hannah spits. "He compares me to you. How long have you been screwing him?"

"Don't be ridiculous. He's my sister's husband."

"Ailsa has been dead for almost ten years, Anita," he says.

"The time means nothing. That's all you'll ever be to me."

He actually asked me out then asked my sister when I said no. I never told her that since she seemed happy. They were on the same degree course at Edinburgh University—politics and international relations. Ailsa was ambitious and hard-working while I fannied about in zoology, no job in mind.

She wanted to be First Minister.

"Am I not also your leader?" Marshall says.

"Fine, so you're two things."

I supported him because he loved my sister. I could have led in the grief and confusion of the aftermath, Ailsa's name enough of a recommendation, but I was never into politics like her. Hannah's right about that.

"Don't forget what you are to him," she says, stalking around the desk. "*Slut.*"

My hands curl into fists. Instead of getting in my face, she stops next to Marshall.

Smart move. She knows I'll fucking take her.

"So rather than talk to me and find out how wrong you are, you push me in a hole and leave me to die? Other factions do that shit, Hannah. Not us."

Marshall cocks one blond eyebrow at her. "Is that true?"

"I told you—she fell," she says in a breathy voice, stroking his arm. "The Embra soldiers were almost on me. I had to run."

"And the part about shooting myself? Wanting me to die?"

She spears me with narrowed eyes. "Lies."

I reach for her and she squeaks, darting behind Marshall. My clenched fingers urge me to rip out clumps of her shiny hair and slam her head into the desk.

Marshall holds up a hand. "Let's talk outside. Hannah, stay here until I return."

He ushers me out of the vestry. A chill wind blows through the broken stained-glass windows and pigeons in the rafters ruffle their feathers.

"She abandoned me in no man's land, Marshall. I can't let that slide."

He nods, his brow furrowed. "I'll deal with her. Does anyone else know what she did?"

"No."

"Probably best. It's nearly the ten-year anniversary. She's jealous, paranoid. Worried about losing more."

"Maybe she's justified. Don't string her along."

His teeth flash in the darkness of the church. "I'm capable of loving more than one woman, Anita."

He touches my elbow but I step away.

"I meant what I said."

He's gotten worse over the last couple of years—watching me, the casual contact. Turning on the charm. I reminded him about Hannah, my friend if not best friend.

And shagging my sister's husband would be gross, even if he is her widower.

"You are more stubborn than your sister," he says, reclaiming my step and brushing a clump of my hair over my shoulder, "but she surrendered in the end."

"Surrender isn't in my DNA."

A spotlight through the window turns his pale eyes to silvered glass.

"We shall see," he says.

Yanking open the heavy door disguises my shiver. I slip through and close it in his face.

Fuck. Is this going to be a problem? Maybe I've been too lenient but he was great after my sister's death. Supportive. Masking his own grief and rallying the party. Seeking revenge.

I had a promise to keep so was fine with that.

I walk down the stairs and frown at the road, heading for the armoury to drop off my rifle plus extra.

Marshall's handsome enough—blond hair, blue eyes, chiselled—but there's something *cold* about him.

And he's far too used to getting his own way.

"Hey, Carmichael," a voice purrs, "you've had a long, hard day. I have something else long and hard that'll help you relax."

As if sex is all it takes to weaken my knees and make my heart go pitty-pat.

Maybe it is, just not with him.

"Reece, perhaps if you channelled your energy into battle tactics instead of trying to hump me, we'd win this war sooner."

"Where's the fun in that?"

"It's not meant to be fun."

"All war and no play makes Carmichael a spinster." He sidles closer. "Let me bang out those cobwebs."

The blade of my flick-knife gives a satisfying *snick*.

"You have two seconds to fuck off or you won't be banging anyone again," I say.

Reece mutters under his breath but disappears down a side street. I wait for the squelch of his boots to fade then sheath the knife.

Speaking of getting worse. I can't tell Marshall since he's morphing from gentleman to creepy stalker and the last thing I need is to be indebted to him. Maybe I could ignore it if it was just one asshole but most of my male comrades treat my virtue like it's a challenge.

Well, challenge goddamn accepted. Sexual repression is preferable to surrendering to the slobbering morons in Calders.

And my frigid bitch act suits me fine, thank you very much.

4

My dreams start with boats and bloody water. The engine fails to catch, trapping me in the centre of the river. Soldiers line the bank and raise their rifles, the black barrels as unwavering as their hatred. They open fire and red drips into biting liquid. I fall to my knees, the plastic of the boat replaced by shattered wood. Blood stains my hands.

But it's not mine.

The air tastes of pulverised stone. Screams echo in the scorched debating chamber, broken bodies tossed between the seats. Ailsa is heavy and warm in my arms. She coughs and crimson speckles the powder on her face. Each breath rattles.

Three bullets to the chest will do that.

"You're going to be okay," I say.

She blinks eyes the same green as mine. "Don't—"

The rattling stops.

An alarm mixes with the howls of the injured and dying. Sparks rain from damaged lights in the rafters. I tuck Ailsa's blonde bob behind her ear.

She said it made her look more mature than a tumble of hair to her ass. Or bum.

My perfect sister never swore.

"I'll find out who did this." I rock her, my promise lost to the noise. "They'll pay for it."

The alarm howls louder, filling the chamber and vibrating in my skull.

I don't remember it being so insistent…

I jerk awake and the wailing trails me from my nightmares.

The blare of our warning siren.

I struggle fully dressed from the warm cocoon of my sleeping bag, the cold stinging raw skin where splashes of burning water have eaten the cloth. I grab my Glock 17 and scramble out of the tent, sprinting to the edge of my private grove of trees. My scuffed boot barely kisses the street before an explosion decorates the sky, somewhere over the boundary fence to the north. A rain of debris crashes out of sight behind the buildings.

I scan the red-streaked clouds, the sun below the horizon. The alarm squawks to silence. A robin sings from the spiked branches of a hawthorn.

A single attacker? Sure, none of us have mounted a major battle in years, content to poke at each other's defences and test the response. Maybe we're all a little rusty.

I crawl into my tent to finish dressing—a flick knife in my pocket and a holster around my hips and I'm presentable. My fingertips rub the embossed words on the gun, polished with use.

Glock 17 Gen6 Russia 9x19.

The sun peeks above the horizon as I head to my mission centre a few streets away, dodging fissures in the remaining concrete. I hop up low steps into a short hallway, waving to the soldiers who call my name, and sit in a chair near the back of the main room.

No Hannah.

Daylight halos the boarded windows, muted by the harsh fluorescents. Shuffling people fill the dusty space with conversation and scraping seats, the babble focused on our rude wake-up call. The overseers of our group stride in, the wooden floor creaking under their glossy black boots.

Brian and James are three years older than me—like Marshall—though the strain on their faces makes them appear closer to ten. Brian perches on the edge of the desk beneath the transparent screen used for strategy meetings. He was attractive, until a bullet tore through his cheek and ripped off his ear.

It's hard not to stare at the mass of scar tissue.

James clears his throat. "Our reconnaissance of the Rebel State stronghold in the Badlands has failed."

I roll my eyes.

Ridiculous name for a ridiculous faction. They should have kept their party name. And to call their territory the Badlands? Come on. The People's Republic are fairer, saner, *right*.

The rest are a bunch of murdering bastards.

"We lost communication with our squadron yesterday. They are presumed dead."

Perhaps their corpses have joined the hundreds ringing Glasgow, impaled on posts. Staked alive, if the rumours are true.

Maybe the Badlands isn't a stupid name after all.

"Let us remember the fallen with a minute's silence." James bows his square head.

I frown at my boots.

Good soldiers lost to the animals. How many more will die before we win?

We *have* to win.

The lights flicker, darkness settling, before pinging back on.

James sucks in a breath. "On a positive note, the Embra reconnaissance achieved its target with no casualties. Though I heard it was a close call on your part, Carmichael."

"Yeah," I say. "Lucky me."

"Marshall is confident Embra will fall within weeks, either by our efforts or from their own dissension. A major assault is planned but we will update you in due course." James paces in front of the desk, swivelling on his heel for each pass. "Do not forget tomorrow is the fitness test. Be assembled and ready to begin at 0500 hours."

A wave of restless shuffling swells around the room, suppressed when Brian pushes himself to his feet and sweeps us with his amber eyes. "We will not tolerate failure this month. You're all under forty now. If anyone else embarrasses us, we will make damned sure your next job is the foulest Marshall can imagine."

Last month's unfortunate soldier was stripped of his dogtags and reassigned to a munitions factory the day after his botched test.

Brian whispers to James. Bodies shift on squeaking metal seats.

"The single plane was from Embra, likely their last one," Brian says over his shoulder. "A foolish and wasteful revenge attempt. Enjoy your rest day. Dismissed."

I follow the bustle into the cramped entrance hall, the wavering screens embedded in the wall listing the names of the fallen, daily assignments and planned meetings. The sun struggles to dispel the morning chill, slanting shadows across the mud and sparkling on frost riming the puddles. I join the queue in the canteen for bland toast, a tart apple and pills for the shortfall. It's barely worth sitting down to eat but a group of soldiers makes a space for me, quizzing me on yesterday's assignment and slapping me on the back for my daring escape.

No one survives alone in no man's land.

They drift away to go to the gym or sleep or whatever other soldiers do on their day off, leaving plates scattered on the table. I stack them in the centre, scooping up the crumbs. A woman hurries over, a cloth in her hand, her jumpsuit dusted with flour.

No dog-tags.

"Soldier Carmichael, you don't have to do that."

"Fiona, I've asked you to call me Anita how many times now?"

Her cheeks pink, a curl of brown hair stuck to tape on the arm of her glasses. "Sorry… Anita."

A soldier clatters his tray on the table in front of Fiona, knocking a cup over and splashing her with water. He salutes to me and strides for the door.

"Hey!" I call after him.

Fiona touches my elbow. "It's all right, Anita."

"They shouldn't treat you like that." I scan the mess left by my comrades. "You're not slaves to pick up after them."

She dabs at the damp patch on her overalls. "You risk your lives to keep us safe."

"It doesn't mean we can lord it over you. I'll talk to Marshall."

"No, please, forget about it." She twists the cloth between her hands. "Are you going to the movie tonight?"

"Course I am."

Her smile peeks through. "Do you not get bored watching

the repeats?"

"Nope. It's the main thing I miss from the world before. And coffee."

We share a nostalgic sigh then she shoos me from helping her tidy up. A block away, I pull open the armoured entrance of a control centre in the old library, the smell of books lingering in the dusty corners. A skinny man slumps at a wall of computers, flipping between camera feeds on the larger screen in front of him. Watery eyes flick to me.

"I could set my watch by you, Soldier Carmichael," he says, his tatty chair squealing as he leans back.

"Just Carmichael is fine. And I'm a creature of habit."

I dodge large cables to a room at the rear and settle at my own bank of computers, though I also have transceivers and amplifiers. I built it myself a year and a half ago. An hour passes. Two. Twiddling the dials produces only static, as it always does. I stretch my spine.

Time to return to my tent and read my torn copy of *Romeo and Juliet*, rescued with a random assortment of other books. Most were burned in the chaotic early years before permanent heating and energy systems.

"Why do you bother?" a voice says from the doorway. "They're all dead."

Kate props her shoulder on the wooden frame, picking her nails with one of her many throwing knives, her tight ponytail emphasising the cheekbones and freckles. Lisa stands next to her, short and curvy, with a cap of auburn hair.

They were Ailsa's friends, alongside Hannah. I enjoyed being a loner since most women treated me like the enemy or wanted me to join their bitchy 'hot girls club'.

But are they still my friends?

"We don't know that," I say.

"Then why the silence? Where are the peacekeepers and the reporters covering our little war story?"

"We're not exactly approachable."

Kate cocks a brow, her sapphire eyes the same colour as the heart of a glacier.

Are there glaciers left? It's not like I can check the internet or go to the coast.

"What are you suggesting—switch off the cameras and open the gate?"

"No, but aren't you curious? What do you think happened?"

"Zombies," Lisa says.

"Jesus Christ." Kate pinches the bridge of her nose. "Not zombies. It could be a million things but it doesn't matter. We've got enough problems right here. The rest of the world can take care of itself."

"Soldiers, sorry to interrupt." The control centre operator bobs behind Kate and Lisa. "Two laser-cameras have gone offline. Soldier Carmichael, you've repaired them before, can you go or should I call the electrician?"

I fix one camera and build my own ham radio and suddenly I'm gadget woman.

"Maybe you should call—"

"Oh, come on," Lisa says, "we're not doing anything. Let's all go. Where is it?"

I trail after them to the wall of computers, two screens dark. The operator jabs a button on his keyboard, toggling a map to his main monitor.

"They're side by side. Sector 44. It's secluded. I'll signal a guard to accompany you."

Kate taps the Glock and knives at her waist. "I think we got it."

"Of course, Soldier, I didn't mean to imply—"

She holds up a hand and his mouth snaps shut.

He has a point, though. Kate and Lisa copy Hannah in actual battle attendance. They have the weapons and the dog-tags but I can't remember the last time they fought or even did recon.

The shriek of a chair punctuates our departure. I collect a bag of tools in an equipment storage shed and flag an approaching jeep. Sun reflects off the mud-splattered window. The vehicle slithers to a stop and I swallow a curse.

"Need a ride?" Reece says, his eyes on me. "You know I'm always happy to oblige."

It's tempting to swear and tell him to keep driving. It'll only encourage him. Who am I kidding? Everything encourages him—abuse, a smile, silence.

Kate and Lisa hop into the rear compartment before I can protest, a pane of glass separating it from the front.

I ignore Reece's leer and climb in. "Could you drop us off at the vehicle depot? Please."

"Anything for you, babe."

"Don't call me babe."

Chuckling, he waits for another jeep to pass before pulling out and heading towards the main street. I frown out the windscreen, refusing to meet his celadon-green eyes.

Pretty colour for an annoying jackass.

"One of these days you're going to realise your mistake and get naked with me."

"Sure," I say and he makes a strangled noise, "if by 'one of these days' you mean 'never'."

"The chase is getting a little boring, Carmichael."

"Then stop chasing. I'm not interested."

"Your mouth says one thing but your body wants another. You like leading men on. Feeling special."

I snap my head around. "You have no fucking idea what I like, feel or want. But it's definitely not you. So leave me the hell alone."

He jams the brake and I brace my hand on the dashboard to stop my face from greeting it. He lunges but I dig my Glock into his ribs.

His lip curls. "Frigid whore."

"That's an oxymoron, you moron," I say, fumbling for the door and sliding out, dragging the tool bag. "You come near me again, I shoot you and call it a tragic accident."

Kate and Lisa barely jump out before the jeep roars away, fishtailing and scattering globs of mud.

"What's his problem?" Lisa says.

"He's an asshole."

Kate pats at her hair in its perfect ponytail. "Nothing new there."

"All men are assholes. They just want to get into your pants."

Kate casts her eyes to the sky. "This again. You had one bad experience, like, fifteen freaking years ago. Are you saying nothing in between has changed your mind?"

"Nope."

"Then you've obviously been shagging the wrong men."

Or shagging none at all.

"Have you two seen Hannah today?" I say.

They share a glance.

"No, why?"

"No reason."

We walk another twenty minutes to the depot—a churned

space thick with the scent of biodiesel and cold concrete. Garages hold vehicles in various stages of dismemberment, one for each sector in the encampment. I take a jeep, driving beyond the buildings and cutting through bare fields busy with tractors planting potatoes and peas. A golden blanket of flowering oilseed rape separates us from civilisation. The fields end in a dense wood, a dirt track continuing along the boundary.

I park the jeep and we step into the gloom. The hush settles on my shoulders, disturbed by the crunch of fallen branches and the rush of my pulse. Goosebumps prickle my skin and shiver down my spine.

The Embra recon has me spooking at shadows.

I unholster my Glock, comforted by the weight of it in my hand. Kate and Lisa follow a step behind, breathing on my neck. I battle tangled bushes and clumps of ferns, the thick vegetation obscuring my feet. The undergrowth thins nearer the fence, the closest plants withered and dead. Metal posts of mottled blue and grey rise out of the greenery, no wires between them, no apparent connection.

But you wouldn't walk through the gap unless you're an idiot. Or suicidal.

So why isn't it shimmering?

The air wavers on the other side of the fence post where the particle beams form an impenetrable barrier, the heat from each invisible stream causing a ripple. It means one doesn't blunder into it by accident.

South Africa used them to protect large estates from looters and food riots.

My tool bag clanks to the ground. "Fuck me, we've been breached."

Cool metal kisses the nape of my neck. Another barrel jabs into my kidney.

"Not quite," Hannah says.

"Drop the gun, Anita," Kate says. "We'd hate to dishonour Ailsa's memory by having to shoot her sister."

"Whatever you're doing, you're way past dishonour."

The barrels grind into my back. My Glock thuds to the dirt, swallowed by the foliage. I slide my hand towards my pocket.

"Search her for knives," Hannah says, circling around, her Glock in a two-handed grip. "She carries at least one."

"Yes, how well you know me, *old friend.*"

She grins. Kate pats me down and removes the flick-knife from my pocket and the five-inch blade I took from the Embra soldier.

Who needs friends? I should have stayed a fucking loner.

"Why are you doing this? You can't still think I'm sleeping with Marshall."

"You are a temptation he doesn't need," Hannah says.

"Did he punish you at all?"

"I'm sure he thought about it but I have ways to help him forget. He came so hard, he almost fainted."

Gross.

Her smile flickers and fades, a sneer twisting her lips.

"It wasn't me he was picturing." She thrusts her Glock at me but stays out of reach. "God, I want to shoot you. But I won't be the one who kills the great Anita Carmichael. I have a better idea."

She puts her fingers to her mouth and whistles a single, short blast. Kate and Lisa keep their guns firmly on my neck and kidney. Hannah turns side-on to cover me and the ragged expanse of no man's land beyond the fence. Scrubby bushes, young trees and a tangle of spiny brambles grow between lopped trunks. A figure appears on the edge of the virgin forest fifty metres away.

"Why are you going along with her?" I say while Hannah focuses on the man approaching our wide-goddamn-open boundary. "I haven't done anything to you."

I feel their shrugs through the guns in my back.

"She's our friend."

"I'm your friend."

"You were adopted into the group because Ailsa felt sorry for you," Kate says, squatting to scoop up my discarded Glock. "We didn't have much choice."

"Fine, we're not friends. But we are on the same side for what they did to Ailsa. She wouldn't want this."

"Too bad she's not here."

Yeah, too fucking bad.

The man crouch-runs from felled trunk to bush to bramble, his silver-plated weapon pointed at the sky. He stays close to the centre of the disabled fence panel, sunlight glistening on the whites of his eyes as they flick between the laser-cameras that should be melting his face. He jerks past the fence posts as if speed will help, his chest heaving, jaw muscles bunched tight. A scar trails across his forehead like the path of a snail.

"Hello, Peter," Hannah says. "How long has it been?"

Peter barely reaches the level of my shoulders but he's

padded out since I last saw him.

"Oh, about six years since you murdered my best friend and your fiancé." He aims his .357 Magnum at her head. "I should kill you for that."

Kate and Lisa take a synchronised step away to include me and Peter in the firing line.

Hannah flutters her eyelashes. "We were estranged on account of him choosing Revolutionary Front and the possibility that he murdered *my* best friend."

"We didn't kill Ailsa Carmichael." Peter's Magnum jitters to Kate and Lisa.

"So who did you kill?"

The Magnum returns to Hannah. "No one."

"That's our party line, Peter, not yours."

Sweat darkens the armpits of his camouflage uniform, the beaded chain of dog-tags visible at his collar. His black boots are scuffed worse than mine.

"I didn't come here to talk about the beginning," he says, eyes the blue of storm-tossed water alighting on me for a second then darting away.

Hannah jabs her gun at me again. "As promised, Ailsa Carmichael's precious little sister. You won't get a more valuable prisoner. Oh, and this."

She drags a woven bag from behind a fern and dumps it close to him, stepping out of reach. The contents whisper as they settle. Peter tucks his Magnum in the waistband of his trousers and removes a small, black handgun from the same place.

He points the weapon at me and pulls the trigger.

Pain blooms in my thigh. I curse and wrap my hand around the metal cylinder. A bead of blood stains the needle when I pull it free.

"How the hell did you arrange all this?" I say. "You had less than a day."

Hannah smirks. "This is one of many contingency plans. You may think spreading my legs for Marshall gives me an easy life but I have skills the great Anita Carmichael does not."

"And contacting Revolutionary Front, what did you use, a goddamn smoke signal?"

"Faction leaders have their own frequency on the comms units. They mostly use it for ribbing each other but sometimes they trade. Though this is a first for us."

"What are you getting out of it?"

"Apart from rid of you?" She laughs, as if that's enough. "John Anders promised me your public and messy execution."

"You fucking traitor," I say.

"Your language is really unbefitting of The People's Republic, Anita. Ailsa would be shocked."

I launch myself at her, the tranquilliser dart gripped in my fist, the needle swinging for her eye. Unfortunately, she splits into three wavering shapes and my blow swipes air. My legs collapse, aided by the butt of her Glock slamming into my temple. I pant into the dirt, my hair over my face.

"If it's any comfort, you will be missed," Hannah says, her voice drifting, "but then it's my turn to be the people's sweetheart."

I try to shove to my feet. My arms twitch. A wave crashes over me and I sink into darkness.

6

Consciousness brings a hint of cow shit and straw, though the metal stalls in the centre of the building are empty and swept clean. Cobwebs tremble in corners, water beaded on the strands. Dull light filters through slatted boards in the upper wall. I clank to my feet, the heavy chains circling my wrists and ankles attached to a bolt in the lower wall. More dangle at intervals to my right. Rain blows in through a large sliding door and speckles my face. Dried blood flakes from the lump on my temple, a sharp ache sizzling to the roots of my teeth. I pat myself down and find I'm mostly intact.

Peter must have parked an armoured vehicle out of sight. No way did he carry me on one shoulder, Neanderthal-like, with a bag of grain on the other.

I wrap the chains around my fists and heave but the bolt refuses to budge from the wall. No hopeful cloud of dust, no wiggle room. I slump against the rough stone and kick it with the heel of my boot. Footsteps scrape on concrete, the feeble light of the doorway silhouetting two men. The taller one approaches with a smile as cold as his eyes.

"Hello, Anita."

I nod stiffly. "John."

"It's nice to see you recovered after our last encounter." He strokes the ivory handle of the knife at his hip. "I've always enjoyed sparring with the Carmichael sisters."

"You knew Ailsa?"

"Oh, I knew Saint Ailsa quite well, back when I was an unappreciated parliamentary assistant. I watched her stride those corridors of power, fantasised about slipping something inside her." He pets his knife again, an olive t-shirt stretched over his chest and shoulders, his combats and boots splattered with mud. "Shame I've only had her sibling to play with, though you are the more beautiful. Seems she got the brains."

Did he just call me stupid?

"Why go to all this trouble to get me? You could have hidden an army in the trees and stormed the fence when the beams were down."

"Hannah warned against such a scenario, though it didn't cross my mind. You are what I want."

Flattering? Nope. Creepy as fuck.

"Execute me and The People's Republic will crush you."

He laughs. The man in the doorway stays blank-faced, his skin tight over his skull and hollow at his cheeks.

"I told Hannah I'd execute you, blame you as the assassin of our party leader. It wasn't you, of course. That's on the Nationless scum." John taps a finger to his chin. "I'm afraid I lied to your friend."

"She's not my friend."

"Clearly not. But you are more useful to me alive. Your people will do anything to get Saint Ailsa's angelic little sister back."

"Don't fucking call me that."

"No, perhaps you're not so angelic after all, though you could be my saviour." He unlocks the manacles from my ankles with a retractable key attached to his belt and unbolts the wrist chains where they terminate at the wall. "I'm sick of being second in command to a recluse who's so paranoid about being assassinated, he hasn't left his house in eight years. If I can turn our fortune around, leverage Marshall, the people will choose me instead of the hermit crab."

"You've not baulked at assassination before."

His blue eyes twinkle. "Oh, Anita, we didn't assassinate anybody."

"Funny how everyone keeps saying that."

He flips the chains over my head and yanks me forward. I walk quickly to lessen the bite of the steel. He drags me past the silent man, whose spindly hands tighten on his Starlight V5 combat shotgun. I stumble into the sucking mud and Silent-soldier follows, like a shadow.

A shadow itching to shoot me full of electromagnetic pellets.

"The only funny thing is, once I've squeezed Marshall for everything I can, I'm still going to keep you." John tosses me a smirk over his shoulder. "You really brighten up the place."

To my right, the road curves to the edge of the main gate. Spikes driven into the ground and spirals of barbed wire prevent a straight run at it from outside. No laser-camera but effective in its own way. A pitted, mud-churned path snakes into the trees beyond the defences.

The encampment is close to the edge of what was once Stirlingshire. Four terrifying hours of sprinting south through Nationless and no man's land would deliver me home.

How are the three back-stabbing bitches going to explain my disappearance?

Drops of rain dampen John's t-shirt and bead in his tawny hair. He appears oblivious to the cold sending goosebumps racing under my tattered combat jacket. I slither down a slope onto a road winding into the depths of the encampment, the main gate behind us. Crumbling, bullet-pocked houses flank the dreary street. Muddy water ripples at the bottom of craters.

Everything is either grey or brown and utterly depressing.

A small crowd at a junction adds no colour, dressed in varying shades of olive.

"Well, guys, what do you think? The famous sister of Saint Ailsa," John says, waving his hand in a theatrical flourish. "Anita, you're a celebrity!"

I raise my chin and ignore him.

"She's not very impressive," one man says, peering behind misted glasses.

"Give me a gun and I'll impressively shoot you through your eye-hole," I say.

The man curls his lip and melts into the crowd.

"Right, back to work," John says. "She'll be more entertaining when she's begging Marshall to save her. Come on, Anita."

He lugs me through the dispersing group, pausing to allow a Raider-3 tank to shudder past, its shell glistening like the carapace of a beetle. The double-barrelled proton cannons aim down the street, their charging portals an eerie blue. A fist over a Saltire is emblazoned on the turret.

Raider-3s were the product of our very own Scottish Army. I remember a line of them thundering through some desert in the Middle East when the news was still reporting the effects of the environmental crisis. They were a terrifying sight.

Revolutionary Front have two.

In a nearby house, John drops the chains to leave me in the middle of an upper room. Rain smudges the window, the wooden frame furred with mould. Silent-soldier stands in front of the door, his frowning face daring me to try something. John fingers his knife and opens a slanted wardrobe. He throws some clothes at me.

"Put these on. Our prisoners wear black. Until they die, of course, and wear nothing at all." His guffaw rattles the glass.

Hard to believe we were all on the same side, once. Sure, there was bickering and some outright hostility between the parties but Ailsa strengthened our rebellion.

She was destined to be First Minister of an independent Scotland.

I cock an eyebrow at John and rattle the metal on my wrists. "Aren't you going to take these off?"

He shakes his head, his eyes glinting, and leans on the wardrobe. The wood groans. I pray for it to topple and squash him. One hand motions for me to hurry up. I resist the urge to show him my back and face Silent-soldier.

Stuck between a rock and a lecherous asshole. Story of my life.

I kick free of my boots and shimmy out of my combats. I pull the black pair on, John's gaze heavy on my skin. The chains catch on my jacket and top. John shoves himself off the wardrobe, his eyes not on my breasts, but lower.

"My, my, Anita, what lovely scars you have."

He traces the silvery lines on my ribs, belly and above my hip, his knuckles white around his knife. He licks his lips and his tongue leaves a bubble of spit. I jerk away and fumble the chains into the sleeves of the black shirt, followed by my arms, and button it closed.

"One day, we'll pick up where we left off," he says, quietly.

I swallow and try not to show any other outward sign of

fear. He's taunting me but… I've been stabbed enough for one lifetime.

He gathers the ends of the chains and tows me outside. Rusted turbines creak in the wind, the rain ebbing to a weak drizzle. Air slithers between the buttons of my shirt and dances chill fingers across my ribs. John marches me into a building, butterfly bushes growing from cracks in the creamy brick. Two metal doors face us across a bare hall, guarded by shotgun-toting soldiers.

I recognise the woman on the left, camouflage fatigues draping her bony frame, her eyes the same colour as her sable hair.

Gayle smiles. "Welcome to Lowkirk."

7

The chuckle of the second guard draws my gaze to his emotionless stare. The man's khaki shirt and trousers strain against his bulk. Unlike Peter, he has the height to suit the mass.

"So, this is Anita Carmichael." His shotgun slides over his shoulder in its tactical sling. He folds his arms, his bulging muscles stopping them from crossing completely. "Not what I expected."

Aren't I just disappointing people today?

"Don't worry, Roysten, if she doesn't behave, I'll let you play with her," John says.

Well, fancy that—the promise of rape fills Roysten's empty eyes with fire.

John hustles me across the threshold guarded by Gayle. Her fingers blanch on the shotgun. A beauty spot attempts to soften her angular features, and fails. Roysten's deep-set eyes track my progress until the door clangs shut.

The rectangular room appears to be for storage and not for anything requiring the presence of two guards. Wooden shelves and brass hooks hold a haphazard collection of equipment: a multi-purpose L1 handgun, a Detector—a black sphere dotted with lenses—particle beam disruptors, and electrical neutralisers in a disjointed tangle of wires.

My hands itch to grab the L1, press it to John's neck and blow a fist-sized hole in his trachea. But the gun probably isn't loaded, or charged.

And Silent-soldier hasn't blinked the whole time he's been watching me.

No other weapons sit on the shelves except the Detector but, similar to laser-cameras, its facial recognition software allows it to recognise friend from foe.

And foe get their faces melted off.

John grips my chains in one hand and rattles through the shelves. He unclasps a black plastic case and pulls something suspiciously like a dog collar out of the protective foam. Polished leather glistens under the overhead lights, knobs of silver metal punched through the strap, ending in flat, circular disks. John pivots towards me. I back up. He wraps the chains around his fist.

"You won't like it if I have to make you stand still, Anita."

He slides the cold collar around my neck and it snicks shut, tightening with a hum. My pulse pounds around the bite of the leather. John uses the key at his waist to unlock the manacles from my wrists and palms a slim remote from the case. The collar buzzes at the push of a button. My hands fly to my throat.

"I wouldn't do that if I were you," John sings, brandishing the controller. "If I press this button, the collar will zap you with enough electricity to make your brain explode."

It doesn't seem physically possible but I'm no neurologist. I lower my hands to my sides and curl them into fists.

"Let me make another thing clear—the range on this is three kilometres. I don't need to be next to your delectable self to press the button. Maybe I'll roll on it by accident and find your corpse so don't let your status as bargaining chip give you delusions of importance. Inconvenience me and I'll kill you."

How does one avoid being an inconvenience to a psychotic sadist?

I hope I find out.

"If you try to remove the collar or tamper with it, it will activate. If you wander out of remote range, it will activate. You're safe within the confines of Lowkirk"—safe, how rich— "but anywhere else…"

John jerks his body and sticks out his tongue then flips the remote between his fingers before sliding it into his trouser pocket with a pat.

I twitch, my pulse jumping against leather.

No buzzing, no blaze of pain. Nothing but the cold weight of the collar, throttling me.

John smirks. "Ah, Anita, I forgot how much fun you are. Such a good little soldier, fighting for her martyred sister."

"At least I have something to fight for."

He frowns and slams the lid on the case, leaving a stumpy wand nestled in the foam.

"I cannot wait to see you and your self-righteous faction crumble to dust. Bellamy!" he barks at Silent-soldier. "Take Anita upstairs. Carol is waiting for her."

The door screeches open. A hand attaches itself to my bicep. I stumble but stay on my feet as Bellamy does his best to yank my arm out of its socket.

John clears his throat. "And Anita?"

I sigh. His parting shot won't be anything good.

He pats his pocket. "Don't forget. Anytime, anywhere—

bzzzt. Maybe if you keep me amused, I'll let you live longer."

"I'm not a performing fucking monkey, John," I say, my lips too slow to fold over the words. "Amuse your goddamn self."

His fist thuds into my jaw, sending shockwaves to the tip of my skull. The blow spins me around and I sprawl into the hall on my stomach, much to the enjoyment of Gayle and Roysten. Bellamy skips out of the way, leaving me eye level with his shiny boots.

Damn, that hurt.

John clamps his hand in my hair and hoists me upright, his hot, minty breath sticky on my cheeks.

"Watch your attitude, Anita, or I will make your stay with us very unpleasant. Do you understand?"

I nod, follicles popping free under his grip.

Maybe one day I'll keep my mouth shut.

John slips his knife from its sheath and presses the blade to my face, the tip close enough to brush my lashes.

"Keep pushing and I will finish what I started all those years ago," he whispers, glancing to the side, a wicked grin curving his face. "I will gut you and let Roysten do whatever he wants. He likes his bedmates slippery and mewling."

Bedmates? Jesus.

"Is that what you want, Anita?"

My eyes burn and blur with tears. I fight not to shake my head in case I stab out my eyeball.

"No," I mumble.

John lets me go and slots the knife in its sheath. My hands flutter over my face for the slick wetness of blood. Bellamy drags me to the stairs. We climb out of sight, John tossing a mocking salute, Roysten's gaze heating my back. The top of the steps opens on a short landing to another metal door, the floor lined with the ubiquitous linoleum.

Bellamy tows me into a large room spanning the upper level. Three tables fill two-thirds of the space, wooden stools tucked underneath. Five battered industrial sewing machines sit on the table to the left. The middle holds scattered pieces of circuit boards, soldering guns bolted to the edge, their cables snaking through holes in the floor. The final table is empty, the surface scratched and pitted with rust.

A brute of a woman stands between plastic drums at the edge of the room and the sewing table, an L1 clipped to the belt on her right hip, a Magnum on her left. She smacks a maroon leather horsewhip into her meaty palm.

Bellamy's boots clomp his departure, followed by the click of the door. I keep my attention on Carol. She doesn't seem impressed.

Another unsatisfied customer.

She points her riding crop towards the table.

"Sit," she lisps.

I sidle around the table to put it between us. She cocks one dark eyebrow. My foot hooks a stool out with a screech. I slump onto the creaking wood, my hands clasped on the table. I try to ignore the collar while John prances about somewhere, the remote in his pocket.

I hate the loss of control. In the end, it doesn't matter how good a soldier I am or how well I fight. If he wants to kill me, there isn't a damn thing I can do.

For now.

Without taking her eyes off me, Carol unscrews the lid of a drum. She scoops a jumble of clothes and dumps them on the table, resuming her original position.

"Repair those," she hisses.

The first garment slips under the presser foot. The machine purrs.

I wonder how easy it would be to remove the needle and stab Carol in the eye.

Probably a long shot.

8

Gayle prods her shotgun barrel into my cheek.

Not one of the nicest wake-up calls but not one of my worst.

Dust motes jitter in the bright sunlight spilling through the door behind Gayle, the promise of warmth appealing after shivering through the night.

"Get up," she says, scowling down her long nose. "You've work to do."

She unlocks the chains using another reeled key contraption. I shove to my feet and stretch, my numb body dulling the throb of bruises and scrapes. The shotgun barrel in my spine guides me to the cream building at a brisk pace. Roysten greets me with a slow, unpleasant smile.

"Go upstairs," Gayle snaps.

I force myself not to stare at her charming comrade and do as ordered. Light floods the smeared glass of the skylight windows. Carol stands at the table, a fresh pile of clothes awaiting my attention, the repaired material whisked away to be re-worn by the grateful soldiers of Lowkirk. I hover in the doorway and she thwacks the riding crop into her palm, the folds of her face crumpled in a glare.

Guess she isn't a morning person.

She also isn't one for idle chatter or pleasant conversation.

More like deathly silence interrupted by commands and threats in two words or less.

She's probably self-conscious of her lispy, little girl voice.

I shuffle the stool closer to the table with an awful screech. Carol narrows her eyes, a green cap pulled low over her forehead, and I hide a smile.

Now I know why John delights in irritating his enemies, and he's the most annoying asshole I've ever met.

I stop scraping the seat and pull the pile of damaged garments towards me, easing into my previous rhythm. As soon as I repair one pile of clothes, Carol dumps another in front of me without a word of congratulations or heartfelt awe at my sewing skills. It's boring and repetitive but, if I ignore Carol's permanent glower, almost relaxing. No one tries to hurt me, barring the threat of the collar. I'm hungry and tired, but what else is new? Meals consist of a bowl of unidentifiable slop and a cup of gritty water but at least I'm indoors. Outside means scampering from one place to another in the cold and wet.

John is manipulating me, letting the dread build. Or maybe he's arguing with Marshall on the secret comms channel.

I use the quiet to plan my escape.

It won't be easy. Carol doesn't take her eyes off me for a second. She never leaves. She looms across the table, her arms at her sides, tapping the horsewhip against her tree-trunk-thick leg.

Beginning my escape from the cream building means less time creeping through the streets. The wand thing in the storage room may be the release mechanism—

The riding crop slaps and stings. I hiss and cradle my hand to my chest, glaring at Carol.

"Get back to work." She manages to make her voice gruff. I bet she practised.

Fighting a sigh, I slide the next piece of clothing under the presser foot. Carol returns to her position of hulking guard. Time blurs to the thump of the sewing machine and a cramp in my leg from working the stiff pedal. When the ground shudders beneath me, I pass it off as a muscle spasm.

Glass rattles.

Not a muscle spasm.

Carol frowns at the door, the loss of her glower leaving me bereft. I leap to my feet, the stool clattering to the floor. Her head swivels towards me. I vault onto the table and throw myself at her, wrapping my legs around her torso and pinning her arms to her sides.

It's like hugging a marble pillar.

She doesn't stagger under my weight, a grunt the only indication she's somewhat taken aback.

She spins and slams me into the wall, pounding the breath from my body. My grip weakens and panic curls in my throat. Carol steps back, her muscles tense, teeth bared. I grip her head with both hands. Her cap falls off, wavy hair springing free and surprisingly soft, like cats' fur.

I jam my thumbs in her eye sockets.

9

Popping eyeballs turns out to be easy. Thick fluid gushes over my thumbs. Carol shrieks and I wince. My nails scrape something solid—the bone at the back of the socket. I swallow bile and push harder. She howls and whirls, jerking her arms to break my grip. I fly over the table, taking the sewing machine to the floor. Carol clutches her ruined face and collapses on her side, her screams dissolving into whimpers.

The door opens on silent hinges. Roysten slinks in, his attention snapping to his comrade. I scuttle under the table and barrel past stools with a scrape of wood. Mewling sounds shiver out of Carol, a line of drool swinging from her gaping mouth. I dive behind her welcoming bulk.

The blast of a shotgun echoes in the room and buckshot patters in a sizzle of electricity. Carol spasms, her hands flopping to reveal two weeping holes. I look away.

I don't need a visual reminder. The slickness of her ruptured eyeballs stays with me.

"Come quietly, whore, and I won't hurt you as much," Roysten says.

That fails to make the prospect more enticing.

I tug at the holster on Carol's hip, sliding the Magnum closer without raising any part of my body above her fleshy cover.

Boots thump on the creaking wooden floor. I grab the rubber grip and slide the gun free, astonished at its weight. My goop-smeared thumb cocks the hammer. I fire at the stomping monster.

The first bullet misses, puffing into the wall by the door but Roysten's gait falters. The bore of his shotgun widens to swallow me. I fire twice—wild, desperate—and drop behind my meaty barrier. The shotgun booms. Blood arcs, painting me in blots of scalding red.

The silence thuds louder than my heartbeat. I peek past Carol's brutalised form.

Roysten's shotgun droops towards the floor. He topples forward and wooden panels shudder under his body.

Another explosion rattles the building, fracturing glass in a musical tinkle.

What the hell is going on out there?

I kick Carol onto her back and pull the L1 free. It's a blocky, grey gun composed of polymer, boxier than my Glock. I check the safety and slip it into the front of my trousers, smoothing the black shirt underneath. The back of Roysten's olive top is a ragged crimson. I tuck the Magnum in my boot and pick up his shotgun, nestling the stock against my shoulder.

No soldiers lurk on the stairs, no Gayle in the entranceway. Gunfire clatters in the street, accompanied by the occasional detonation. Blurred figures race past through the fogged glass bordering the front door, their voices raised. I cross to the storage room.

The back of my neck itches and I finger the collar.

John could activate it at any moment, believing I'm better dead than loose in the confusion. Or someone may bump into him and trigger it.

I drag the familiar case off the shelf, scattering devices to the floor. I place the V5 to the side and tear open the lid, waiting for the building to crumple as a missile slams into it, or for electricity to buzz from the collar. I scoop the stumpy wand from its bed of foam and search for a switch. Nothing but smooth black, cold and heavy in my fingers. Sweat drips into my eyes. The floor quivers under my knees.

I wave the wand at the leather, feeling ridiculous. Seconds tick away, taking pieces of my sanity. The locking mechanism releases with a soft click. The collar loosens and I rip it off. Ridges mark my chafed skin where the leather has pressed.

Thank god. Slipping from John's clutches again will be more than an inconvenience, the bastard. If he's alive in the aftermath.

I pray he is not.

Outside, I crouch in the shadowed vestibule. The empty street darkens, the sun dipping behind the buildings. To my left, the road continues past a junction and curves sharply, heading deeper into the encampment, bordered by trees and decrepit houses. To my right, the track leads back to where I met the crowd and on to the barn-slash-prison. A building collapses in a cloud of dust and fractured brick. Centipedes emerge from the haze, the three-segmented vehicles undulating over the rubble on manoeuvrable tracks. Mounted laser turrets scorch the streets of Lowkirk, soldiers following in their wake.

My heart leaps.

Am I being rescued? Maybe everyone saw through Hannah's bullshit or Marshall decided to rally the troops following John's taunting call.

The insignia of a silver dragon with blood-red eyes decorates the side panels of every Centipede.

My surge of hope dissolves.

Nationless.

It's more interesting than other faction emblems, I have to admit. Thistles, Saltires and rampant unicorns get a little boring.

An increasing roar batters the smoking buildings and I tuck myself deeper into the gloom of the vestibule. Three Darter FA-2 jets speed over the roofs, like huge dragonflies with their double wings and bulbous cockpits.

Nationless claimed a majority share of aerial vehicles in the armament battles, the rest of us squabbling over the scraps. Their dominance of the sky served them well.

For a while.

A deep boom and a flash of white too bright to look at comes from beyond the houses opposite me. It streaks across the sky, hitting the wing of the closest jet in a burst of fire and smoke. The Darter wobbles, engines whining, and falls out of sight somewhere along the main street, the impact shuddering through the soles of my boots. Another burst of white flares, striking the middle jet. It trails its companion by a millisecond to crash in the depths of Lowkirk. The remaining Darter continues unmolested, lost from view between one blink and the next.

One more jet shrieks overhead but the blaze of light does not return.

The defence system probably shorted out, as usual. Lowkirk likes to flaunt its volatility, daring enemies to gamble their survival on whether it will function.

A stupid tactic and another reason why Revolutionary Front are a shithole on the brink of collapse.

The throb of an approaching helicopter bleeds into the vacuum left by the Darters.

Now they're just showing off.

Explosions and gunfire ripple, burning and ozone tainting the sunshiny air. Infantry and Centipedes pour from the direction of the main gate, pummelling the houses into powder.

A green-patterned Tricopter lowers into the ruined street on three horizontal rotors. The precision hovering system allows it to float half a metre off the ground. Vehicles and soldiers group around the war machine, hunched against the backwash. A man unfolds himself from the front compartment, his black gaze sweeping the gathered crowd, strands of hair whipping his weaselly face.

Daniel Wick. The only party leader in the debating chamber to survive assassination. Now leader of Nationless.

A long finger jabs at four men, who step forward with brisk salutes, SA80 rifles slapped to their shoulders. The thwup of the Tricopter buries their voices.

It's Revolutionary Front's problem and nothing to do with me.

I bolt out of the doorway.

<h1 style="text-align:center">10</h1>

An explosion tosses me into the soft dirt. The throb of the Tricopter pummels the air. I duck into the corner of a garden and press my back to the creaking wood of a ramshackle fence. Swaying grass obscures my hiding place. The vehicle rises over the rooftops and angles away to sweep the encampment, its departure heralding an increase in gunfire.

A Darter roars above me, firing missiles into a building across the street. Smoking bricks splat into the mud of the road and rain into the garden. I cover my head and wish for a helmet. The jet thunders away with a graceful roll and a belch of pineapple-scented biofuel.

The pilot appears to be enjoying himself. *Bastard.* I want the freedom of the sky. To be untouchable in my war machine, not huddled in a garden, enemies on every side. I want to go home and see my three traitorous friends punished as they deserve.

And if Marshall baulks again?

I am Ailsa Carmichael's little sister. I'll tell everyone what they did and start a fucking coup.

I plough through undulating grass into another garden, wisps of cobwebs stuck to my shirt. I swing my leg over a chain-link fence. No movement from within the buildings but footsteps squelch in the mud of the street. I dive into the next garden and tumble across a yellowed lawn to end in a crouch, my shotgun steady.

The four soldiers who stepped forward at Wick's command march in a line twenty metres away. One man points towards me, the unfastened straps of his helmet swinging. The group aims for me in a confident lope.

Blind idiots.

The V5 kicks against my shoulder. The gesturing man stumbles, smoke curling from his sizzling face. His comrades scatter, protected from the worst of the peripheral shot by bio-electric armour beneath their dark green uniforms.

I jump to my feet and hurdle fences. The cul-de-sac ends in a block of blackened woodland. My boots stir ash and I burst from the trees trailing a pall of charred wood. I skirt the crumbled ruins of a church, avoiding shin-shattering gravestones concealed in the grass. A gate in the wall opens into a road. I sprint across and through another crooked gate, the second section of the cemetery much the same, minus the church. At the rear, a moss-furred wall blocks the view of the boundary fence.

No one seems to consider it a potential route for anyone who wants to get *out* rather than in.

The roar of the two circling jets merges with the boom of explosions and the rattle of gunfire. And the occasional scream.

My pursuers enter the cemetery and I throw myself behind a gravestone, rough flakes of lichen catching my shirt. I fire the shotgun at the soldier in the middle. A praying figure splinters into pieces. The men separate, using other gravestones for cover.

Cloth scrapes on stone. An angel marker disintegrates in a hail of marble fragments and a man yelps. Bullets pummel my hiding place, stone pattering on the other side. I return fire at a thick clump of weeds, my spent cartridges disappearing into the grass in a flash of red. Pieces of broken vegetation flutter. The bolt of the gun locks open.

Shit.

I dump the Starlight in the dirt and pull the Magnum from my boot, the sight scraping my ankle. Three empty chambers, four bullets. Not great. I want to avoid relying on the L1 since it's old and temperamental.

Knowing Lowkirk's laissez-faire attitude to the state of their weaponry, I bet it won't even fire.

I spin the Magnum's cylinder to a loaded chamber and click it closed, cocking the hammer and peeking over the gravestone.

The fighting draws closer. A Darter blasts by, its slipstream tugging my hair and bending the grass. The Tricopter hovers at the far side of the encampment, its machine guns raining bullets. It looses two missiles in a burst of flame.

A blur of movement catches my eye and I fire.

No cry of pain or crumpled body.

A flash of green between two granite stones pulls my attention to the opposite side. I fire again but the man dives out of sight.

The assholes are playing with me, wasting my ammo. They have all the time in the world while my seconds melt away.

The rest of their army must be almost on us.

The soldier on the right rolls from one marker to the next. My bullet misses him by inches and puffs into the dirt.

One round in the Magnum.

How many are left—two men, three? The cry of pain could be a ploy.

Another streak of green. I ease out a breath, my finger cramped on the trigger. The soldier changes position again, diving between markers. The man on the right springs to his feet and charges, teeth bared. I flinch and adjust my focus, insignificant details branding my brain: a wispy goatee, the helmet strap digging into his jaw.

My bullet opens a dainty wound in the pale slab of his cheek. He thumps to the dirt. I toss the Magnum and pull the L1 from my waistband. My burst of bullets forces the soldier on the left to lunge behind a gravestone drowning in ivy.

Silence falls.

Is there one left, or two?

I wait.

And wait.

Are they bluffing?

A Centipede zips past the gate of the cemetery, its laser turret blazing at something down the street. The driver hollers before the high wall swallows the vehicle.

Reinforcements mean death. Or capture. I can't bear to be taken prisoner by another damn faction, not this close to escaping the first.

A second Centipede zooms past the gate.

"Balls," I hiss, tucking the L1 into my trousers.

I press my ass to flaking lichen and concentrate on a pink marker at the base of the wall.

All I have to do is break from cover and launch myself off of it.

Oh, and not die.

11

I sail over the boundary fence through a prickling wash of heat, my boots scraped raw from levering myself on top of the wall. The greenery of no man's land stretches ahead.

Pain flares in my back. I yelp but land on my feet, the impact flaming in my ankles and knees. I attempt a roll and slam onto my face.

Is the bullet in my lung? Am I breathing?

Gasping, I scramble upright. My questing hand, expecting wetness, dislodges something near my shoulder blade. A dart falls into the plant litter. Drops cling to the inner surface of the plastic cartridge, the puff on the tail a bright splash of orange in the brown.

Does every faction own a goddamn tranquilliser gun?

I spin from the fence into a shambling trot, aiming for the emerald gloom of the forest. My heavy boots scuff up a pile of leaves.

I can make it, even if I crawl the whole way.

Lopped trunks transform to ancient trees. Ferns brush my thighs and encourage me onward. Two thuds come from behind me but I fix my gaze on the next tree and the next and the next.

"You have about thirty seconds before you collapse," a man

says almost gently. "You might want to stop before you hurt yourself."

Thirty seconds? I could run for hours.

The ground tilts. I blink and find myself on my knees. Footsteps crunch but turning my head takes an age. Two soldiers stand in the shade of the woods, one man's hand resting on a long-barrelled tranquilliser gun tucked into his waist holster.

The assholes were bluffing.

I fumble for the L1 and jerk it from the clinging material of my shirt but it slips between useless fingers. The men stride forward. I slump to all fours, frowning at my hand on the gun but unable to grip it. My hair trails in the dirt. My heart rate slows and I struggle to care. A branch pokes my cheek, the damp earth plugging my nose.

Why am I lying down when I should be running?

My eyes close.

Don't lose consciousness, don't lose—

* * *

Consciousness brings another headache.

The ground rocks under my back, swaying my head in tandem. I slit my eyes and wince at the sudden light.

A narrow corridor of weeping stone and fizzing bulbs. I face the thin back of a man carrying me on a stretcher, the line of his vertebrae like a mountain range. Wick precedes him, clothed in black. He looks over his shoulder. I squeeze my eyes shut but a sharp bump rattles my teeth and snaps them open again.

Human remains occupy one corner of a dank room, rats scrabbling between the flaps of cloth. Wick sneers, his lips too full for such a narrow face.

"Hello, girlie," he says after a period of silent regard. "I believe we'll have fun together if the way you fought during your capture is any indication." He turns to the stretcher-bearers. "Chain her."

The men bend, quick to comply. I try to crawl away. The stretcher-bearers grab my arms and drag me upright to rust-speckled chains.

What is it with encampments and shackles? Can't they lock me in a room and leave me free to pace like the caged animal I've become?

The men deflect my feeble struggles and clamp the manacles around the red marks already decorating my wrists. I sag against the moist wall, sluggish and spacey from the drugs. The skinny stretcher-bearer kneels at my feet. I kick him in the face, not particularly hard but he grunts and falls on his butt, his blue eyes sparking over clutching fingers.

"Keep fighting, girlie," Wick says. "It'll be more amusing when you break. Hurry up and fasten her legs."

Wick swivels on his heel and strides into the corridor. Warmth floods the space, fear trailing him like the ghosts of his victims.

The other stretcher-bearer grabs my legs, cold metal encircling my ankles. They leave, the stick figure throwing a glare over his shoulder.

I yank at the chains for the illusion of resistance.

It didn't help me in Lowkirk and it doesn't help me now.

I almost want to be back there.

But the rumours of how Wick treats his captives can't all be true.

Right?

I suck in a breath and slither to a seated position on the gritty concrete floor.

Basic training covered how to resist torture but everyone succumbs to pain in the end. What scares me is becoming a creature no longer me—broken by agony and lost to madness. No awareness in the tattered shell that remains.

My nails dig into my palms.

Not helping. Think of something else.

I'm probably in Livingston, the stronghold of Nationless. A bit of an unknown. Their aerial attacks dwindled in correlation to the strengthening of our defence systems. They also prefer to squabble with Lowkirk and the rest of Revolutionary Front, sandwiched between our territory and theirs, blaming each other for the atrocities of ten years ago.

Perhaps tomorrow will give me something to use. Anything to escape from Wick before he directs all of his malign interest at me. The brief periphery of his attention was enough.

Chilled and alone, I count the bones of the ill-fated souls who preceded me.

12

Wick stands in the room, watching me with his bottomless gaze. I swallow a gasp and lever myself from the floor, waiting for the sting of raw flesh where the rodents have nibbled me in my sleep. Desiccated mud flakes off my crumpled clothes. I meet Wick's stare, aiming for cool and unconcerned.

I don't pull it off.

"Good morning, girlie, my name is Wick. Yours is of no interest—my prisoners don't last long."

His laugh chills me worse than the damp, rat-piss-splattered stone of my bed.

"Let me offer you a quick tour then we'll get down to business."

Why are other factions led by psychotic assholes? I guess power does corrupt. John acting like the true leader of Revolutionary Front and planning a coup. The urge to shit myself whenever Wick's black eyes fall on me.

He strides over and I edge away but the clanking chains end my escape attempt. He grabs my left hand, unlocking the manacle and digging his long nails into my palm. He spins me into the rough wall and binds my arms behind my back. Using his shoulder to pin my legs, he unlocks the chains from my ankles. Only then does he release the final manacle from my right wrist.

Goosebumps prickle wherever he touches me.

I need to run rather than discover what kind of business brings such an anticipatory glint to his eyes.

His fingers curl around my bicep and jerk me off the wall. "Walk, girlie, if you know what's good for you."

I stagger on trembling legs and send a bone skittering across the floor. Furry bodies slither from within the pile in the corner. Wick's loud footfalls follow me into the corridor of weeping brick, still uninviting despite leading outside.

I'd rather be left in my cell, blissfully ignorant, to be eaten by rats.

A flight of concrete steps rises to a rusted gate. I squeeze close to the wall and Wick barges past.

Rain pours from an ominous sky and whips into my face. Two women emerge from the gloom, identical twins with blonde hair in pert ponytails, water darkening their camouflage fatigues. Both wear a shoulder holster holding a 9mm Browning Hi-Power Mark IV. The handle of a machete extends above one twin's head, caressed by the bob of her ponytail. They take an arm on either side, each no taller than my chin but muscular, and power me along the treacherous road.

The deluge obscures the surroundings, turning buildings into blurred shapes. My world narrows to the quagmire and the bruising grip of the soldiers' hands, the presence of Wick stabbing between my shoulder blades. My boots slip. The fingers on my arms tighten, crushing muscle against bone.

A woman hurries across our path, her head bent, black hair plastered to her skull. Bulky waterproofs hide her petite frame.

"Janine!" I blurt.

Her head comes up like a hound scenting blood. She squints through the windblown rain, her careful steps slowing, sharp cheekbones accentuating her elfin face. She glares at me and jogs into the murk.

We worked at the same recruitment company, where I made real good use of my zoology degree. She hasn't changed much in the intervening years, though her hair was longer.

Short suits her better.

Hard hands slam me into the mud. I struggle not to drown in the gloop, bitter grit crunching between my teeth.

"No one is your friend here, girlie," Wick says, the softness of his lips brushing my ear. "My soldiers will shoot you if I tell them to so shut up, get up and keep walking."

He pulls me to my feet, and shoves. I almost fall right back down.

A large glass dome looms out of the dimness after half an hour of sullen trudging. Water beads its smooth surface and runs in meandering streams. Wick bends over an access hatch indistinguishable from the ground and throws it open, mud spattering our huddled group. A boot planted in my butt propels me into the space beyond the ladders. I hit the floor feet-first and tuck into a moderately successful roll, landing on my back rather than greeting the concrete with my face. The twins yank me upright, my new aches added to old.

Our footsteps echo in a long, cream corridor lined by grey doors. The corridor ends at a balcony within a massive, round room. Weak light filters through the opaque dome, the rain drumming on the glass. The two females manhandle me to the railing.

People in white lab coats mill between workstations in a

hubbub of voices and operating tools. Sets of ladders stretch down through gaps in the balcony. Despite the bustle, the machine on the other side of the chamber is the central star in the galaxy of the room.

I gasp and Wick smirks.

"Breath-taking, isn't she?"

She?

"That's not possible," I say.

"Anything is possible with incentive. I've been working on her since the beginning." He steps to the railing, his chest puffed, and the blonde twins ease back. "My earliest prisoners were chosen specifically for their knowledge. People will do anything if they believe they can win their freedom. There is nothing more exquisite than watching that hope shrivel in their eyes when they realise I lied."

I manage to close my mouth and look like less of a drooling idiot.

A dragon-shaped machine of silver material crouches on the floor of the chamber, its great head level with the railing. Sharp teeth, eyes black and unforgiving.

It explains the mythical insignia of Nationless, apart from the eye colour.

What fantasy world is Wick living in?

I dig my nails into my palms to confirm I am, indeed, awake and not in a coma. "But how…"

"The external surface is quite straightforward—her skin is graphene-based and her muscles are composed of carbon nanotubes, making her an indestructible machine. As for the *how does she actually work*"—he imitates my voice as an irritating whine—"simple. A brain-computer interface."

Right.

His brows furrow over the dark pits of his eyes.

Exasperated by my poor response to his magnificent creation? Must think of something clever and complimentary.

An empty cavity of white noise fills my skull. And warning bells, lots and lots of warning bells.

Wick tuts.

"A helmet containing electrodes 'listens' for brain signals. When different areas of the cortex activate for specific parts of the body, it creates a unique pattern of electromagnetic waves. The dragon is controlled by detecting these patterns. For example"—his face shows a hint of animation, his black eyes like those of the machine—"when your brain thinks *move right hand*, the electrodes read and transfer the signals into moving her right hand. Do you get it?"

He scowls at me. I nod dumbly.

Best not to admit I still have no idea what the hell he's talking about.

He turns away, apparently satisfied.

How many people have listened to this spiel? None have escaped to tell their story. News of this magnitude would've spread through the factions like an Ebola bomb.

"She also has sonar and cameras feeding data into her operating system, giving her shared control."

And what on earth does that mean?

"But a dragon? That is ridic—" I clear my throat. "Why a dragon?"

Keep him talking. While enlightening me, he isn't hurting me.

"I suppose I could produce the technology in something mundane—a jet, a tank—but why not a dragon? A legendary beast wreaking fire and destruction. She is a killing machine.

Nothing will stop her, not even your faction. A final battery of tests and she will be combat-ready. The war will be won in *weeks* after all these years. And what little is left of the world will bow to me."

Ice solidifies in my chest.

By creating the ultimate weapon, his domination seems inevitable.

Unless I stop him. I can't let him slaughter and reign over the remains. That life would be a nightmare, more than it already is.

So… I need to steal the dragon. On the bright side, it'll make an excellent escape vehicle.

"I hope your limited intelligence can grasp how useless your struggles are. I could free you to scuttle back to your faction, bleating like a lamb, and destroy you later but I'd rather keep you." Wick brings his face inches from mine. "You will die here when I've squeezed as much fun out of you as I can get. When you are broken and all you know is despair."

I lock my trembling knees.

No doubt he's right—he'll break me into a million pieces.

But I will fight, and *hope*, until the thing remaining is me no longer.

13

In his role as gracious host, Wick lets me wash up before he defiles my body. At a featureless grey door in one of the many corridors, he removes the rope from around my wrists, his sharp nails caressing the reddened marks.

His expression promises worse by sunset.

He steps away and I stumble into a white-tiled bathroom after an encouraging shove, expecting him to follow but the door locks behind me. One corner contains a glass shower cubicle, a pile of clothes on a chair beside the toilet.

No windows.

I'm too cold and wet to be defiant, even if the thought of getting naked with Wick so close chills me further. I strip off my soiled clothes and twist the shower on full. Tepid water sputters.

Nice to see they also have a problem with hot running water. Our rainwater-collecting system always clogs.

I scrub harsh soap smelling of creosote over my blue-mottled skin, rivers of dirt swirling down the drain. I wait for Wick to burst into the room, drag me out by the hair and rape me on the slick tile floor, but the door stays shut.

Unable to stretch the interval out, I turn the water off and dress in ripped blue jeans, my battered boots and a baggy jumper, leaving the other clothes in a sodden heap on the floor.

Lowkirk's prisoner garb looked smarter but I'm warm and dry.

Small mercies.

I steal a few more minutes of unmolested, pain-free time to examine my reflection above the cracked sink. Purple bruises bloom at jaw and temple, the lump on my head reduced from a plum to the softly meandering gradient of a poached egg.

I must be hungry.

I have no scars on my face, and all of my teeth. My eyes are striking, possibly my best feature, but I don't understand the obsession of the slobbering morons or Marshall's increasing interest. Hannah is beautiful—buxom—and jumps into bed at his crooked finger. I guess that isn't the point. I said no and am not unattractive.

An intoxicating combination for someone used to getting his own way.

Will I look the same if I live through Wick's plans? People might lose interest if I'm disfigured.

Is that optimistic or depressing? I can't decide.

I glare at myself.

You will be strong. You will survive this, as you have survived everything else. For Ailsa.

But I want to go home.

Fear fills my eyes and I drop my gaze instead of watching myself crumble. I wipe my face and rap a knuckle on the door. It opens to reveal Wick's thick smile.

Not an uplifting sight.

"Good," he says. "Now we can begin."

Is it naive of me to still be surprised by the depths of human depravity?

Probably.

I've never been tortured. Hurt, beaten, attacked, but never systematically pulled apart and destroyed.

A heaviness settles in my stomach. The two female guards slide into the room and grab my arms. They force me to walk on quivering legs, Wick laughing softly behind.

14

The lessening rain speckles my face, glorious on my flushed skin. The greyness recedes to reveal red-bricked buildings bordering muddy roads and pools of water.

My captors guide me to an old veterinary clinic, the sign split in half. Missing tiles gape, cracks snaking up the walls. The stunted bushes around the border cling to life, their branches scraping in the wind.

They struggle to survive, just like me. Stubborn and resolute.

Man, companionship with foliage? I really am scared.

Sometimes I crave the touch of a gentle, loving hand so much it hurts to breathe past the longing. Or a cuddle. Christ, how long has it been since someone held me and didn't try to hurt me?

Fucking *years*.

My boots drag on the shattered concrete steps to the warped plywood of the front door. A ginger-haired woman sits at a large desk in the reception area, barking into a phone clasped between neck and shoulder, one finger stabbing at a tablet. She pays no attention to my entrance, my feet hoisted clear of the floor.

Does she manage the appointment system for their many

69

torturings? Can't make Tuesday? Not to worry, there's an opening on Thursday.

How can she listen to the screams?

Two stony-faced guards stand on either side of the desk, cradling Heckler and Koch MP5A6s. They salute Wick and sweep my body with a single, burning glance.

"Welcome to our torture chamber, girlie," Wick says, his breath moist in my ear.

I stumble deeper into the building, past what used to be three consultation rooms. I risk a peek and immediately regret it.

Curiosity disembowelled the cat.

Gleaming instruments line the walls and shelves surrounding a table with thick leather bands in each corner. Rust splotches the silver surface. No, not rust—dried blood. My feet trip over themselves, my eyes fixed on the smears, the stink of a slaughterhouse creeping up my nose and onto my tongue. I realise I'm panting and stop.

Strong. I must be strong.

Wick turns me to his sneering face.

"I notice you examining my excellent little room. Usually, there would be someone to introduce you to but, alas, he did not last as long as expected. *You*, however..." Dark eyes assess my vulnerable flesh with stomach-clenching familiarity. "You I have high hopes for."

"You'll get nothing from me. I won't betray my faction."

"What valuable information could you possibly give me? I have the weapon that will win. I need nothing from you but your screams."

My lips mash together. Wick wants me to mewl and beg and cry, reduced to something inhuman. He may get my screams but I won't beg for mercy. He'll be denied the satisfaction if it's the only option, the only power left to me. I promise this to myself.

But do I have the strength to keep it?

"Do not doubt me, girlie—I could make you talk if I so desired but the days of torturing for secrets have passed." He shoves me, tearing my gaze from the room. "I've simply developed a taste for the act itself."

We swish through a set of pink, rubber-lined doors into the surgical preparation area. A black mat and four leather straps top the metal table in the middle. Shelves stacked with tools cover the walls. The guards drag me down a passageway and into a rectangular room. Propelled into a cell, I stumble, bracing my hands against the rear wall. The barred gate clangs shut.

"I'm going to hurt you," Wick says in a soft voice, "so you'll wish for death. Reflect on that and the many ways I can break you."

"You fucking *bastard!*"

He laughs and retreats, the two females on his heels. The door to the prison room snicks shut, the heavy silence filled by my rasping breath. I shake the bars of the cage but the cold metal is solid under my palms. I slump to the ground, my head in my hands.

Part of me—the fatalistic, resigned part—wants to get it over with, even if death comes sooner. It's preferable to imagining the terrible things he can do to destroy my mind and body with pain.

I chew on a knuckle. The ache distracts me for a second before I return to the thought of Wick rearranging my flesh like a jigsaw puzzle.

15

An object clatters into the bars and yanks my mind from thoughts of shrieking, blood-splattered death. A man-boy a whisper from his teens clasps a metal dish, greasy hair curling to his shoulders in a blizzard of dandruff. He hawks and spits a glob of yellow into the cage, sliding the bowl through a small gap in the bottom of the door.

He—predictably—sneers at me. "The People's Republic, pah. You don't look tough."

He produces another wad of phlegm that splatters the toe of my boot. I shove to my feet, tired of being dismissed as nothing.

Anger is good, anger I can mould. Better than fear.

"Neither do you, *Nationless*," I say with a sneer of my own, "unless fat little pigs are tough in this shithole you call a stronghold."

I gob in his face and he flinches, swiping at his jowls.

It's hard to tell if his expression is perplexed or furious under the layer of blubber.

"You bitch!" he roars, slamming his palms against the bars. "You're fucking dead!"

He's right—I'm dead, or about to be. But if I'm going to die, it'll be fighting, like a soldier, not grovelling. I am not weak.

The man whips around and storms off, his buttocks jiggling like ferrets wrestling in a bag.

"See ya' later, fat boy!" I say to his broad back.

It's fascinating how my insults are more immature when I'm scared out of my mind.

The outer door crashes hard enough to rattle the bars of my cage. I wait for him to stomp back in, accompanied by Wick to punish me. Though no self-respecting warrior would allow himself to get overweight.

Maybe it's puppy-fat.

Nah, definitely just fat-fat.

I lift the bowl and wrinkle my nose. A brown protein ball rolls in the bottom but my stomach growls, unperturbed.

The morsel will give me nutrients, vitamins and energy for the next day at least. After that, I probably won't feel much like eating.

Sighing, I scoop up the ball and bite into it. Sniffing it would make it harder to eat. The consistency is akin to dried pastry dropped in the dirt, the flavour sour and metallic. It tastes like it looks—shit.

I eat the whole thing.

I place the empty dish on the ground upside down and stomp on it. It screeches to the side unscathed. Repeating the action delivers the same result but it's cathartic to be doing *something* instead of worrying about the future.

Even if it's failing to make a weapon out of a bowl.

I scrape it against the bars and run my thumb along the roughened edge but it's nowhere near sharp. I doubt I'll get the luxury of time to mould it into a serviceable blade.

Conjured, Wick enters the room and smirks at the dish. "Your efforts are entertaining, but pitifully wasted. You have, nonetheless, disrespected one of my soldiers. I promised him your begging squeals as reparation."

"I don't beg, not for anyone."

"I love a challenge, girlie."

He unlocks the door of my cell and I tense to brain him with the bowl. It's certainly solid enough. The Guard-bitches crowd into view, the machete twin seemingly keen for any excuse to pull it from its sheath. Wick grabs the wrist of the hand holding the bowl. I drop it without encouragement and it rings off the floor. He squeezes my wrist anyway, grating the delicate bones together. I smile instead of squirming. A slight frown puckers his forehead.

I will not beg. I'm strong, a soldier. We die with dignity, not pleading and snivelling.

Screaming in the face of heart-quivering torment is, however, perfectly acceptable.

Wick tugs me into the surgical preparation area. An emergency exit mocks me through a strip of glass in a far door.

"Take a good look, girlie. Each object is capable of causing pain in wonderful, magical ways."

Magical? Not the way I'd describe it, but I'm not a fucking psychopath.

"Bring it on," I say.

"So you're going to be tough and die with honour? You'll beg like the others. I know it, as I know the sun will rise tomorrow."

He, quite obviously, doesn't know shit. I open my mouth to reply with something about me begging when the sun rises out of his—

"Strap her down," he says.

Hands fasten around my arms and propel me towards the table. I lash out at the knees of the Guard-bitches. Their grip weakens and I twist to face them, my fists ready to do some damage.

Maybe being hacked by a machete isn't such a bad way to go.

An object catches me in the temple, a starburst of white imploding in my eyeballs. I collapse and rough hands hoist me into the air. Stiff leather fastens around my wrists and ankles. The swish of the double door heralds the departure of the Guard-bitches. Wick looms, slapping a truncheon into his palm.

Smack, smack.

"*Coward!*" I say, thrashing against the bonds despite the nausea burrowing through my skull. "Face me in a fair fight, we'll see who wins."

"Fair? You are quite stupid. I will tie you to this table every day and torture you. You won't be able to escape. You will lie there and suffer, until your poor little heart gives out."

How can he hurt me for no other reason than enjoyment? Torture is barbaric but I understand its use for information to keep people safe, to improve our chance of winning. But Wick doesn't care about that. Nothing I say will encourage him to stop unless I beg.

And if I beg, I'll never forgive myself.

He leans across, continuing to slap the club into his palm. Foul breath caresses my face, as though he eats the flesh of his victims and leaves their meat to rot between his teeth.

"Now this"—he indicates the object captivating my attention—"is made of rubber. It will bruise but it won't break any bones. The bone-breaking comes later. I want to tenderise you first."

The truncheon swings. I tense and suck in a breath. The bat hovers an inch from my collarbone then lowers to prod at my dog-tags, freed from the baggy jumper during our tussle.

"Carmichael?" Wick says, his head cocked. "I knew your sister."

His narrow face softens, the dark eyes lightening as they meet mine. My heart thuds under the truncheon resting on my chest.

"She was a wonder in the debating chamber. A real sharp intellect. She cared about everyone."

People seemed to like my sister. Respect her. Even Wick.

So who the fuck killed her?

Wick brushes his hair back, his fingers trailing across a scar above his temple.

Did the same person shoot him and my sister? Head and heart—different locations but equally vital.

He frowns at the truncheon in his fist. "I feel as if I've been sleep walking for a long time."

He scans the room, the display of deadly instruments, the blood dried into the grooves of the wall.

"Who am I?" he says.

I lick my lips. "Daniel. Your name is Daniel."

"Daniel, yes," he whispers, bowing his head. "But there's a monster inside me."

"Untie me. I can help you."

He winces, pressing a hand to his scar. He raises his head and his eyes are as black as a shark's.

"I'm going to enjoy this, girlie," he says.

He slaps the truncheon into his palm then starts whacking it into me.

Smack, smack.
The noise is the same.

I'd like to say I'm stoic. That I endure the pain and treat Wick to withering disdain.

That's what I'd like to say.

But I scream. I scream and yell *a lot*. I yell his name—Daniel, not Wick—desperate to jolt him from monster to normal human being. His wide lips twist in his narrow face and the rubber truncheon sings through the air.

All he does the first day—*all*, as if it's nothing—is beat me with the club. Half-way through, the Guard-bitches return and he commands them to flip me on my stomach, providing a whole undamaged surface to whale away on to his satisfaction.

Oh, and how content he is, whistling as he works his personal magic. He describes his plans for the next few days and estimates my survival time. It's not long. He has faith in his ability to reduce a person to a mewling shell, its mind a shattered thing.

The war provides a medium in which to perfect his art.

Night creeps to the narrow, frosted glass windows of the prison room when the Guard-bitches drag me to my cell and dump me in a heap. Wick's tall frame barely fills the barred doorway.

"My name is Anita Carmichael," I croak. "You knew my

sister."

He blinks at me, his brow furrowed. His eyes dart to the Guard-bitches who watch him with identical expressions of adoration.

He shakes himself. "See you tomorrow, girlie. I shall dream of your screams."

Wick leaves, still whistling.

I fear Daniel may not return.

My body throbs, my mind in shock. I thought I could tough it out.

What a fool.

I'll be lucky if I survive the next day without falling to my knees and pleading for mercy, telling him I will do anything—*anything*—if he stops.

I curl into an aching, miserable ball, and cry.

* * *

A blast of light and high-frequency sound jerks me awake, adrenaline jack-rabbiting my heart. A camera on the roof outside my cell watches my tears, my despair. I turn my back and try to rest, shame prickling my skin hotter than the swelling bruises.

The night lasts an eternity. Time enough to watch the bruises coalesce, my abused tissues pulsing under my fingertips. They flare on touching the ground, or another part of me, my clothes scraping me raw.

All from a rubber truncheon.

There are harder, sharper implements to come.

* * *

A cheery Wick collects me the next morning. I blink stinging eyes and will my body to move. Stubbornness alone brings me to my feet rather than submit to being hauled by the muscle-bound soldier replacing the Guard-bitches.

Wick sweeps his arm towards a metal chair, his plump lips twisting into a grin. I refuse to sit like a good little prisoner but the guard forces me. He outweighs me by at least fifty kilos and could palm my whole face in his giant hand. He straps me to the seat at ankle and wrist, stepping away to the double doors, his piggy eyes lingering on me. Wick lifts my jumper to expose my bruised belly and tightens a chunky belt around my stomach. His pointed nails pinch and squeeze and caress.

"Daniel," I whisper. "Let me speak to Daniel."

"Daniel died ten years ago, girlie." A remote appears in his hand from out of his pocket. "Let's test how you do with electricity."

I discover what John hoped I'd feel from his damn dog collar—like someone is ripping my muscles apart with a fork.

I faint after a few seconds and have no idea how long I'm out, consciousness returning in a jittery wash.

A pitying smile graces Wick's lips. "I'll dial this back a little. Passing out is too much like escape, and you're not going anywhere."

He presses the button again.

My spine bows, threatening to snap. If my tongue was in the way of my clamping teeth, I would've bitten it off. My skin ripples and shivers and burns.

Whispering hisses through my daze. The goliath guard talks to someone through the double door before disappearing into the reception area. Wick's black gaze drinks in my twitching body.

"Tell me about my sister," I manage. "Tell me about Ailsa Carmichael."

"Oh, how I would love to have her here, strapped to my table, your screams complementing hers."

I shake my head hard, my hair whipping across my face. "You liked her. Fight it, Daniel. You have to win."

He stays quiet so long I risk a peek. Turmoil lightens his eyes from merciless black to ebony.

"Are you a dream?"

Aftershocks quiver on my tongue but I herd it into forming words. "You want to let me go. You want to help me."

"I think I've done bad things."

"You don't have to anymore."

He slips the remote into his pocket and I go limp. His fingertips graze the strap around my wrist. The double door flaps open.

"Sir, I know you don't like to be disturbed but it's The People's Republic." The Goliath hands Daniel a comms system. "She says her name is Hannah."

Oh, shit.

Daniel taps the screen, his eyes flicking to me. "This is Wick."

"I believe I have some interesting news about your prisoner, Mr Wick, if you haven't already killed her," Hannah says in her best breathy voice.

Daniel winces and rubs his scar.

I strain against the straps. "Haven't you done enough, you bitch?"

"That's a pity. For her." Hannah's laugh tinkles from the shiny oblong.

The Goliath reclaims his position by the double door.

"This line is not for casual conversation," Daniel says, turning his back on the guard. "Get to the point."

"My point, Mr Wick, is the person you have in your clutches today, the great and honourable Anita Carmichael, is the one who shot you in the head."

My eyes widen. Daniel presses his scar so hard, his fingers threaten to pierce his skull.

"She killed her sister, too," Hannah continues in a grave voice. "She betrayed us all."

"Why would she do that?"

"Jealousy. She's always wanted to lead."

"She's lying! I'm not even the leader of The People's Republic. Why would I wait so long to take power from Marshall?"

Daniel stays silent, his black eyes unreadable.

"Snakes are patient," Hannah says. "Everything you've suffered is her fault. Everything we've lost is—"

Daniel's thumb swipes the screen. We stare at each other, my harsh breathing the only sound. He slips his hand into his pocket.

"Daniel, she's—"

Pain seizes me and sizzles through my nerves. The spasms wrench my head back, the edge of the chair digging into my shoulder blades.

"Did you shoot me?" Daniel says, quietly. His eyes swirl black on black.

"No!" I gasp. "I didn't kill anyone that day."

"Let's see who's the liar."

He jabs the button again. Again.

"Did you make me this monster?" he screams.

It continues for the rest of the day. He lets the shock ebb and presses the button, catapulting me into agony. Somewhere around the fifth time, my bladder and bowels lose control. Hot, thick fluid soaks my jeans.

Wick sneers and presses the button. He asks no more questions.

I'm less than human. Humiliated and debased and utterly worthless.

Stop. *Please* stop. No more.

The words clog my throat.

* * *

I have no recollection of returning to my cell. The sleep deprivation techniques resume beyond a numbing layer. I lie and breathe, my muscles spasming, heart hitching, my own waste crusted on my legs.

Not thinking has its advantages. Thinking leads to despair.

I enjoy the haze, my pain a dull ache, my life a distant memory.

* * *

That changes the third day when Wick pulls out my toenails. They detach with surprising ease. He kneels, a fine mist of blood on his hands, the ghost of my shrieks bouncing off the walls. He stares at the pliers then raises his head.

"Anita?"

"Daniel?" I croak.

His slow smile stretches the width of his narrow face.

"No," he says.

The pliers clatter on enamel to the back of my throat, bearing a metallic taste similar to blood. I gag, roots separating from gums in a gush of warm liquid and a sizzling spear of pain. Wick tosses my wisdom teeth and they skitter across the floor. Another dose of the rubber truncheon and electric belt punishes my lack of grovelling.

I yell, I cry, I soil myself. I don't beg, though the words long to be free.

But then, I will be lost.

* * *

On the fourth day, delirium transforms Wick into a scaly, pulsing-eyed monster and the room into a tilting carnival ride. I'm half-aware of being stripped of my stinking clothes, my abused flesh unrecognisable.

Wick plunges my body into a tub of water. Ice cubes rattle, the cold aching in my bones and remaining teeth, liquid nipping my exposed nail beds. He holds me under, his arms locked though I don't struggle. The water caresses fevered skin.

It's the most peaceful I've been in days.

I lie in the freezing darkness and think about inhaling.

The pain will stop, the torture will end. It would be effortless.

I open my mouth and Wick pulls me, gasping, into the light. Water cascades from my hair and beads in my eyelashes. He shakes me, snapping my head back and forth.

"Get Gibson," he barks at the faceless guard on the door. "I want this bitch awake and aware of what I'm doing to her, not smiling like a fucking simpleton."

I struggle to focus on Wick's hateful face, blinking the watery film from my eyes.

"You know what, Daniel?" I manage to whisper through cracked lips. "You were always a fucking monster."

"There are monsters in all of us, girlie."

I cough up enough phlegm to spit in his face. His fist slams into my jaw, his weaselly features a feral mask as the beast slips its leash.

17

I find myself in my cell, naked apart from my dog-tags. A drip bag one-third full of yellow fluid hangs from a small hook on the wall beside an empty bag.

The liquid has worked wonders, my mind clear and whole. Fuck.

I sit up carefully. Fresh red bruises cover shades of violet and green, the rainbow of abuse painting my skin. Weeping blisters circle my waist from Wick's overzealous use of the stun belt. Dark fluid cakes the nail beds of my feet. My tongue explores my savaged gums, pulsing pain down my jaw and tasting the copperiness of blood. My stomach roils at the stink of my dirt and blood-encrusted body. I vomit stinging bile close to a rusted drain in the corner and wipe a shaking hand over my mouth, the drip pulling uncomfortably in my arm.

I can't take another day. I've barely coped with what Wick or Daniel or both have done already. What happens when he chops parts off? Or fractures my bones, one by one?

I swallow hard and fight another wave of nausea.

I can't do it. I need to escape or force him to kill me quickly. Anything else is too gruesome to contemplate.

The tape on my arm catches on silken hairs. A tiny bead of blood shimmers where the catheter slips free. I press a filthy finger to it and hope to die of septicaemia, though it would be too slow a death.

Wick could still harvest my organs while I watch.

The sun gilds the frosted glass of the prison room.

A whole night of blessed unconsciousness—what a reprieve.

Summoned, Wick strides through the door, his gaze roving over my body. I hunch at the hungry anticipation in his dark eyes.

"Now, this is better," he says. "Lucid and defiant—just what I need for the day I break you into pieces."

I bare my teeth. He beckons me out and I use the wall to lever myself up. His gaze never leaves my nakedness.

How can he look at me, considering the state I'm in and how ripe I smell, and feel anything sexual?

He forces me to brush against him. I dig my nails into my palms and stumble into the torture room. A different guard stands at the door. Horrified recognition sweeps across his features even with my battered appearance. He gulps and drops his gaze.

I met him at several independence rallies when the rebellion was young, Ailsa heavily involved and cajoling me along. Sparks of attraction led to teasing conversations, shared glances and nerves rippling in my belly.

But I wasn't ready to trust men yet.

Stig hasn't aged well—dark shadows, thinning hair. He was tall but now stoops over, an old man despite his lack of years.

Maybe he'll intervene.

I try to capture his attention, beseeching him silently with my back to Wick. Pallid eyes meet mine but dart away, the last hint of colour leaching from his face.

The *coward*.

I scan the shelves around the room.

Running is not the only option.

I lunge for a metal bat, scattering torture implements to the floor and coaxing my muscles into mimicking normal function. Wick grabs my arm, spinning me around. I grip the club in my hand, somehow, and swing it at him. He plucks the bat from my fingers.

"Still got some fight in you, girlie? I'll gladly beat it out of you."

He backhands me, holding me in position, and continues to hit me until my knees buckle. He drags me to a patch of wall with a hook, unhampered by my feeble struggles, and binds my hands to hoist me aloft. My arms stretch above my head, my back to the room.

You getting a nice view, Stig? He's probably staring at my ass. Well, I'm not at my best with shit caked on my skin.

Wick rummages among his toys, ignoring the ones strewn on the ground in my desperate attempt to arm myself.

I don't like what he selects after much deliberation.

The end of the whip snakes onto the floor. I turn to the wall and bow my head.

Please, no more. I just want it to end.

A loud crack splits the room. A scalding line sears my back and rips a yelp from my mouth. Wick laughs. The whip lashes a second time but I clamp my lips shut. The leather bites a third time, tugging on the hair falling down my shoulders and tearing it in chunks from my scalp. Lashes scorch delicate skin. I squirm against the wall, my skin bathed in stinging sweat. Wick finally stops and I sag in the ropes, lank hair sticking to my face and chest. Blood trickles in rivulets to my buttocks and thighs.

"Why—don't you beg—you cunt?" Wick snarls.

I grit my aching teeth.

Speaking is impossible without the pain seeping into my voice or words of pleading spilling out.

Boots slap linoleum. Wick yanks my hair and appears disappointed, somehow, his hatred gleaming in eyes as black as tar.

"I know what will make you beg," he whispers, his breath sour on my cheek.

He unhooks me but keeps my hands bound. He smiles and it's the most terrifying thing I've ever seen. His fingers wrap around my throat. Squeeze hard.

How does he expect me to beg if I can't breathe?

18

I choke and scrabble at Wick's hands. His hold crackles in the delicate cartilage of my throat. My bare feet aim for his kneecaps but get no response. Stars explode prettily, my head as distended as a hot air balloon. Colours blend and turn grey. Wick and the torture room float away.

All my fighting was for nothing. Wick has crushed my dreams of avenging my sister and claiming victory for the only faction that deserves it.

Will the murderers ever pay for what they did?

The pressure eases. I crumple to the linoleum, heaving gulps of air. Each precious inhalation chars my starved tissues and eclipses the pain from my other wounds, my entire focus on relearning the art of respiration.

Wick sneers.

He does it a lot.

"We're not finished yet, girlie."

He kicks me onto my flaming back. I shriek at the fresh assault and try to roll on my side. He sits on my legs. One hand grabs my bound wrists and pins my arms above my head. My shredded flesh mashes into the unyielding floor. His other hand unbuttons his trousers.

A flash of panic energises weary muscles and I buck.

No, I can't take the violation. Ram other things into my body but not him. *Not him.*

Wick backhands me and my eyes blur. He finishes stripping off his trousers while I lie stunned, the voice in my head screaming for me to resist, attack, do *something!* Stained cotton briefs land on the floor. Wick uses his knees to spread my legs and pin them, the weight bruising me further. A faded black dragon with crimson eyes crawls the length of his thigh.

He smells musky. Fungal.

Bile spurts into my mouth. Wick squeezes my breast in his free hand. I squirm at the crushing pain. His erection juts from his narrow hips.

"I'm going to enjoy this, girlie." He leans closer to expel his rotting breath in my face. "I forced myself to wait and I'm about to explode. After I'm done, I'll give you to my guards. When they drag what's left of you back to me, I'll remove pieces from your once lovely body. Starting with these."

He gives my breast another vicious pinch and begins to sit up. I slam my forehead into his nose, breaking it in a crunch of bone and hot, splattering blood. He howls and jerks backwards, red dripping between his fingers to speckle his white t-shirt and patter on the floor between my legs.

"Not so great when it's your pain, is it?" I wheeze.

His fist smacks my cheek.

Maybe now he'll kill me.

His hand uncurls and he slaps me until my vision swims. He stops and awareness floods back.

There's no escaping his brutality.

"Valiant struggle but worthless," he says, his teeth smeared crimson. "You and your life are worthless here. I will do whatever I want and you can do nothing to stop me. You can do nothing but wish for death. And beg, of course."

He's right. I'm worthless. *Weak.* Tired of fighting him.

I shut my eyes. Tears pool, slipping free to burn my cheeks.

Please, let it be over soon.

Wick removes his knees from my weeping muscles. The tip of him pushes against me and I bite my lip to keep from screaming.

"Oh, girlie, your sweet tears are the best aphrodisiac."

Sobs build in my chest. It hurts too much, it's too much.

A dull thud shivers through the torture room and the foul pressure disappears.

19

Stig blinks at me down the body of his gun, the MP5 reversed in his grip. "I couldn't—watch him—with someone I *knew*."

I wriggle out from under Wick and curl into a ball, my face buried in my bound hands. Shudders ripple from my shoulders and torment my wounds.

Is there no end to the torture?

"It's all right, Anita, he's unconscious." The heat of Stig's hand hovers over my arm. "But you have to get out of here."

It hurts too much to move, let alone run, but I nod my head.

I want to go home so badly, my stomach aches.

Stig slips a knife from his boot and cuts the rope between my wrists. I ease myself into a sitting position and scrub my face with shaking hands. His weary eyes dart away to frown at a patch of floor somehow free of blood.

"I'm sorry, Anita. Should have intervened before now. Before you. He tortured so many."

I coax my trembling mouth into a smile. "This war is littered with regrets."

"This won't be one. Let's get you out of here."

The ghost of his younger self smooths his weathered face and hope flutters in my chest. Foolish, unquenchable, glorious hope.

My fight isn't over. How am I going to challenge Hannah, Kate and Lisa in this state? But the rest of The People's Republic will be shocked by their behaviour.

I'm the goddamn faction sweetheart.

Stig helps me to my feet despite my wobbling knees. I bow my head, my matted hair swinging, and concentrate on breathing.

"Can you stand by yourself?"

I doubt it if my wavering vision is anything to go by.

"I think so," I say.

"Wait here. Need to check on the other guards."

He crosses to the double doors and edges one open. Holding a finger to his lips, he disappears through the single door leading to the emergency exit.

Wick groans. I jump, pain spearing through my back.

The bastard is waking up. Stig will return to find him raping me, smeared in my blood, my eyes glazed.

I retreat on quivering legs and nudge an object with my foot. The metal bat rolls to a stop. I crouch, my gaze fixed on Wick. His fingers twitch. I snatch the club and straighten too quickly, the floor tilting beneath my feet.

Oh god, don't faint.

Air wheezes through my bruised throat. I force myself to stumble over to Wick and kneel beside his head.

I raise the bat.

His dark eyes open.

20

Wick's bloodied nose disintegrates under the bat. I hit him again. And again and again and again. Bones cave, muscles tear, red droplets arc on each swing.

I can't stop. Can't leave him breathing. Turning a corner to be confronted by a sneer on his grotesque lips and a, "Hello, girlie."

He has to die so I can live.

I slump, panting hard, my vision clouding to black. His face no longer resembles a face but a concave lump of meat and glistening shards of bone. Blood drips from my hand and drenches my skin.

I doubt he'll recover from this head injury.

I giggle, a shrill bleat more mad than happy, and the bat slips from my fingers. I stare at the red mess of my tormentor, unable to raise my head.

Footsteps stutter to a halt. "Anita... *Jesus.*"

"He—woke up. He—"

My stomach rolls and I shut my mouth to keep from vomiting.

Stig's boots appear beside me. "It's okay. He can't hurt you anymore. He can't hurt anyone anymore."

I sob over Wick's corpse, whining at each muscle spasm.

My pink tears patter on the ruin of his face. I want to crawl into a corner and pass out.

Agonising relief, agonising pain. Equally debilitating.

Stig tucks a bedraggled strand of hair behind my ear. "Come on. The guards are occupied. You need to go."

I shake my head. Chattering teeth inflame my gaping sockets.

"Please, Anita. You have to go."

He's risked everything to help me. His punishment will be brutal if he's discovered.

Traitors aren't tolerated.

Get up, you snivelling wretch.

I peek at him through tangled hair. "Can you help me stand?"

His fingers skid on the blood smearing my arm. He flinches but doesn't let go. I climb to my feet, my legs quivering, and he guides me through the single door. We enter a staff room where uniforms hang from hooks on the closest wall, five blue chairs lining another. An electric kettle and a chipped mug sit on a counter next to a sink.

Did Wick come here for a restorative cup of tea between sessions? Sipping and sighing with pleasure while I shivered and moaned in the next room.

Stig lowers me onto a chair, immediately ruining the upholstery. He pulls dark green combats and a matching jacket from the hooks, his movements hurried, his eyes flicking to the door. His anxiety nibbles my skin and sinks claws deep in my gut.

Wick is gone but one of his guards could take his place. The Goliath will break my bones with his bare hands.

Stig dresses me in the proffered clothes, my shaking fingers useless. I lever my butt off the chair and try to ignore how bad I smell. It's amazing not to be naked, though the fabric scrapes my battered skin. Stig hands me a helmet and I fasten it, pulling the collar of the jacket higher to disguise the bruising.

Do I resemble a Nationless soldier?

Maybe one who's had a very crappy day.

Stig holds out my own scuffed boots.

How nice. Wick kept a memento.

Stig attempts to slide the boots on. My exposed nail beds shriek and my foot jerks out of reach. The boot hits the floor and I stifle a sob.

People will question a soldier stumbling barefoot, her nailbeds a cluster of maroon scabs.

"Wait," Stig says, scrambling to the cupboard under the sink. "There should be something here…"

He slams a green first aid kit on the chair beside me and wrenches the lid up. I swallow a laugh.

It'll take more than a sticking plaster to fix me.

Rolls of gauze bounce on the linoleum, a plastic box of safety pins rattling as Stig tosses it aside. He grabs a small glass bottle topped by a long nozzle.

"This'll sting."

I snort.

Why is everything so damn funny?

Cool spray mists my toes. It nips for a second and fades, replaced by a pleasant numbness.

Can he drench my whole body? A tormented zombie shuffle may also give me away.

My boots fit snug, the shriek of my toenails reduced to a whimper.

"You'll need this, too." He brandishes a dull brass syringe

gun, the needle winking in the overhead light, white liquid filling the barrel. "Tilt your head."

"What—"

"A stimulant. Wick's own blend. Caffeine, amphetamine, god knows what else." His watery eyes jitter to the door. "Intravascular."

I want to argue—refuse—but I tilt my head. I need some serious medicinal help or I'm going nowhere.

"Oh, um, let me just…" He fumbles for a square packet and scrubs my neck. "Ah, maybe one more."

Two stained alcohol wipes flutter to the floor. The needle pierces my throat, the syringe hissing as the trigger depresses. Heat spreads towards my chest and my heart kicks, sending ribbons of fire to my muscles.

Stig offers me a Browning. I stop myself from lunging for it and slip the barrel into the front of my trousers, tucking the jacket over. I limp to the sink and wash my face and hands to avoid potential questions on who I slaughtered.

What do I know? Perhaps it's normal in Livingston.

I leave the ceramic pink-splattered, pieces of bone and tissue clogging the plughole.

Stig hustles me into the short corridor and unbolts the emergency door. "The effects should last an hour, maybe two. I can't go with you from here. Ask for a different detail and I'm stuck between this cursed place and my house. I'll be reported if I'm seen and once they search for Wick…"

No, he has to come with me. I can't make it without him. I need him.

Shut up.

"I'll hide his body. Give you more time. You shouldn't be recognised. We move between encampments, not amalgamated like your faction. Always new faces." He sucks in a breath, glancing over his shoulder towards the main room. "Take the dragon. You'll need a pass off someone to get close to it."

"You're telling me to steal the dragon?"

"Only way you'll escape."

"But if it's as powerful as Wick said, my faction will win."

He shrugs one stooped shoulder. "Someone has to end it. Does it really matter who?"

"I… Thank you."

"Just try not to kill all of us, okay?"

My mouth opens, closes.

There's nothing more to say.

I grab the handle of the metal and glass door and a blast of crisp air hits me in the face. The exit of the torture chamber shuts behind me with a quiet sucking sound, like a tooth pulled from a socket.

21

The air sparkles as if ground diamonds dance on the wind. Hints of spilled biofuel and gunpowder sweeten the taste. I stretch my hand out to brush my fingertips on the rough, pitted stone of the building next to me. The sensation tingles up my arm.

Christ, I'm high.

Voices seem too loud, the squelch and splash of footsteps echoing inside my head. People march along roads, purposeful and confident, their sphere of existence as it should be.

Dazzled joy transforms to hot anger.

Do they care how their psychopath of a leader abuses his prisoners or do they ignore it, like Stig did?

I clench my fists and step away from the building.

If any of them smile, laugh, I'll punch them.

But I'm greeted by an army of expressionless mannequins.

My boot slips in mud smelling rich enough to eat. The movement jerks my wounded back and I swallow a cry, Wick's wonder blend not enough to dull all of my pain.

How dare the minions of Nationless hide behind their ignorance. They deserve to share a fraction of my suffering.

And righteous fury is preferable to dwelling on the past five days.

I enter a deep shadow cast by a large screen, one of many dominating the rooftops.

Did Wick use them to address his subordinates, his terrifying weasel face stretched four metres high? Maybe he entertained his people with old movies, like Marshall.

Head down, I join the tail of a group of soldiers wearing similar uniforms to mine. They trudge towards the domed building arching above the surrounding structures. I match their pace, jittery energy twitching my muscles, bidding me to hurry, my mind uncomfortably alert. Horrific replays flicker behind my eyes. I focus on the Browning digging into my stomach instead of dropping to my knees and howling.

Get home to safety then fall apart.

The soldiers continue around the curve of the domed building. I lift the trapdoor and inch down the ladder, my teeth gritted. Every movement pulls at the lash wounds and aggravates my other injuries. I lean against the wall at the bottom, already out of breath, my heart unsure whether to race or stop altogether.

I can do this. Grab a pass, steal the dragon, fly home. Easy.

The third door of the corridor opens onto a small lab, white tables lining the room, microscopes in a neat row. Vials fill a glowing glass fridge in the corner. I perch on a stool to wait, praying it won't be long. The seconds settle on my shoulders, burdening me with the threat of discovery.

Footsteps. One person.

I stumble out of the doorway. "Oh, thank god! He's having a seizure. Quick!"

The man in a white coat gapes at me.

"Please, he needs help!"

I spin into the room. My brain keeps spinning. I slap a hand on the edge of a table to steady myself.

The man rushes in and skids past. "Where—"

The butt of the Browning smacks the back of his head. He sprawls on his face. I dig my nails into my palms and the pain from my sudden movement fades. Tugging the white coat from his body almost makes me throw up. I pull it on, smoothing my fingers over the pass clipped to the lapel. A datamatrix code and shiny hologram wink in the light of the fridge. I slide my gun into a pocket and toss the helmet.

Shutting the man inside the lab, I hobble into the bright space of the main room. Workers continue to swarm, typing on computers, chatting to neighbours or scurrying about clutching files. None of them appear to have weapons. One person stands half-hidden under the dragon, examining the interior. Armed guards circle the machine between bevelled black posts with winking red eyes.

Scanners. Does an alarm sound if someone tries to access without a pass? Is mine even the right one?

I descend in the nearest lift, willing myself to keep breathing. I jump at a loud *ping* and the doors whoosh open. The closest guard glances at me but returns to scrutinising the room, somehow unperturbed by my battered face and filthy hair. I ease past a black post, expecting the squeal of a siren and hard hands bruising tenderised flesh. I almost walk into the person peering into the beast's belly, my concentration on not looking over my shoulder, certain my incredulous eyes will give me away.

I tap the scientist on the back. "Sorry to disturb you but my orders are to—"

Shit.

Janine's mouth drops open. I fist my hand in her lab coat

and tug, stepping behind her to face the room. Her petite frame offers little cover. I press my gun to her temple and back us towards the dragon.

"Stop her!" she shrieks. "The prisoner is free!"

Equipment clatters to the ground. The guards slot rifles into their shoulders. An alarm wails, booted feet thundering down multiple corridors.

"Drop your gun, you're surrounded," a man shouts near the front of the gathering crowd, one flap of his lab coat tucked into his trousers. "Someone tell Wick the prisoner has escaped."

"Wick is dead," I say.

"You're next, you bitch," Janine says, her pulse fluttering against my hand at her throat. "You won't get out of here alive, *Anita*. And if you do, we'll hunt you down, no matter the cost."

Huh, she remembers my name. The rest I choose to ignore.

I continue to reverse, crouching lower, hoping no one sneaks up behind me. Blackness beckons through the hatch. I shove Janine and she flies to the ground, her lab coat flapping like the wings of a dove. I haul myself through the hatch, shots ricocheting off silver skin and tugging at my trousers. I yell and slam the hatch shut. The gunfire, shouting and general mayhem hushes with the sealing of the rubber-lined door. I slide the bolt and collapse to my side, my breathing loud in the cosy space. The darkness of the interior is a desperately needed sensory deprivation chamber.

Nausea rides waves of pain, dried blood catching on the inside of my clothes. Swallowing hurts, breathing hurts, moving hurts. *Thinking* hurts. I want it all to go away.

I open my eyes without realising I've closed them, my cheek

cushioned on spongy material.

Is Wick's potion wearing off already?

I fight against the pull of unconsciousness and sit up. Tiny bulbs embedded where floor meets sides cast a muted light. The front of the machine doesn't contain the complicated buttons and levers I expect. Three cables ending in padded loops dangle from the roof, hung in an equilateral triangle, the point directed at the tail and suspended to about waist height. I crawl closer, distrusting my ability to stand. Wires trail to a helmet and a pair of goggles hanging on a hook. I cradle the eyewear in my hands and slide them on, the elastic band snagging my hair. They settle around my eye sockets, pressing into my cheekbones and brows. I jerk and regret it, my torn back protesting.

The domed building surrounds me, the dragon's snout where my nose should be. I move my head for a better view but the picture stays the same. The dragon stares at a curve of wall above hurrying people, their nervous glances jittering in my direction. Soldiers with MP5s form a loose semi-circle, gripping their weapons and fidgeting.

Since a person hasn't climbed in and shot me, there must be no external unlocking mechanism for the door. Perhaps Wick believed no one would steal his secret weapon.

Now who's the moron?

I remove the goggles and struggle to adjust from sunlit space to dark cave. I stand slowly, one hand on the side to steady me, and examine the cables.

The parallel two end in smaller loops. Maybe they go around the wrists of the controller, the larger loop around the waist. I pull on one and it lengthens. Released, it returns to its original position.

21

If the dragon works by listening to a person's brain, mimicking the outward body position could give smoother control. If she flies, I fly, supported by the cables.

She? Sweet Jesus, I'm as bad as Wick.

Muffled banging on the side stifles that happy thought.

Do they expect me to open the hatch and invite them in? They're going to be disappointed. If the dragon is as invincible as Wick boasted, there's nothing they can do to get me out.

What if it isn't ready? My choices are surrender or starve, sacrificing myself to prevent Nationless from reclaiming control of her/it.

Ultimate killing machine to shiny mausoleum.

Sweat coalesces in my palms. I shed the lab coat and slip the cables on, manoeuvring the one for my waist over my head instead of bending to step into it. The padding chafes my raw skin and will only get worse as the cables hold my weight when—if—I get the contraption to fly.

It'd be undignified for me *and* the dragon if I stomp back to Calders like a winged Godzilla.

I fit the wired helmet on my head and tighten the chinstrap. Cool metal presses against my scalp, helped, no doubt, by my numerous bald spots. I ease the goggles on, my mind rushing over the steps to get home. Nothing happens and a knot of fear twists my gut. I quiet my chaotic brain.

One action at a time.

I think about bending my right leg. The floor tilts to the left then violently to the right. The dragon topples and my body swings in the cables. Soldiers and scientists stagger back.

I hear everything in the room as though standing in it rather than enclosed in my silver cocoon—frightened voices, rushing feet, the wail of the alarm.

I/we turn my head at a creaking noise. A bulbous dissolution ray trundles towards us, pushed by grim-faced men. Others watch, frustration plain on their features. Wick designed the dragon to be indestructible but I choose caution. I open my mouth and roast the group with a blast of fire from sharp-toothed jaws. They sizzle and scream.

The dragon works if I don't over-think it!

I push onto my haunches and bunch my legs, launching through the roof in a flurry of wings. The smash echoes, glass exploding in a twinkling shower. People stare as their secret weapon hovers in the unmarred blue of the sky.

How can I fly if I've never had wings?

I dip but catch myself, silencing the excited babble in my head. Nothing like revenge to clarify one's thoughts.

It's sustained me this last decade. What's a little more?

The shattered domed edifice is the first to go. Two missiles loosed into its depths fold the rest in a slide of debris. I fly swiftly to the torture chamber and land on the roof, tearing at it with claws and teeth. Slate cracks, wood splinters. The bored receptionist is gone, probably scuttling away at the first sign of danger. Three male guards remain, including the Goliath who forced me into the metal chair to be electrocuted. A fourth, one of the Guard-bitches, lies dead on the floor, her chest crushed under falling rubble.

I hope it's the twin with the machete.

A blast of fire cleanses the evil from the place. In the crackling flames, I destroy the building, breaking it apart brick by hateful brick.

No one else will suffer in this hellhole, Wick or no Wick.

A rocket smashes into my side in a puff of smoke. I swivel my head. The flabby man-boy struggles to balance a launcher on his shoulder.

How many prisoners has he taunted, aware of their awful fate? Maybe the soldiers of Livingston gathered to watch recordings of the torture sessions on the giant screens. Laughed at my screams, sneered as I soiled myself.

They deserve to be razed to the fucking ground.

My lasers fry the man-boy, sparking in his globs of fatty tissue. My furious roar vibrates in the dragon's chest and rattles the rubble of the torture chamber. I stomp away and blast helicopters and planes, other armoured vehicles in the minority. Thinking 'fire' or 'bullets' or 'laser' activates my selected weapon from wherever it exists on my body and jettisons it to my target. Buildings burn, whole structures collapsing into the mud in a cloud of red.

Pain and terror turn to wrath. Everything is Livingston's fault. They're an extension of Wick—they forced me to feel weak and wish for death but in their dragon I am strong. Unstoppable.

And there won't be enough of them left to hunt me down.

Golden afternoon light softens the smouldering remnants of the encampment by the time I bound into the air. Survivors cower under my shadow. Stig watches with sad eyes from a pile of broken concrete as I swoop overhead.

Bet he regrets it now.

I squash the ridiculous pulse of guilt.

They let a psychopath torture countless prisoners for nothing but enjoyment. If there's no honour in war, why the hell are we fighting? Maybe they had no choice. It wouldn't have changed a thing. They needed to be destroyed to keep them from building another dragon. The survivors can regroup in the other encampments of Nationless, select another leader.

And submit to the might of The People's Republic. The faction that refused to strike first will be the one to end it. *I* will end it.

For Ailsa.

I push higher into the sky, aiming south-east in the direction of Calders.

Going home. I'm really going *home*.

Each beat of my wings numbs my brain and smothers other insanity-inducing thoughts. I shove the memories deep, where examination is impossible.

No need to relive it. Once is enough.

The countryside opens beneath me in the sprawl of no man's land between Livingston and Calders, close to an unassuming place once called Carlops. Abandoned villages surrounded by rank agricultural fields slowly crumble to dust.

Should I see if England still exists?

My smooth flight wobbles.

The border control is no barrier to the dragon. We constructed a fence as a 'screw you' to England for continuing to refuse another independence referendum despite it being almost a decade since the first.

Soldiers of the Lost weaponised it.

But the defensive barrage won't harm the dragon.

Are the Moderates still in power? Is anyone? They could imprison me as a terrorist, submit me to endless interrogations.

They probably won't torture me.

Unless the whole damn world is at war. It explains the silence, the lack of intervention. Crackles of static over normal communication channels. Enough time has passed since the loss of the internet for their economies to stabilise. They must have experienced their own societal collapse from something else. The news from the Third World was pretty bleak—drought, famine, freak weather, the movement of refugees causing hostilities in Africa and the Middle East. Maybe someone lashed out and the rest blamed each other, the violence escalating until there was no going back. Unity a forgotten dream.

Sounds familiar.

I swoop closer to the ground, my shining reflection chasing me across the surface of a reservoir.

The water has been toxic for years—some kind of deadly nanoparticle.

One heavy wingbeat propels me over the hills and moorland into a wide, flat valley we claimed as ours.

Excitement curls in my stomach, more nourishing than food. Home. Safety. I want to be horizontal and up to my eyeballs on morphine when whatever Stig injected me with wears off. No time for gallivanting to England or the rest of the world out of morbid curiosity. What would happen if I faint thousands of feet in the air? Or the minute I open the hatch? I'm too vulnerable to take the risk.

I hover over Calders, my wings slicing the air. The alarm stays silent, the defence system apparently unable to detect me. Another of Wick's brilliant additions to his fantastic killing machine.

Pity he was a psychopath.

My roar settles on the maze of muddy streets, buildings and patches of green. Crowds mill like cattle. Missiles and rocket-propelled grenades explode in bursts of orange flame and smoke. Lasers refract as someone manually overrides the radar guidance of the inoperative aerial defence system.

A fireworks display to celebrate my return.

I hover for a heartbeat more and tuck my wings, plummeting towards a large area of weeds and grass close to the edge of our territory, the boundary fence shimmering beyond it. The ground rushes to greet me and I spread my wings to avoid a spectacular nosedive. I stand tall, head high, and wait for my people.

22

The Raider-3s arrive first, the rumble of their passage scattering loose stones. They fire volleys at me, their charging portals blazing, but I don't budge, explode or disintegrate. The swirling smoke parts to reveal my undamaged hide and the hulking machines power down. A crowd assembles, led by Marshall and his second in command, Weir. My comrades gawp at the unbreakable dragon machine in their domain, their SA80s levelled.

I'm so glad to see their faces.

I lower my head. The crowd edges backwards but Marshall and Weir remain unmoved.

What right do they have to be unafraid when I spent my days drenched in fear and pain? A prisoner at the mercy of someone who had none.

Rage is the only thing keeping me from falling apart. A boiling fury to rival the shrieking torment inside my head.

I want to lie down. To pull my meagre possessions around me like a shield and cry until it doesn't hurt so very much. To wake in my own space instead of a cell.

"Can you hear me?" I say, my distorted voice spilling from the dragon's mouth.

Surprised recognition registers on pale faces. Whispers

shiver through the pack, bright eyes flicking to neighbours.

"Anita?" Marshall says, striding closer, a hand on the Glock at his waist.

"You expecting someone else?"

"No, it seems about right for you to appear in a fantastical machine, though I'd be more comfortable if you got out of it." He glances over his shoulder at the crowd, a mixture of soldiers and non-combat personnel. "Your disappearance raised some interesting questions."

"I'll bet. But the answers can wait."

I scan the group and see no sign of Hannah, Kate or Lisa. Lucky for them.

I remove the operating equipment, a bleat of sadness in my chest. The last of Wick's power juice leaches away. I slip outside and lean on the dragon, my knees threatening to buckle. A woman leaves the crowd and hurries to my side. The sunset burnishes her glasses, the golden disks hiding her eyes. Gentle fingers wrap around my arm.

"Are you all right, Soldier Carmichael? What happened?"

I coax my mouth into a smile. "Bit of a long story, Fiona."

"Of course. Sorry. Let me help you to—"

"Southwell!" Marshall barks and Fiona jumps. "You're meant to be guarding the main gate."

Something tightens her face—something like anger—but her expression smooths and it's gone.

"I'm glad you're back, Anita," she says and inches closer. "Be careful."

Be careful?

Her long legs spirit her into the crowd before I can ask what she means. I sag harder against the dragon, too depleted to hide my exhaustion. My boots slosh as if filled with water.

Thankfully, I still can't feel the mess of my toes.

"Weir, get this thing into the garden centre; use the timber lorry," Marshall says. "Anita, you and I have a lot to talk about."

"In case you haven't noticed, I'm in a great deal of fucking pain," I say past the burning in my throat. "We can talk after I get some medical attention."

A coughing fit practically drives me to my knees and I end with my hands on my thighs, spitting blood into the grass.

How much damage has Wick done?

I straighten and don't faint, puke or start coughing.

Hooray for me.

"Quit the act, you traitor," Hannah says, stepping boldly beside Marshall in figure-hugging combats and a shirt, her skin healthy and unmarked. "You killed your own sister because she outshone you and look how you capitalised on it—perfect soldier, perfect in her grief."

I'm too fucking damaged for this shit.

"You started the war that's claimed so many of us," she says. "You ruined our dream of independence."

May as well blame me for global warming, environmental catastrophe and the internet collapse while she's at it.

I blame my exhaustion for letting her prattle on.

She opens her mouth to spout more lies. I shoot her in the forehead. My bullet jerks her backwards and she collapses in the grass.

Traitors aren't tolerated. Particularly ones who betray my sister's memory.

"Rest in peace, *old friend*," I say into the silence.

Have the guns always been pointed at me?

A smirk flickers over Marshall's face.

Not exactly the response I expected. I should have thought

how it would look—me disappearing for a week to return in a strange machine, killing Hannah during her accusations. Out of context, I *am* the traitor.

"She deserved it," I croak.

My statement doesn't alleviate the stony expression of the crowd.

They can't believe Hannah over me. Everything I've done was for them. For Ailsa. This is all a misunderstanding. We'll laugh about it once I've recovered.

"Drop the gun, Anita," Marshall says.

I slide the safety on and the Browning thuds to the ground. A greasy ball settles in my stomach.

"Reece, take her to the medical centre."

Just what I need—another slobbering moron to torment me when I'm fragile.

Reece heads for a jeep parked on the road. The eyes of the crowd follow me. My clamped lips cage the whimpers produced by each step, each movement of muscle, each breath. My name floats on the air. Reece jumps lithely into the vehicle. I reach it without collapsing to my knees and sobbing. I lever onto the seat, unable to stop small pain sounds. He twists the key in the ignition and the engine roars to life. I brace a hand on the dashboard.

If he peels away and forces me backwards, I'll punch his face in.

Once I awake from my screaming faint.

The vehicle accelerates smoothly but bumps, holes and rocks mar the dirt track. The jostling worsens the ache in my abused muscles. The wind through the open top caresses my hot skin, familiar buildings passing on each side.

Home but the relief is hollow.

I'm too hurt to enjoy it.

The jeep hits a pothole and I hiss. Reece glances at me.

"I always knew you were a slut, Carmichael," he says.

I force myself not to grind my teeth. My jaw and violated sockets throb.

"What are you talking about?"

He snorts as if it's obvious. "You've spent the last week whoring yourself to the enemy."

I'd laugh, but it's terrifying. If everyone believes it, I'll have to run before they execute me like I executed Hannah. Into no man's land to be taken captive again and tortured by someone crazier than Wick.

After what I've been through, it's too much.

I vomit out the side of the jeep, retching saliva and foul-tasting stomach acid. Each heave tenses the muscles in my back. My lash wounds screech, making me retch, tears streaming down my cheeks. I want to sob but that will hurt, too.

"Sure," I wheeze, wiping snot and tears from my face with one hand, "and one of them just got a little rough."

"Or you got more than you bargained for. You're stupid to come back here, as if batting your eyelashes will convince us of your innocence."

My stomach roils and cramps. I swallow hard, fighting not to gag.

"You're the one who's going to look pretty stupid when you find out what really happened."

"I doubt it. You're a sweet piece of ass, Carmichael, but it won't save you this time."

"Shut the fuck up and drive."

He delivers me to the medical centre and allows me barely

enough time to lower to the ground before roaring away in a cloud of dust. I stand for a minute, breathing and swaying, gathering dregs of energy to move the last few steps. Dragging myself into the building, I pray the medics are immune to Hannah's lies. I need to focus on recovering, on forgetting all about Livingston, not on worrying if they'll smother me in my sleep.

23

I spend a week of unsmothered recovery in the medical centre and pass the first couple of days in complete unconsciousness, my traumatised body escaping from pain and horror into blessed darkness.

When I wake, one wrist is cuffed to the bedrail, the rest of me hooked to drips and machines. The medics treat me for malnutrition, seizures, cardiac arrhythmias, shock and exhaustion, tending to my injuries professionally, if not lovingly.

I miss them lavaging the detritus of the torture room out of my whip wounds.

They ignore my repeated insistence to be set free.

Marshall's orders. Seems I'm a danger to the people.

They sedate me after I thrash so hard against the cuff, I start to bleed. Nightmares plague me in my drugged state, visions of being in the torture room, brutalised without end. I open my eyes, bathed in sweat, certain to find Wick standing over me, ready for another day. My glorious flight nothing but a figment of my imagination.

I throw up, reliving my surrender. Anything catapults me back: a scent, a sound, the cuffs on my wrist winking silver in the light. I try to be stoic but worry some innocuous sight will shatter me into a thousand pieces. Ironic, having survived torture relatively intact, to lose myself to the memories. Though, if I go insane, I won't be coherent enough to bemoan the unfairness.

I'll be babbling in a corner until someone puts me out of my misery.

* * *

Weir eases his rangy frame through the doorway, whistling between his teeth.

"Marshall requests the pleasure of your company," he says.

"Then why isn't he here? It's not like I've been inundated with visitors."

How dumb are they? If it was a ruse—the dragon, my captivity—I wouldn't have been injured to the point of fucking collapse.

"They're afraid of you. You murdered Hannah in cold blood."

"It wasn't cold."

"So you say."

"Who says different?"

Weir rubs his face, stubble rasping under his too-big hands, the knuckles prominent.

"That's one of many things Marshall wishes to clarify this evening." He unlocks the cuff from the bedrail. "Give me your other wrist."

I cuddle my arm to my chest. "You're not cuffing my hands."

"You're under suspicion, Anita. You might want to cooperate."

"I am cooperating. This will all be cleared up before the

night is over."

Weir's mouth twitches. "How nice to see your confidence isn't as damaged as the rest of you. But you've gotten too comfortable as faction sweetheart. Give me your wrist."

"Give me the key."

"You don't give the orders here, Anita."

I slice him a smile. "Neither do you."

We glare at each other. His knuckles bunch around the metal.

"Are you saying you can't keep me under control without the cuffs?"

"Maybe I like my women tied up."

"I'm not your woman."

"You might wish you were."

There's no fucking way I'll let him touch me. *No one* gets to touch me.

Weir flips the key onto the sheet and spins on his heel. I unlock the manacle and trail after him, shivering in my thin clothes and unsteady on my feet.

Analgesic-infused bandages protect my nail-less toes, my boots stuffed with cotton. Fading bruises cover my body, my lash wounds reduced from an inferno to a campfire. Dissolvable stitches seal the deepest lacerations where the whip bit almost to scapula and vertebrae. The dressings are gone, an antibiotic patch on my arm guarding against infection.

Weir never looks over his shoulder, his shadow chased ahead by the soft internal glow from the building. Two figures walk down the quiet street towards us and nod at Weir.

They're in a different squadron and their names escape me for a minute.

One of them spits on the ground at my feet.

"You deceitful cow," he says.

The woman shakes her head. "Your own sister. Your own *comrades*."

Comrades? I've only killed one traitorous bitch. The other two are still breathing.

The soldiers hurry away before I can respond.

"Life is quite different when people aren't kissing your ass, eh, Anita?"

I drag my gaze from the couple. "You seem to be confused, Billy. It's your ass they kiss. People actually respect me because I worked for it."

"Yet how swiftly it crumbles."

"It's temporary."

He climbs the concrete steps of the church and heaves open the door, sweeping his arm out. I take a deep breath and squeeze past him, the mould an insidious contrast to the crispness of the night air. The sweep of spotlights sparkles in the broken glass of the clerestory windows. Through them, the dead branches whisper in the dark. Weir's footsteps dog mine, thumping as loud as my heartbeat. I keep moving, my body stiff, injuries complaining. Water drips from somewhere in the arch of the ceiling, collecting in slicks of black on the floor.

My knuckles rap on the solid gate of the vestry. At Marshall's confident command, I twist the cold handle and the wrought iron hinges screech.

He sits at his desk, hands clasped on the battered surface. Weir closes the door and flits to Marshall's side, one giant hand atop the chair.

"I trust you are sufficiently recovered to answer my questions now, Anita?" Marshall says, blond hair curling in the exposed triangle of his shirt, sparser over a silvery scar. "What happened during the week you were missing?"

"We have more important things to talk about, like why I went missing and whose fucking fault it is."

He holds up a hand. "We'll get to that."

I gloss over the torture, except Hannah's part in it. My fury at her helps ease the nausea.

"The dragon is Nationless's secret weapon and will win the war in weeks. You saw how our weaponry didn't scratch her—it. I've already destroyed Livingston."

Weir's lips part, the leather of the chair creaking under his fingers.

Marshall sits forward. "Livingston is gone?"

I nod.

"Then Nationless will fall." He rushes around the desk and grips my arms. "This is why you're my favourite soldier. Attack you or those you love and you are merciless."

"Speaking of attack—what is this bullshit about me being a traitor?"

I try to pull away but his hands tighten.

"Anita, you shot Hannah in front of everyone."

"She abandoned me in Embra, traded me to Revolutionary Front and incited Wick to torture me. She got off lightly."

"The people don't know that."

I tug out of his hold. "So tell them."

He flashes the charming smile that captured my sister, and returns to his chair.

"It may take a lot to save your reputation. The people believe it was you who tried to trade Hannah, Kate and Lisa to Revolutionary Front. Hannah was most distraught."

"Hannah didn't give two shits about me. Why did you let her lie to everyone?"

"How did I know it was a lie?"

"Because she already tried to kill me once and you didn't bother to punish her for it!"

The softness melts from his face. "Do not raise your voice to me, Anita."

I swallow hard, unease prickling my spine.

"I'm not the traitor. I didn't kill my sister or start this war."

"I'm aware of that."

"So what's the problem?"

He places his elbows on the desk and tents his fingers, tapping them against his lips.

"You are the one with the problem—isolated, abandoned by your support network. Hated. But there is something you can do."

"What?"

He grins. "Me."

I blink at him and glance to Weir but his smug expression is far from inspiring.

"Partnering with me will do wonders for your damaged reputation. I am the leader, my endorsement means every-thing." Marshall's gaze drops to my thin vest. "Now, head to my rooms and get comfortable. After all this time, I'll show you how good I can make you feel. How good I made your sister feel."

You have to be fucking kidding me.

I lick my lips but my mouth is dry. "We've been over this."

"Do I have to order you to my bed, Anita? Is that what it will take for your surrender?"

I shudder at the leer on his face.

23

I can't bear anyone's touch after…

Not going there.

"There are some orders even I won't follow."

"You do not have a choice."

I brace myself, my chest tight. I'll fight, but two against one—one who is injured and weak—will result in me pinned to the floor, Marshall free to pillage what he's coveted for decades.

How did I mistake coldness for this calculated psychopath?

If he attacks me, I'm going for his carotid with my teeth. And his eyes. How easily they pop under the pressure of thumbs.

I clench my hands behind my back to hide my shaking.

"The People's Republic do not rape," I say with only a slight wobble. "We do not murder or torture. We are not cruel."

Weir and Marshall share a laugh. Marshall thrusts to his feet, his hands on his desk.

"You are as self-righteous as Ailsa. Always so certain of your place, but your place relies solely on me and I am tired of pretending. Please me, and I'll welcome you back into this faction. Refuse, and you will be executed as a traitor. You have one day to think it over." He flutters his fingers. "Take her below."

Weir strides around the desk. I back up. My mind scrambles as ineffectually as my hand on the door, the movement pulling my stitches.

"You can come quietly or I can drag you," Weir says, sneering at me. "Your choice."

"Oh, so now I get a fucking choice?"

"Only for this."

He reaches past me to tug open the door. I jerk away, hurt rippling through my healing wounds. Instead of leading me outside, Weir kicks at a rug in the corner, almost invisible in the black. He repeats his sweeping gesture over the gaping maw of a hatch. I hesitate, panic swirling in my stomach.

"I'd be more than happy to manhandle you, Anita," Weir says.

I fumble down wooden steps. A click floods the space with harsh light. Bars separate one side of the concrete room. Weir's breath moistens my hair. I clench my fists and stalk into the cell. The door shuts with a clang that punches into my gut.

"Why does Marshall have a cage beneath his office?"

"Maybe we're crueller than our manifesto suggests." Weir turns, one foot on the lowest stair. "You should be glad you have a bed for the night. Hannah and her buddies trashed your tent. I hope you didn't own anything precious."

He hits the switch and leaves me in the dark.

24

Ten years ago today, someone murdered my sister. Or I think it's today. It's hard to tell if the sun is up since I can poke my own eye without seeing my finger.

God, I wish Ailsa were here.

My muscles ache, the trauma of the rubber truncheon penetrating deep. I no longer suffer seizures or cardiac arrhythmias as a side effect of Wick's stun belt.

Just as well. If I needed specialist medication long-term, it would've run out with no means of replenishment, death following from a catastrophic seizure or heart attack.

But I'm still here. Still breathing.

Shame that's all I have to measure my life at the moment.

My back hurts the most, my brutalised tissues slow to heal. The resulting scars will forever remind me of the worst days of my life, alongside my badly repressed memories.

And the nightmares.

I shake the distress away. My gums are healed. I have fewer teeth, but not enough to cause impairment. My toes are crusted, the medics assuring me the nails will regrow over the next six months.

If I have six months.

Marshall can't shoot me for refusing to sleep with him.

Right?

"We don't do this shit," I whisper to the dark.

I'm more useful to him alive than dead, even if he can't get into my pants. Look what I delivered yesterday—certain victory for The People's Republic.

He should think about that instead of thinking with his dick.

Hell, he can brag to his buddies I'm terrible in bed and I'll keep my mouth shut. It's preferable to being a traitorous whore.

I need to convince him it's his own idea. A better idea.

If only I were as manipulative as everyone else appears to be.

Damn my kind and innocent nature.

I lie on my side in the lumpy bed and count the hours, the chill of the concrete seeped into my bones. Hunger claws at my stomach. The light sizzles on and blasts my retinas to cinders. By the time I blink the blindness away, Marshall stands in front of my cell, sliding a tray through a slot in the door. A bowl of porridge, a beaker of strawberry juice and the requisite nutritional supplements in their paper cup.

My last meal. Is it breakfast, lunch or dinner?

"Did you sleep well?"

I pause in chewing a mouthful of bland porridge and give him the glare he deserves. His mouth twitches.

Is he smirking at me?

"No, I suppose not." He curls one hand around a bar. "Is submitting to me really so terrible? All this unpleasantness will end. You might even enjoy yourself."

I surrendered to Wick, would've been raped without Stig's intervention.

Never again.

"Can we just say I did and get on with our lives? You make the lies disappear and I'll crush the bastards who started this war."

His eyebrows threaten to disappear into his shorn hairline. "Oh, Anita, it's hardly that simple."

"It's exactly that simple."

"You know what I want."

I shake my head. "Hannah was telling the truth—you are obsessed."

"Her jealousy certainly came in handy. You were too well-protected as faction sweetheart but Hannah destabilised that, with some encouragement, of course. And the effect you had on her…" His gaze slithers across my skin. "She tried so very hard to make me forget you."

Gross. Men are insufferable, sex-crazed morons.

"I'm a soldier, Marshall, not a whore. This can't be all you want."

"I've waited *decades* for this."

The porridge congeals in my stomach.

Sleep with him and get it over with, you stubborn bitch.

No. The thought of him touching me… My chest squeezes tight, bile bitter on my tongue. I struggle to conceal my panic.

"I'm not fucking you, Marshall. Pick something else."

He tuts. "I gave you a choice."

"You gave me two ways to destroy myself. That's hardly a choice."

"Only you would choose death over sex."

"Are you surprised?"

His teeth flash. "Not in the slightest."

He pulls his Glock from its holster. I leap to my feet, catapulting the bowl across the cell, the flimsy tray held in front of my chest as if it can stop bullets.

"Your death will not be that easy, Anita," he says, opening the door and flicking the barrel to encourage me out. "At first, I thought of a public execution but Southwell has been making a nuisance of herself, rallying all your little worker friends."

I stagger up the steps, the clomp of his shiny boots marching close behind. Moonlight silvers the broken shards of stained glass and bejewels the floor.

"I hope she enjoys gate duty, because she will be on it for the rest of her life. But I have something special for you. Something that will give you enough time to truly regret your decision."

Nervousness builds—not butterflies dancing in my stomach but snakes, their muscular bodies writhing, wriggling, biting. Goosebumps flare as I step outside.

"Tonight," Marshall says, his voice ringing with glee, "you will be dropped into Fellhill on a sensitive mission. You volunteered."

Soldiers of the Lost are the most radical faction, though they've gone quiet the last few years. They, too, amalgamated their encampments into one—Fellhill. And no one who approaches comes back. Worse than Rebel State. Sending me there is like banishing me to no man's land.

He might as well kill me himself.

Why didn't I choose the sex?

"Care to change your mind, Anita?"

I clear my throat, aiming for unruffled while screams bounce around my skull.

"Go fuck yourself," I say.

A slow smile spreads across his face. "Well, you're not going to."

I fix my gaze forward, my teeth clenched so hard, my jaw aches.

I'm not ready to die. To be captured or hurt again. I have no strength to run. I'll land in Fellhill and fall to my knees, my hands high in surrender, hoping for mercy.

What an optimistic fool.

It takes thirty minutes to reach the landing pad but none of it registers. My boots shuffle over dew-dampened grass towards a matte-black Silencer V12 helicopter on the central concrete area. Its blades turn in a hissing blur, the dark coating absent of insignia. A group of Marshall's cronies have gathered to one side.

The bastard knew what I would choose.

I stop beside the open sliding door of the passenger section. Marshall smirks, his eyes drinking in my pale skin and the sheen of my sweat.

I hate him more than Wick. Wick was an enemy and enemies are cruel. But Marshall is on my side.

I won't die in Fellhill. I'll make it back to wipe the sneer off his face with a bullet. I will survive. I *will*.

Pity I possess the intent but not the stamina.

Marshall reaches into the helicopter. "Put this on. I wouldn't want you to die of cold."

He thrusts a black military jacket into my hands. Ignoring his grin, I shrug it on, grateful for the fleece lining. The retractable wings he passes me are nanocellulose. I thread the straps over my shoulders and clip them around my chest, finding a position that doesn't hurt my lash wounds.

The nanocellulose provides a high strength to weight ratio, produced using algae from our biomass processes. The jet engines give an extra boost when gliding won't do.

"You're not just going to kick me out the helicopter?" I say, my voice more squeak than growl

"Too easy, Anita."

"What about weapons?"

A smirk sparkles in his eyes as he offers me a rose-pink L4 handgun. One lousy bullet. The weapon disappears into my fist and I ache to raise it and shoot his cold, despicable face.

"Get in the helicopter," he says, his Glock pointed at my heart.

I grab the flexible handle on the roof of the passenger compartment and haul myself inside, acclimatising to the encumbrance of the wings. The pilot performs his pre-flight checks, his features lost in the dimness. I settle my hand on the door to slide it shut and seal me into my black, black hearse.

"While you're there," Marshall says, failing to mask his grin, "ask which one of them killed your sister."

The door slams on mocking laughter. Kate and Lisa gesture at the head of the group ranged on the grass.

God, I hate them. *Everyone.*

I turn my back to their gloating and perch on a seat. The pilot speaks into a headset, craning his head to leer at me.

Weir.

I smother my surprise. It seems reckless for Marshall to risk his second in command's life. Or maybe Weir volunteered. The Silencer bristles with stealth and noise abatement technology but it isn't invisible. Fellhill could have anti-covert machinery.

I guess we'll find out if we burst into flames and plummet to the ground.

Weir engages the controls and the helicopter lifts. Soon

we're high, swinging towards Fellhill, my heart hammering.

If I could fly the damn Silencer, I'd club Weir and get the hell out. Calders isn't home anymore. Maybe I'd be better taking my chances in the unfamiliar chaos of the rest of the world.

It can't be worse than this.

I wipe the damp pools of my hands on my trousers, surveying the blackness below. My stomach churns, a headache zipping between my temples and down my spine. The straps of the wings squeeze my chest.

I'm going to die. Everything I've suffered in Ailsa's memory was for nothing. She'll never get justice.

And neither will I.

Where are those horrible gasping sounds coming from?

Oh. Me.

I shove my head between my legs, my pulse thundering behind my eyeballs. My vision darkens into a long tunnel and the inside of the helicopter drifts away, Weir in his pilot's seat as distant as the moon. The sensation is similar to five days of Wick's hospitality, minus the disturbing hallucinations.

I shriek inside my skull and struggle to hold myself together. This is not the place to reminisce. The thought of what Weir will do to my unconscious or gibbering body slows my breathing from hyperventilation to a pant. I stare at my scuffed boots, painted in a subtle green glow from the instrument panel.

"It'd be more fun if you put your head between my legs, Anita."

The spike in my blood pressure jolts my settling heartbeat, air rushing out from the tightness in my chest. It takes a few seconds to unclench my jaw and speak instead of growl.

"Don't you ever get tired?"

"Don't you ever put out?"

"No, I fucking don't."

"Then you only have yourself to blame."

"Me?" I say, my voice bordering on shrill. "For not wanting to be treated like a walking sex doll? For hoping you might actually respect me saying no?"

"I'd respect you a lot more if you put my dick in your mouth."

"If your dick goes anywhere near my mouth, I'll bite it off."

"You know, it's funny," Weir says, gently panning the joystick. "Marshall ordered us to approach you—me, Reece, a few other guys. He thought he'd look the gentleman and be your shoulder to cry on like he was before."

I should be shocked by the insidious bastard but I don't have the energy.

"I guess you can drop the act."

"Who says it's an act?" Weir stretches his long body in the pilot's seat, his hips thrust forward. "How about you be nice to me and I take you back to Calders? Marshall won't touch you if you're mine."

I suppress a shudder at the thought of his large-knuckled hands bruising my skin. There would be no tenderness, no reciprocity. A man demanding to be satisfied by his whore.

What the hell is everyone's obsession with sex? I'm not getting any but it doesn't turn me into a raving lunatic.

"I belong to no one," I say.

"Suit yourself. We're almost there."

Terror chases the heat and tingles to my fingertips. I force myself to slide the door open, grabbing the roof handle when my knees wobble. The blast of cool air soothes me a little, whipping my hair around my face.

I just have to stay alert, not panic. I'm a good soldier. I don't need to shag people to win my battles for me.

One bullet, one bullet, one bullet, moans the voice in my head.

The Silencer slows and hovers as quietly as a hunting owl. Lights encroach on the blackness, tinting the landscape bronze.

When did Fellhill become so huge? Their energy generation and defence systems must be strong to have so many lights running at night. Weaker encampments huddle behind blackout screens, praying the dark will shield them.

"Last chance, Anita," Weir says, grinning. "Swallow your pride—and something *much* bigger—and I'll turn this chopper around. You won't have to step one foot in Fellhill. Just get on your knees and open wide."

The edges of the L4 bite into my palm. "You can't possibly think I'll say yes."

"Makes no odds to me. Marshall should have taken what he wanted but he was too scared of Ailsa's saintly influence. You had the power to incite a revolt, but no longer." Weir straightens in his seat, adjusting the Silencer with a deft tilt of the joystick. "Either way, we have the weapon to win the war. And you're about to be chewed to pieces by the crazies in Fellhill because you won't spread your legs for your betters."

And he laughs. He laughs, confident in his position. He fought in few skirmishes, safe behind the lines with Marshall. Claiming the spoils without bleeding for them. He doesn't have to ward off unwelcome advances or mourn a murdered sister. He stands at Marshall's right hand, doing whatever the hell he wants.

Fury explodes white and hot.

"Fuck you, Billy."

"I wish you would, you frigid ice queen."

The back of his skull pops in a messy spray on the console, his lips still twisted in a smirk.

Did I pull the trigger?

Weir's corpse slumps against the harness, globules of tissue smearing the control panel. A perfect bullet hole decorates the centre of his forehead, its copy drilled into the glass of the cockpit.

I peel off the covering strip on the L4 and stick it to the back of my neck, hiding the gun under my hair. The Silencer yaws. I haul myself out of the door, launching into the night to avoid the slicing rotors. I risk a glance and spread the wings. They catch the air, slowing my descent from a freefall to a glide.

The tumbling black shape of the helicopter blocks a patch of cloud, its blades turning uselessly. It plummets to an expanse of grass on the edge of Fellhill and shatters into a starburst of smoking fragments that burn in the rough sward. Searchlights blaze in columns of white. An alarm wails, loud and long and plaintive, similar to our own.

Shit. What is wrong with me? Worse has been said by other smug bastards and I didn't shoot them in the face.

I guess I am good at killing my comrades.

I ignore my roiling stomach and dodge the sweeping searchlights.

Time to get my feet on the ground until they're switched

off. Who knows if I'm invisible to Fellhill's other detection systems.

Banishing the unhelpful image of my body erupting into a fireball, I focus on reaching the roof of a building without delivering myself into the arms of the frantic people filling the streets.

Continuing out isn't an option—with the encampment's extent, I won't have enough altitude to clear the laser-cameras on the boundary fence, and firing the jet engines to gain height will highlight me in the sky like a firework. I have to conserve fuel to avoid dumping myself in the middle of no man's land in the dark.

The wilderness is abomination territory.

Details sharpen as I drift closer, cool tendrils of air snapping my jacket. Trees and fields flank the side of a sports centre, a biomass plant on the opposite side where the running track used to be. Parking areas to the front and rear hold an assortment of military vehicles, not the cars of exercise enthusiasts using the gym.

The sports centre looms and I flap to slow my approach. My boots crunch on loose dirt and stone. I stumble a few steps on the shadowed roof, falling to my hands and knees. A second block soars above me, the building resembling two rectangles glued together.

Weir's blood clogs my nose. I retch, drooling bile into a clump of moss.

Why didn't I ignore him and jump out of the Silencer? I wasted my only bullet and alerted Soldiers of the Lost.

Unarmed, injured and vulnerable is no way to survive in Fellhill.

Even if the asshole deserved it.

Anita Carmichael—protector of the people.

I pass a shaking hand over my mouth. Best to worry about my decaying moral fibre later when not deep behind enemy lines.

Maybe Fellhill are unaware of me, the intruder in their midst. The helicopter could be a single attacker on a recon mission. Certainly not there to drop someone off. That would be madness.

Yeah, *madness.*

I secure the wings and crawl to the edge of the roof. A darkened alley separates the sports centre from the hulking biomass plant. Silver ducts curve from the roof of the factory and into the wall, like flumes in a swimming pool. A swathe of solar panels glitters in the moonlight.

No guards on the side door of the sports centre.

I dangle out, my hands clutching the edge, and lower myself, brick catching my clothes and scraping my skin. Stitches stretch and threaten to rip. The toes of my boots scuff the wall, scrabbling for purchase. My muscles tremble and I smother my unease.

Still so weak.

I release my hold and drop the last two metres. My knees, ankles and toes protest, the burning implosion slow to fade. Pain ripples between my healing injuries, my back particularly unhappy.

The side door gleams white in the darkness. I sneak past it towards the rear of the building. Voices approach. Loud, louder.

No time to run for the other end of the alleyway.

I curl my hand around the plastic handle of the side door and pull, expecting resistance but it swings towards me. Electric light emblazons across the concrete. I dive into the sudden brightness and pause in a small entranceway, a wooden bench nestled in a recess, a decaying mat covering the floor. Grey double doors lead into a corridor of blue linoleum. No security cameras.

Most factions look outward rather than in.

The voices stop on the other side of the wood.

Please don't come in. Please don't.

Soldiers of the Lost are fanatical. They bombed London and probably planted the explosive in the debating chamber. Rumours vary on what they do to all the people who disappear in their territory—eat them, torture them? They'll torture me. Whip me, beat me, *rape* me. Livingston on repeat, with an ending Wick would've enjoyed—my twisted, blood-soaked corpse, slaughtered after begging for mercy but receiving none.

The door stays shut. I wait one minute. Five. Ten. The voices continue to murmur.

Maybe they were pulled outside by the wail of the warning siren and have decided to enjoy the night air. They could come in any second.

Great. Now I'm trapped in a building in the middle of fucking Fellhill.

No bullets. No hope.

I hug the wall to keep from scraping my wings along the rough, white-painted brick. The first two rooms in the corridor contain chairs and desks, each with an embedded screen. No windows. The next two have steel benches and cupboards, sheets of silicone stacked to the side. I finger a pile of neat rectangles no bigger than my palm.

Data slides, freshly cut and ready to be imprinted.

25

I search the cupboards, rifling through boxes of safety goggles and snatching a black cylinder from a shelf. Cutting laser. Not exactly a weapon but I'm pretty sure it can do some serious eyeball damage.

I slide it into my pocket with a pat.

The corridor branches to another set of double doors leading into the reception. Through the vertical windows, a heavyset woman sits in a Perspex box talking to two soldiers, her eyes flicking towards the main entrance.

I dart past and melt against the wall. No shouts of alarm or running feet. The heating and ventilation system sighs from a grille above my head, the warning siren muted by layers of brick.

I sidle to the final door in the corridor and scuttle inside, dragging a short filing cabinet behind it, wincing at each scrape on the ribbed carpet. The room is cramped and dim, light filtering through the glass panel above the door. Battered filing cabinets line three walls leaving a glass partition free, yellowing blinds blocking my view. I pull one aside with a finger.

Moonlight through high windows silvers rows of chairs filling a hall. A basketball hoop hangs sad and disused, thickened with dust. The green glow of a peeling sticker floats in blackness.

Maybe I can make it.

Not that Marshall expects me to return. He'll be picturing my corpse paraded through the streets of Fellhill.

I imagine sauntering up to the gate, the expression on his slack-jawed face. Unless he removes me from the database, watching, instead, as I shriek and sizzle.

I frown and lean on a filing cabinet.

The logical option is to flee as far from Calders as possible. But I don't have enough equipment to survive alone in no man's land. Can't risk begging the savages in another faction for sanctuary.

I need to return to Calders. The dragon is *mine*. I suffered and bled for her. She and I will make The People's Republic great again. We'll win the war and find who murdered Ailsa.

That's all it's ever been about.

I push away from the cabinet. The wounds on my back throb, the dusty air tickling my throat. I kneel beside the partition, holding the blinds out of the way. The laser cutter detaches a neat rectangle of cool glass. I wriggle through the gap like a cockroach, my wings scraping the edge. My boots squeak on the scarred but polished wooden floor. The emergency door eases outward on oiled hinges.

Clear.

I step into the chill embrace of the night and meet the startled eyes of a man behind the door.

26

Time solidifies like frost on a blade of grass. The man blends with the shadows, the barrel of his SA80 swinging in a mesmerising arc. I smack it away from me and shove him hard in the chest. He sprawls on the ground, his rifle clattering to the concrete. I plough into the darkened woods beyond the path, cursing Marshall for not giving me a torch.

Or a machete. Or a machine gun.

"Hey!" A scrape and the crash of pursuit. The piercing shriek of a whistle blasts my eardrums. "Intruder! *Intruder!*"

Fuck.

A streetlight through the trees illuminates bristling branches, a path and a circle of grass. Unseen twigs scratch my face, tugging my hair and the wings on my back, aggravating my lash wounds. The ground dips and knocks me off-balance but I stumble on, thorns taking a bite out of my knee.

I need to lose the whistle-blower and get closer to the boundary. I'll fly the hell out of Fellhill, never to step foot in the place again. If the jet engines fail to deliver me to Calders, I'll at least be free.

Sprinting past slavering beasts in the dark seems a better choice than facing Soldiers of the Lost.

The soldier hounds me, blowing his whistle and shouting.

The attack alarm rises and falls in a goosebump-inducing howl, supporting a cacophony of people and dogs from every direction.

Please let it be the acoustics, not reality.

A root grabs my foot and I sail into a clump of bushes, my mouth full of pine and leaf mould. The soldier thrashes closer, his breathing as harsh as mine. I wait for the crack of a shot but the blast of his whistle swells and fades. I raise my forehead from the cool mulch, my hair tangled in the web of branches above me.

No one in sight.

I unravel from the shrubbery and limp to the tree line. Two crowds of soldiers and dogs advance along the path in a pincer movement. Voices echo behind me, the flicker of torches bright among the trunks.

Goddamn flanking manoeuvre.

I explode from cover and bolt over the path. Two steps and my boot finds grass covering a field of solar panels. Beyond it, streetlights show a canted chain-link fence, buildings and a road.

I plan to be airborne at the fence. It's too risky to head further on foot given the number of people chasing me. The searchlights have been turned off so I'll propel to a quieter, preferably higher, area and fly to freedom like before, albeit less spectacularly.

There will be no dragon's roar or smoking ruins in my wake.

"There she is!" a voice shouts.

I dash into the central aisle of the solar field followed by shouting people and barking dogs. I spread my wings and flick the protective plastic bubble on each handle to expose the ignition buttons for the jet engines.

Too late to worry about my visibility. I'll hug the roofs and hope their defences can't lock on at low altitude.

I'll be a stealthy firework.

Right.

My thumbs tense over the buttons.

A shot shatters the night.

A hard shove bowls me onto my face, reigniting the pain in my back. I scramble onto hands and knees, unclipping the wings and shrugging them off. Fragments tinkle to the grass.

Nanocellulose is strong but not impenetrable. Whatever they fired was armour-piercing.

I jump to my feet and whirl to face the advancing soldiers, both groups converging in a wave of humanity. German shepherds, freed from their leashes, bear down on me in a flurry of black and tan. I tense for the boom of another shot and a punch to the chest lifting me off my feet. I'll drown in my blood, watching my heart slow.

But I'll not go meekly to my death.

I rip the cutting laser from my pocket and target the closest dogs, dodging between the solar panels. Shrieks of pain shiver up my spine. A waft of roasting meat and scorched keratin confuses me somewhere between hunger and nausea.

The crowd pounds after me in a bellowing mass. I vault the fence at the edge of the solar field in one gazelle-like bound and dart between buildings into a narrow street, my mind empty of options. I focus on sprinting and not tearing myself apart.

Run and hide then think and plan. Escape will be easier

once things have calmed down.

Sure.

I stumble off a kerb and into the road, my boots crunching on loose gravel. Cracks lace the concrete as if heavy vehicles pass this way. It and the lack of cars are the only signs of irregularity. There are no scorched buildings or sucking mud, the pock-marking of bullet holes absent from stone.

The street dead-ends in a chain-link fence topped with barbed wire extending from the buildings to a row of garages. Paint-peeling metal doors mock me as I slam to a stop and hop from foot to foot.

Caught. I'm caught. Again.

Only if you stand here tap dancing like a fool.

The shadows of the last house obscure a black wheelie bin coated in grime and merging with a tangle of ivy. I grab the handles and drag it to the nearest garage, banging it into the door, scattering paint flecks to the concrete. The lid buckles under my weight but I boost myself onto the roof.

The crowd surges around the corner. I totter along the solid edge of the garage, avoiding the rusted corrugated metal in the centre. Below me, a path bordered by swaying grass leads to an underpass or deeper into more buildings.

A bullet whizzes past my ear. I flinch and slip, twisting in the fall, my arms flailing at the sky. I thump onto the path and slam my hands down but my head still hits the ground. The stars swirl between the gathering clouds and sink into my eyeballs. I open and close my mouth, too stunned to feel the pain in my back yet.

It'll be bad.

Footsteps scrape on the garage roof. Faces push against the creaking fence, pale fingers curled in the chain-link as if they're the prisoners and I'm free.

I wish.

Sitting up, I heave in a gasp and it becomes a shriek, my back hot and wet. I fight not to puke and collapse in it.

That would be embarrassing.

"Jeez-*Louise!*" a woman says, no doubt sneering at me.

Five soldiers stand on the edge of the garage, their faces bronzed by a nearby light. My eyes strain to focus on much beyond flashes: the fall of a woman's black hair, a mole on a man's cheek, the glint of dog-tag chains in an open shirt collar.

Maybe I have a concussion.

I climb to my feet and sway, my hands hanging at my sides.

What do they see as they judge me from their vantage point—an enemy to dispatch? Another prisoner to torment for entertainment?

Maybe I should ask if they know who I am.

I straighten my hunched shoulders.

I won't be tortured again. I'll run and force them to shoot me. Die while trying to escape, not insane from agony.

We stare at each other and their weapons droop. No one breathes. Perhaps they expect me to surrender.

Clearly, they don't know me.

I race towards the underpass, the blur of movement fracturing our unnatural tranquillity.

"Hey!" a second woman shouts. "Stop!"

So they can rip me apart with their bare hands? No, thanks.

I dive into a pool of blackness and burst out the other side. The path splits around ornamental stones perched in the middle of a circular area. I select the left path without altering my pace, dashing between barn-like structures onto another street. I turn left again at a wide road but don't stay on it. I climb the stone barrier of a bridge and drop onto a slope, crunching into vegetation and slithering down. My ankle twists, spilling me onto a concrete path. I clamber to my feet and limp into an underpass. Boots pound in the distance.

The route continues to a wasteland of churned earth and broken glass. Pillars support the road overhead, cracked slabs angling to the underside. I boost onto the gritty incline and scramble up, wriggling through a haze of sticky cobwebs into a damp space formed by broken slabs beneath the overhang. Blood trickles down my back, the material of my vest clinging beneath my jacket.

No voices tail me into the underpass. It's just me and the spiders under the bridge, panting quietly. Me, not the spiders. They tickle their merry way through my hair, covering me in a veil of shimmering silk.

The dogs may follow my scent and drag me from the shadows with their teeth but it doesn't keep me from enjoying the lull. It feels good to stop running for a moment. And losing the crowd buoys my flagging courage.

Now to concoct a brilliant escape plan leaving Soldiers of the Lost awe-stricken at my ingenuity.

I manoeuvre more comfortably into my hidey-hole.

The main gate is my only option. It's too risky to search for ancillary gates, the concealed tunnels used to escape an attack besieging the encampment.

When all is lost, there's no choice but to flee and regroup. To seize any chance at survival.

I smile in the dark.

Ah, the irrepressible hope of the human condition. I'm not the only one afflicted.

28

Groups of soldiers stomp and shuffle through the underpass, preceded by the clink of weapons. No one explores the darkness where road meets slope.

Fellhill's siren stops its caterwauling after ten minutes. Probably to avoid attracting other factions.

I don't kid myself that it signals the abandonment of their hunt.

Sheets of rain dampen the ground and make paste of the dust. Fifty minutes crawl by with no sign of people.

I scoot down the slope in an avalanche of dirt and stones, my filthy hands wiping the cobwebs from my face and scattering the branches tangled in my hair.

Have to look somewhat presentable. I am a professional.

I pat my weapons—one useless, one surprisingly effective—and creep to the end of the underpass, peering out over the waste ground lit from the road above.

It's too open to cross to the hulking factory buildings beyond.

The road at the top of the vegetated slope stretches empty in both directions. I jog to the next row of houses, skirting walls and ducking behind bushes. I avoid exposed, lighted areas, searching for transportation.

I need something big and armoured. Laser-cameras are less effective against a vehicle. The laser won't activate against a tank, having nothing organic to shoot at, but the camera warns the encampment of an imminent attack.

Someone is always watching.

Stealing a tank will be unlikely but awesome. Windowed vehicles aren't infallible, the lasers scanning through the glass.

I'll have to resist the urge to wave when driving out of Fellhill.

The streets stay deserted. My footsteps echo in the avenues, the thudding of my pulse loud across dark spaces.

I sneak along a hedge bordering a disused car park. A stone skitters behind me. I dart away, heart kicking, and veer towards a pub with boarded windows, the fruity-sweet hint of beer leached into the pavement. Two options greet me around the corner—a cluster of ancient commercial buildings, shuttered tight, or a field of tangled grass to a clump of trees. A shape flits from one trunk to another. I spin in the direction of the buildings and enter a square bordered by squat concrete structures, a paved zone in the centre. A footstep scrapes from my destination. I swerve for a corner appearing to be a way out. A shadow looms.

Oh god, I'm surrounded. My second escape attempt barely begun and already blown.

I scurry into an alleyway. LED bulbs along the edge of each roof carve a slice of artificial daylight in the narrow space and reflect in the puddles pooled on the uneven concrete.

What an arrogant waste of energy.

The roughcast of the commercial buildings ends in a high wall.

Maybe it's not too late. Maybe my stalkers have no clue

where I've gone.

I move to turn back and footsteps enter the alley.

"Put your hands on your head and turn around slowly. Any sudden moves and I'll shoot."

29

I've been manipulated into a trap, like herding a dim-witted sheep.

My fingers flutter over my pocket. Dying in a hail of bullets seems preferable to a future at the mercy of Soldiers of the Lost.

Who am I kidding? I want to *live*.

I raise my hands and link my fingers on top of my head, banishing the despair trembling across my face.

Show no weakness, only defiance and withering disdain.

A man stands with a .357 Magnum held at his side.

What the fuck. He's not even pointing it at me. How arrogant are Soldiers of the Lost?

Still, the gun reminds me of the moment I started on this awful path—when Peter aimed the same model at me over two weeks ago. Such a short but horrific space of time now coming to an end. Shame my passing will go unnoticed and unmourned.

No one grieves for traitorous whores.

My facade of nonchalance slips but I straighten my spine and meet the gaze of the man without flinching.

All is not lost, not until I stop breathing.

God, my hope and optimism are exhausting.

"What's your name?" my captor says, his chocolate-brown eyes curious rather than hateful. He towers over me, a navy t-shirt and jeans moulded to his broad chest and narrow hips.

He looks *good*.

My heart skips, surprising the hell out of me.

Perhaps I hit my head harder than I realised when I fell off the garage roof. Or the stress of the evening has pushed me into an insanity so profound I'm unaware of it.

Wait. How long has it been since he asked the question?

I clear my throat and say, "Anita."

"Okay, Anita, my name is Gizzy. Are you hurt?"

I stare as if another head has sprouted from his muscular shoulders.

"Sorry—what?"

"Are you hurt?"

Is this a trick? If I say no, will he hit me to prove me wrong? Or is he concerned about my well-being?

Nah, that can't be it.

I brace for the inevitable punch or slap. "No, I'm not hurt."

It's not entirely truthful but I'm not listing my wounds for his delectation.

We'd be here all night.

He doesn't seem angry, no hint of a derisive sneer. I try to keep the confusion off my face.

This is new.

"Why do you assume I'm going to hit you?"

I open and close my mouth to avoid a condescending response. He's being calm. I don't want that to change.

Check me out, all mature and sensible.

"Enemies aren't normally treated with delicacy," I say.

"Have you been a prisoner before?"

"Yes."

He tilts his head, his hair mussed and sticking up in spikes. "And they hurt you?"

"Of course they did."

Who is this guy, the Dalai Lama?

Interest bubbles in his expressive eyes.

Maybe he's pretending. When he gets to the torture, shattering my fragile trust will hurt more.

"What have you done to all the people who've disappeared in Fellhill over the years?" I say.

"Most joined us."

"They what?"

"Most of them joined us."

Yup, I'm trapped in a delusion. My body lies in the alleyway, twitching and slavering, driven mad by the pressure of capture, conjuring dreams of peace and love and goodwill between men.

"What happens if they don't want to change sides?"

"Hasn't happened yet."

Why would anyone choose to join Soldiers of the Lost? Their stupid bomb started the war in the first place. Who knows how many party leaders they assassinated.

Maybe they were the ones who shot Ailsa in the heart.

"Where are you from?" Gizzy says.

"Calders."

Respect sparks in eyes as warm as a mug of hot chocolate. "The People's Party?"

"Republic. That was when we were a party. When we were all parties. Now we're..."

"Lost?"

We share a bitter smile.

"Your attack was unusual. Buxton is very concerned."

"Buxton? I thought your leader was Simmons."

"We, ah, staged a coup a few years back. His methods were becoming a tad bloodthirsty." Gizzy takes a deep breath and rolls his shoulders. "I'm going to search you for weapons now. I don't want to shoot you but I will if forced."

"I don't have any weapons."

He laughs as if I've said something funny.

Our whole conversation is funny. He asked my name, wanted to know if I was hurt and was shocked when I expected him to hit me.

Maybe Soldiers of the Lost will turn out to be compassionate, honourable human beings instead of monsters.

Bomb a few thousand people and others think bad of you. Go figure.

Gizzy closes the gap between us, never taking his eyes off me. I fight the urge to squirm. He stops in a waft of applewood scent and holsters the gun.

"I'm going to pat you down, okay?"

Is he asking permission?

At my nod, he runs his hands down my cramping arms to my military jacket. He smiles when he pockets the cutting laser. I stay motionless. He crouches to slide his fingers into my boots and up my legs but he doesn't stray. His hands slip inside my jacket, caressing around the underwire of my bra. He moves to my sides and over my stomach, his skin separated from mine by the thin material of my vest. I lean towards the press of his fingers.

For fuck's sake. Apparently, I'm so starved of human affection, I become a slobbering moron to the first man who shows me the slightest kindness.

How embarrassing.

His questing hands pat my back. I hiss and he jerks away.

"What did I do? You said you weren't hurt."

"It's nothing. An old injury."

"What's wrong with your back?"

"I told you—an old wound. It flares up."

He ignores my narrowed eyes. "Turn around."

"No. It's nothing."

I keep my hands on my head. He circles but I face him and we spin.

"Let me see."

"Why?"

"I need to know how badly you're hurt. And, I want to know what's wrong. You've obviously been treated poorly. That won't happen here."

Treated poorly—understatement of the year.

Gizzy's gaze searches my face, his Magnum in its holster.

Why is he being courteous instead of slamming me to the ground and digging his gun into my head? I'm an enemy, a security threat.

He must be playing me.

I curl my lip and yank my clothes up, wincing as dried blood tugs at the wounds. "Fine. *This* is what's wrong."

He sucks in a breath. "Jesus! Who did that to you?"

"I don't want to talk about it."

No need to re-experience the misery. I'm content to pretend it never happened, that I'm not a victim.

"Who did that to you?" He clasps my arm, turning me to face the horror and sympathy in his eyes.

Well, damn.

Apart from my nightmares, I avoided shining a light on the

darkest period of my life, lest the memories shatter my fragile recovery. Other events, like being judged a traitor and booted into Fellhill, diverted my mind. But Gizzy is dragging it out, malicious intentions or not.

Shame bubbles up and stoppers my throat.

No, goddamn it, no crying. I've humiliated myself enough by mooning over him—not that he's noticed, hopefully—I'm not going to break down and complete my mortification.

"Anita?" he says, still holding my arm in a gentle grip. "Who?"

"Livingston," I choke past the bowling ball lodged in my trachea.

"Nationless? Weren't they destroyed a few days ago?"

"Just Livingston. Destroyed it when I escaped."

"I thought it was Revolutionary Front. They must have moved in to finish the other encampments after you left. Nationless are gone."

Christ, my actions led to the obliteration of an entire faction. So many people who had nothing to do with my torture. And nothing to do with Ailsa.

Sickened, I bow my head.

"We've heard stories of Wick and his torture chamber. *The twisted bastard.* Whipping wasn't all he did, though, was it?"

"No," I mumble into my shoulder, my hair a welcome curtain. "Don't make me talk about it. I don't want to remember."

Arms wrap around me in a careful hug and press my face into the warmth of his neck where his pulse jumps. I stiffen but the tenderness drowns the last of my defences and I start to cry. Gizzy murmurs soothing nonsense, stroking my hair.

It takes a while for my hitching sobs to abate but I feel better, lighter, despite bawling over an enemy. It doesn't mean I'm weak. I needed to let my true emotions show for an instant.

Even if everything goes to shit in the next few minutes.

I sniff and rest my forehead on Gizzy's collarbone. "Thank you."

Those two words seem pathetically little.

He steps back and smiles. He has a nice smile. I ignore the giant wet patch on his t-shirt, the evidence of my tears soaked into his clothes and damp against his skin.

"You can talk about it later when you're ready."

Later—the promise of a future where we can be close enough and trust enough to talk about the worst time of my life.

As if that's possible.

"Soldiers of the Lost haven't tortured a prisoner since Simmons was removed. You won't be harmed." Gizzy grimaces at his Magnum. "I need to take you back. Buxton wants to meet you. You've impressed him, which is pretty hard to do."

He smiles again. I manage the ghost of one in response.

Gizzy can't guarantee fair treatment, no matter what he says. He's not the leader.

I know what they're like.

Gizzy pats his jeans pocket. "You weren't lying about the weapons. What are you doing here without a gun?"

"Trying not to die."

"I'm sure we can help with that." He walks to the entrance of the alleyway, his back to me.

Either he's extremely arrogant or he trusts me already.

But I can't trust him.

30

The L4 yanks the delicate hairs from the back of my neck. I fist one hand in Gizzy's t-shirt and hold the gun to his head, wobbling on tip-toes. Warmth pulses off of him. He tenses and I expect him to rage or call me a cold-hearted bitch. I hope he doesn't struggle because I have no fight left in me.

Oh, and no bullets. Mustn't forget that.

"I lied," I say, "sorry. But you can't guarantee I won't be harmed, as much as you might believe it."

He relaxes in my grip. "Buxton's a good leader—fair and strong and rational. He's not cruel. He won't hurt you unless you hurt one of us."

"All leaders are cruel. Some are better at hiding it."

Gizzy turns his head, his eyes sending a shiver through me. "One day I hope you'll trust me enough to tell me about it."

Trusting someone makes it too easy for them to hurt you.

"Maybe one day," I say. "Right now, I need to get back to Calders. Put your hands on your head."

I ease away, reclaiming the cutting laser plus his Magnum. He watches me—all interest, no bitterness.

"I'll never live this down."

"Don't beat yourself up. It was very small and I'm very good."

Heat fills his eyes. "Yes, I see that."

Shit, maybe he noticed my response to him and just showed better self-control.

I drop my gaze when I find myself staring at his mouth.

Great. My repressed sexuality chooses this moment to haunt me. Thanks a lot, libido.

I put the L4 into a pocket of my jacket, the glue no longer strong enough to stick. I hold Gizzy's Magnum at my side.

"Do you have a plan to get back to Calders?" he says.

"I'm pretty much winging it. Oh, you can lower your arms."

"I don't want to upset you but no one has ever escaped. Buxton won't open the gate and if you injure or kill anyone to encourage him, he'll execute you. Won't you stay? Come with me and I promise you'll be safe."

"I need to try. I have unfinished business." There's a dragon to take back and a faction to rescue from a lying snake of a leader.

We're The People's Republic. We didn't strike first but, by god, we will strike last, motherfuckers.

That can be our new motto.

Gizzy sighs. "Okay, I'll help if I can but you won't get far. I don't want you to get hurt."

"I've been hurt before."

He looks sad. I drop my gaze a second time.

"What about ancillary gates? Can you get me to one of them?"

"We don't have any."

I frown. His face appears open, honest, but I'm not the best judge of character right now. I guess it's implausible but not impossible. It says a lot about Fellhill. Soldiers of the Lost must be pretty confident in their defences to forgo escape routes.

"Okay, what about an armoured vehicle?"

"There's one in my garage. It's not far."

Better than strolling, unprotected, to the main gate.

"Lead the way. Hopefully, we won't meet anyone else."

"And if we do?"

"I'll worry about it when it happens."

"Winging it?" He smiles.

I smile back, fighting a warm glow in my chest.

This stupid girlish crap is really inconvenient.

We walk out of the commercial square and into the empty streets. He leads me through darkened trees and fields of slumbering cows. We climb a slippery footpath beside a burn, guided by the moon among the clouds. Buildings surround the hill and we pick our way onto a road.

"How many times have you been taken prisoner?" he says between breaths.

Does being locked up by your own faction count?

"Twice," I say. "The first was Revolutionary Front."

We seem to be heading for the sports centre. I try not to be mesmerised by the slide of muscles under his t-shirt, the bunch and flex of his ass.

"How did you destroy Livingston?"

He looks over his shoulder and I yank my gaze up, hoping the night hides my blush.

"Stole their secret weapon and ruined them with it."

I picture the dragon sitting in the dusty garden centre awaiting my return.

"What was their secret weapon?"

"You won't believe me unless you see it for yourself."

"Try me."

"A dragon."

"Come again?"

"A dragon. A mechanical dragon."

He frowns.

"Told you," I say. "Nationless built themselves an indestructible weapon controlled by a brain-computer interface."

Wick would be proud at my final understanding of his great beast. Too bad he's dead.

"Sounds amazing. War-ending, in fact."

"She is. She's the best thing this war ever gave me."

"She?"

I duck my head. "Um, yeah. You can't call her an *it*."

We walk a little further, following the main road deeper into the encampment.

Is he herding me into another trap? I doubt it, but I'm not myself. Especially since I can't stop gawping at his butt, framed perfectly in his jeans.

Jesus. Bring back the sneering bastards.

"I'm confused. If the dragon is unstoppable, why not flatten us with it, *everyone* with it? Why send you into Fellhill? Marshall did send you, didn't he?"

Like I'd choose to come on such a mission all by lonesome.

"Marshall and I no longer get on." Another understatement. The evening is awash with them. "He wants me dead."

"Why?"

"He thought he could coerce me into his bed. I said no."

"He wants you dead because you won't sleep with him?"

"Pretty much."

"That's crazy. I thought he was a decent leader?"

"So did I. But he helped convince most of Calders I was a traitor."

"Because you wouldn't sleep with him?"

"Yup."

Gizzy grins. "You must be good."

A surprised laugh bursts from my throat. "He'd be bitterly disappointed after all the expectation. But he gave me a choice—sex with him or this. Like I said—leaders are cruel."

"Most women would've said yes to the sex."

"I'm not that easy."

"So I'm beginning to understand. What're you going to do if you get out of here?"

If, not when.

"Take back my dragon and burn the cancer out of The People's Republic."

"Then destroy the rest of us?"

"I'm not interested in destroying the country or ruling the world. I just want some answers."

And destruction was Wick's ultimate plan. Anything he considered a valid attack strategy is abhorrent.

Gizzy leads me down a quiet street to a modest semi-detached house, the road overlooking a school. We crunch up the gravel driveway to a garage at the side. He unlocks it and I help pull it open, rust flaking onto my palms, the Magnum scraping metal. A forest-green Venus-DR sits in the darkness, a rampant unicorn prancing on the drivers' side door. A PA speaker and four round lamps on a roof bar wink in the glow of the streetlights, in front of the dissolution ray.

Gizzy produces another key and dangles it in front of me. "You want me to drive?"

I nod. He climbs in. I hesitate, my hand on the open door.

"Can you drive out if I hide?"

"We keep a log. Buxton informs the guards of any movement. We don't leave often, and not at this hour."

I glance at the dashboard—one o'clock in the morning. Exhaustion swells as if an awareness of the time is enough to make me realise how tired I am.

I settle into the leather seat, gingerly leaning back. The engine purrs and Gizzy pulls out of the garage. The passing streetlights silhouette him as he concentrates on the road. I force my gaze out the window to the blurred landscape slipping by, the interchanging blackness and lighted streets. My eyelids droop, lulled by the motion of the vehicle.

But I'm a seasoned warrior. I won't fall asleep. Only a little rest to recharge and prepare myself for the next battle. No longer—

"We're coming to it now," Gizzy says.

I jerk, my gaze flying to the clock.

Shit. I dozed for over thirty minutes. He could've done anything.

"Okay," I say, and scrub my face. "Drive as close as you can."

How could I relax my guard? He's my enemy, not my friend, despite his kindness.

The Venus-DR turns a corner and the main gate of Fellhill slithers into view.

31

The road curves to a foreboding structure of metal bars and electrified wire, the shimmering of the particle beams on either side difficult to spot in the dark.

Our vehicle won't ram through the gate nor will the dissolution ray dissolve it, according to Gizzy. It turns people into puddles, nothing inanimate.

More technology from the friendly Africans who brought us flesh-melting, semi-invisible fences.

Opening the gate will be no easy feat. A fingerprint and retinal scan plus a numeric password unlock the first horizontal bolt. A key releases the second. The third bolt only functions when the first two disengage. Compounding the fancy trickery, five guards stiffen at our approach. One man speaks into a headset.

Damn. It's about to get crowded.

Gizzy halts a few metres away and yanks the handbrake.

"Turn the roof lights on," I say, shifting in my seat.

The soldiers squint into the white glare, their faces pale but their Uzis steady.

"How do you work this PA thing?"

Gizzy leans over, flicking a switch and handing me the black microphone. A curled wire attaches it to the main system mounted under the dashboard.

I depress the button on the side. "I have Gizzy. Drop your guns and put your hands up or I'll shoot him."

My voice, though tinny and crackling from the speakers, is somehow calm and authoritative. I lower the window a crack to hear their response.

The three men and two women stare.

"Tonight would be nice," I say while they pretend to be statues. "Drop them *now*."

The Uzis clatter to the ground. The guards clap their hands on their heads and scowl into the light.

"Okay, one of you use the scanner. And quickly, please, I don't have all night."

No one moves. I sigh.

"We don't have clearance," a woman says, her crimson hair bleached almost pink in the beams.

I turn to Gizzy. "She's bullshitting, right?"

"Carrie-Anne is our finest bullshitter."

He smiles. I smile back. Aren't we getting along fine?

"Nice try but I'm not stupid," I say. "Do it."

They remain motionless, their faces set. The microphone box hisses and pops.

"Fine. I hope you're not fond of Gizzy."

"Ouch," he whispers.

I snort and raise a shushing finger to my lips. I juggle the items in my lap, holding the gun beside the microphone and pulling the hammer back to produce a satisfying *chuck* through the speakers.

Gizzy blinks serene eyes at me.

A short guy skips forward, sweat beading on his forehead. I sag a little in my seat.

If they call my bluff, it's over. My opportunity to flee will vanish when confronted by an enraged crowd and their—maybe fair, maybe not cruel—leader.

Gizzy won't sit placidly while I liquefy his comrades with the dissolution ray.

"Thank you," I say to the short guy. "Go ahead."

Manners may make them aid my escape out of politeness. Or not.

The guy spins to the control panel and stabs at the buttons. A small light on the console changes from red to green. He hops back into line, putting his hands on his head.

"Now the password."

Does my voice travel in the still air? How close are the crowd?

"We don't have the password," Carrie-Anne says, arching a perfectly plucked eyebrow.

I turn to Gizzy.

He grins. "Bullshitting."

"Carrie-Anne, punch in the fucking password or kiss your lovely face goodbye."

Time is too short for pleasantries.

Cheeks flushing, she whirls and jabs at the control panel. A thump signals the unlocking of the first bolt.

Close. I'm *close*.

"You won't get away," Carrie-Anne says, folding her arms and re-joining the line. "Since you're apparently not stupid, you must know that."

"Oh, I know it."

"Then why bother?"

"I have to."

She shrugs. My headache returns, hammering the centre of

my forehead. The back of my neck tingles.

"The key, please, people."

I glare at Carrie-Anne, though she probably can't see me through the blaze of lights. Her eyes glitter and she purses her lips.

"They don't have the key," Gizzy says. "Buxton does."

My fingers tighten on the microphone box.

Why the hell didn't he tell me earlier?

"A heads-up would've been nice," I say, releasing the button.

His eyes remain steady. "I told you no one has escaped. I had to stop you from concocting another desperate plan. I meant it when I said I didn't want you to get hurt."

My anger deflates, leaving me hollow.

I'm not going anywhere. Not getting out of Fellhill. Forced to be a prisoner in another faction for the third goddamn time.

Three's lucky, right?

I open my mouth to instruct Gizzy to ram the bars but doubt his helpfulness extends to wrapping the vehicle around his main gate like a pretzel.

Shouting cuts across our happy gathering and a crowd swallows the Venus-DR. A tall man steps from around Gizzy's side of the vehicle, his blond hair shaved close to his skull. A single diamond flashes in his ear.

"Drop the gun, intruder, and release Gizzy." He holds a hand over his high forehead, shading his face against the glare. His eyes are a light colour, maybe blue.

"Buxton?" I say.

Gizzy nods.

"Sorry, Buxton, no can do. Not until you open the gate. I have other places to be." I pause. "No offence."

Aren't I hilariously adorable? Now, let me out the damn gate.

"No can do," Buxton says, quirking his mouth.

"Why not? Open the gate."

"Let Gizzy go."

"I'll let him go when you open the gate."

"I will not let you escape, intruder. Put down your weapon and exit the vehicle. You won't be harmed unless you hurt one of mine."

"Open. The. Gate. Or I shoot Gizzy."

He must recognise the bluster. I can hardly shoot Gizzy and climb over his body to reach the pedals before the crowd drags me from the vehicle and stomps me to death. Slaughtering the one man who showed me compassion would be cold, even for me.

"You're alive because you haven't shot anyone. If you shoot Gizzy, I'll kill you myself."

Frustrated tears burn my eyes.

Maybe it won't be so bad. Soldiers of the Lost are strong, secure, and Gizzy appears to like me without being creepy, like most men.

I sigh, loud in the intimate confines of the Venus-DR.

Gizzy shifts in a creak of leather. "You'll like it here and you'll become one of us. You could've done worse."

The People's Republic to Soldiers of the Lost? I guess I am a traitor.

But I can't leave Marshall to ruin my sister's legacy.

"Give yourself up, you have nowhere to go," Buxton says.

I hold the Magnum out to Gizzy and force my fingers to release it. He turns the engine off and slips outside. The night seems blacker with the loss of the headlamps, the inside of the vehicle chilled. I square my shoulders and pop the handle. The door slams, harsh in the silence of a thousand staring bodies. Gizzy waits at Buxton's side, his eyes fixed on me.

"Relieve her of her other weapons, please, Gizzy. The rest of you return to your quarters."

Gizzy holds out his palm with a half-smile. I place the cutting laser and the L4 on it. Buxton cocks an eyebrow as if to say, "That's all?"

Yup. That's all.

The crowd disperses, casting curious glances at me. Buxton, Gizzy and the five guards stay behind. The sentries reclaim their Uzis and resume their positions. Carrie-Anne favours me with a 'told you so' eye roll. I resist the urge to give her the finger.

"What now?" I say.

Buxton re-cocks his eyebrow. "Now, we talk."

32

Buxton's office is in the old school near Gizzy's house and contains the bare minimum of furniture, the decor utilitarian. My reflection watches me from the windows in one wall, the glass free of smudges.

Excitement over, my body reminds me I'm a slave to some of its basic functions.

I clear my throat. "I need to use the bathroom."

Buxton nods at Gizzy from behind his spotless desk. "Take her but be quick. There's a lot to talk about."

Ignoring the ominous undertone, I follow Gizzy into the darkened corridor, the office lights spilling across grey linoleum and magnolia walls. Windowed doors are squares of black into multiple rooms. Our footsteps echo, our shadows increasing as we move further away. I peek at Gizzy then frown at the scuffed toes of my boots. He stops at two wooden doors, one with a faded sticker of a figure in a dress. I go to enter and he places a hand on my arm.

"I'll be right out here."

What's he implying? He'll hear if I try to run? Or he's close if I fancy a quick shag on the bathroom floor?

I swallow. "Okay."

He squeezes my bicep and the door swings shut. Five

cubicles sit opposite three porcelain sinks and a large mirror. The sharp tang of bleach sears my nose. Misted-glass opens into the night, too small to shimmy through. I use the facilities and flush the toilet, washing my hands under the sputtering taps, the pipes clanking in the walls. I soak a paper towel and wipe most of the mud off my face, picking a leaf from my hair. Dark circles ring bloodshot eyes when I muster the courage to meet them.

What if a husk stares back, like Stig? Wearied by the things he's seen and done.

I pray that day of hopelessness never comes but I can't go on like this.

Turning around, I lift my jacket and vest. Scabbing welts slash my back in raw, crisscrossing lines, blood dried in flakes. The purple sutures are harsh against my pale skin. The sight of it depresses me and I start to lower my clothes but Gizzy pushes inside the room. His eyes search my face.

"I wanted to know what it looked like," I mumble.

His expression softens and my heart does a disconcerting flip. He takes my hand, settling the jacket at my waist and entwining his fingers in mine. I freeze while he tucks a straggle of hair behind my ear and traces my jaw. His thumb strokes my palm, firing nerve endings and fluttering in my belly.

Oh god, say something. Stop him.

I don't want him to stop.

The gentle caress continues down my neck, shoulder and arm, his hand ending on my hip. Our bodies nearly touch. I close my eyes, too dizzy to meet his gaze. His breath warms my lips.

What if I've forgotten how and slobber like an enthusiastic

dog? He'll shove me away, wipe his mouth and storm out, leaving me to curl under the sinks.

Or what if it's amazing?

I tilt my head back. The heat of him surrounds me and sizzles to my fingertips.

The door bursts open. We jump apart.

"Time is passing," Buxton says.

Gizzy glances at me. "Sorry, sir, we were, ah…"

"Come on then."

Buxton disappears back into the corridor. I force my wobbling legs to walk, my cheeks burning.

Without the interruption, would I have shown restraint? Nice to think so. Preferable to the suspicion I was one second from climbing Gizzy's body and demanding he fuck me.

My pulse steadies by the time I ease myself into the chair facing Buxton's desk.

Back to toughened soldier instead of panting nympho.

What was I doing, almost letting Gizzy kiss me? He could have murdered Ailsa, though it was more likely Simmons.

"What is your report?" Buxton directs at Gizzy sitting beside me. He ignores me despite his insistence for my presence.

"Anita is from Calders, sir. The People's Republic." Gizzy glances at me then recounts the main points of our interaction in a calm voice.

"This dragon," Buxton says, gracing me with his attention, "it's indestructible? Nothing can damage it?"

I jerk, struggling to keep my gritty eyes open. "Nothing I've seen."

He rubs his fingers over his mouth, a deep frown between his brows. I hide a smile.

He's right to worry. The dragon means annihilation in the wrong hands.

And she is in the wrong hands.

Buxton leans back in his chair, the relaxed posture at odds with his sharp grey eyes. Gizzy shifts in his seat, his fingers drumming the arm rests. I wait for Buxton to speak. He takes a breath and lets it out.

Here it comes.

"You are our prisoner," he says, stating the blatantly obvious, "and an enemy from one of our greatest rivals. I cannot accept you into the Lost without proving yourself. After you've been tested, you can join us."

"I didn't realise entry into your faction had conditions. Have you tested everyone this way?"

"No one else brought news of such a valuable machine. To keep Fellhill safe, I must secure it. In order to do this, you will return to your encampment tomorrow night, steal the weapon and come back here, to be welcomed as one of us. Consider it your initiation. Now—"

"No."

Surprise registers on his austere features. Gizzy goggles at me.

I guess no one refuses Buxton's orders.

Funny, I'm getting a taste for insubordination.

Buxton composes his face but I keep speaking. "The dragon belongs to The People's Republic."

"Your loyalty for your faction is commendable but misplaced."

"We just need a change in leadership. I'm sure you understand."

He barks a laugh. "Look where you are, Anita. This is not a negotiation."

"It kinda is when I have something you want."

"Something you will bring me willingly"—he leans back in his seat, his face smug—"for I know who killed your sister."

I flinch, my hands gripping the arm rests.

"Oh, yes, I recognise you. Your reputation as Ailsa Carmichael's vengeful sibling precedes you."

"Who killed her?"

"All will be revealed when you return with the machine."

"Fuck, no!" I leap to my feet, my fists clenched. "Tell me now or I'm not going anywhere."

Buxton stiffens, spots of red colouring his cheeks. Gizzy sends a pleading look my way.

"Let's cut the bullshit," I say, and plant my knuckles on the desk. "You want the dragon but won't risk your ass to get it. You don't care about sending me in because it doesn't matter if I die. You dangle this convenient titbit and expect me to bubble with gratitude instead of demanding the truth. I refuse to be your goddamn delivery girl unless you prove it's not a lie."

A battle rages across Buxton's face. "I do not lie. If you refuse to do this, you are useless to me and will be shot."

Useless? I am not, and will never be, useless.

"Who murdered my fucking sister?"

Gizzy cringes in his seat as our conversation degenerates into growls, like two wolves snapping at each other. Buxton yanks at a drawer and palms a small, unfamiliar handgun model, his fingers curled around it.

"You do not speak to me like that. Now sit *down*."

I cock an eyebrow. "I've been threatened by guys with guns for the last millennia. Excuse me if I don't pee in my pants."

"Then you should know how this goes. You do what I say, or I shoot you." Buxton's hand tightens on the gun. "Sit. We are not finished."

I wait long enough for his jaw muscles to bunch then I lower myself into the chair.

He clasps his fingers over the weapon. "Do you always have to be coerced at gunpoint before you'll do anything?"

"Do you always drop bombshells to manipulate people into doing your bidding?"

"Anita, don't," Gizzy says, holding out his hand as if sheer force of will can stop me from mouthing off.

He'll be lucky.

Buxton swallows, hard and loud, like it hurts. "I cannot let you go and I cannot leave the machine where it is. I want it because I want to win."

"You don't deserve to win."

"And The People's Republic do?"

"It wasn't our bomb in the debating chamber ten years ago."

The smugness returns to his face. "Are you sure?"

Why do people keep asking me that?

"We are the good guys," I say through gritted teeth. "We didn't strike first."

"I know your little mantra quite well, thank you."

"And what's yours? Some shit about chaos."

"Only true chaos brings great change."

"Well, congratulations—you did it. Shame it wasn't a change for the better."

He shakes his head. "Ten years is long enough to be blamed for someone else's crime, especially when party squeamishness banned us from the debate in the first place. The dragon finally gives us the means for justice."

"Tell me everything, right goddamn now, and maybe I'll get her for you."

"You will get her, whether I tell you or not."

We glare at each other across the desk. Gizzy attempts to dissolve into his seat.

How has he survived this long if confrontation makes him uncomfortable? We're in the middle of a bloody war zone.

"*Maybe* I'll get her, but if you want me to risk my life, you can send me with a team—no, a goddamn battalion—of soldiers. Dispatching me alone is a suicide mission and I'm fucking *sick* of those."

"Don't be ridiculous. You're returning to your faction, how is it a suicide mission? I will not jeopardise my men to make you feel better."

I curl my lip to snarl something abusive when Gizzy interjects. "Marshall wants her dead, sir, that's why she's here. You would be risking her life to send her alone."

Buxton frowns at Gizzy, barely a wrinkling of the brow, but Gizzy bows his head.

"Regardless, it is not worth the gamble or up for debate. I don't want you to die but I cannot send anyone with you. I won't risk my men for you." He sweeps the gun into the desk. "In a few minutes, I believe nothing will keep you from returning. You will, in fact, be eager to go."

"So quit being a tease and spit it out."

His nostrils flare but he slaps a tablet onto the desk. I peer at the dark screen.

"Some say ignorance is bliss, Anita."

"Ignorance is for the weak. Show me."

Buxton swipes his finger on the screen and selects a video file. The image shows a semi-circular array of chairs facing a podium, wood-panelled walls and people frozen in place. The date stamp in the bottom corner says 30/04/2030.

The day Scotland was lost.

"How did you get this? The security footage was wiped."

"We stole it."

"Why, for god's sake?"

"Chaos. And validation."

"If you didn't want to be excluded, you shouldn't have bombed London or weaponised the border fence."

His finger hovers over the tablet. "Our exclusion is what saved us."

The video fast-forwards, people zipping to their seats. Ailsa steps behind the podium.

"Play it. I want to hear her."

"There's no sound."

"Play it anyway."

Buxton prods the play icon. Ailsa addresses the crowd, her face bright with enthusiasm, her blonde bob tucked behind her ears.

She talked about unity. Our exciting future. The establishment of our independent government and the slow removal of the border fence once England accepted the new status quo.

I cared little for independence. She inspired me to care.

I try to find myself in the gallery but the camera must have been mounted in the gantry above me. The video shivers. Stone, wood and smoke billow into the air.

So much smoke.

"Smoke bomb," Buxton says, "though packed with enough explosive to kill the leader of the Green Party. Before they became Guardians of Scotland, of course. May they rest in peace."

He closes the video, the screen filled with grey, and selects another. Nearer to the podium. Ailsa uses it to pull herself to her feet, dust powdering her clothes.

I remember my panic, scrambling through and over the

desperate people fleeing from the gallery. Soft flesh under my shoes. The wail of the alarm. Screaming.

I had to get to my sister.

A figure drifts from the swirling smoke. I sway in my seat, the blood not just draining from my face but all the way to my toes. I barely feel Gizzy's hand on my shoulder, my nose pressed to the tablet.

Marshall's hair is longer. I forgot it had a curl to it.

He shoots Ailsa three times in the chest and withdraws into the fug, leaving his wife gasping on the floor.

I can't breathe, either.

Buxton eases the tablet away. "They planned it meticulously, each kill different so it looked as though several parties were involved. They murdered anyone else who saw them but there were few since they moved through the smoke like ghosts."

The image opens to Weir and a garrotte.

"Leader of Alba gu Brath, née Scottish Libertarian Party."

Daniel Wick sprawls on the ground, his crimson halo bright in the smoke. Reece stands over him, gun pointed down.

"Leader of the Lib Dems," Buxton says, clicking on another file.

"Leader of Embra, née Scottish National Party."

A slender figure with a perfect ponytail plucks a throwing knife from a body on the floor.

"Leader of Revolutionary Front, née National Front."

Lisa. A hammer. Globs of skull and tissue.

"Enough," I whisper. "Enough."

Buxton slips the tablet into his magical drawer. My fingernails bite into the wood of his desk.

"So you see, Anita," he says, "The People's Republic have never been the good guys. You may have to find a new motto.

Nos occidit eos perhaps?"

He graces me with a pitying smile and I vomit all over his carpet.

34

Soldiers of the Lost are the good guys. God, that leaves a bitter taste in my mouth. They bombed London, weaponised the border fence and destroyed the transport network to cut off the flow of refugees, marooning everyone in this nightmare created by The People's Republic.

But *I'm* the bad guy.

I've killed so many people in the name of vengeance, the blaze of my self-righteousness blinding me to everything else. Nothing mattered except finding my sister's killer.

The motherfucker was in my faction all along.

"We'll get who did this," he said when I cried on his shoulder. "They'll pay for what they've done."

He turned me into a monster.

I pace in my cell from the single bed to the archway that opens into a smaller room with a toilet and sink, the air heated by the purr of a boiler. The mattress and pillow are stuffed with down instead of scraps of random material or nothing at all.

It's the nicest cage I've ever been in and a luxury compared to my tent and the metal slab I slept on.

We evacuated Buxton's office after my stomach trouble the night before. He dismissed Gizzy, who saluted and marched away without argument, flashing me an apologetic glance. Buxton directed me to a cell in the basement of the building and I was too numb to protest.

I woke to the faces of everyone I've killed. And the faceless. The ones I murdered for following a psychopath of a leader.

Oh, the irony.

It has to stop. I have to stop killing before I become just another sociopath. Every person I slaughtered was innocent. Okay, maybe not innocent.

But the war twisted us all.

How do you apologise for a decade of misplaced blame? A gift basket won't quite do it.

The least I can do is tell the truth and end the war with the minimum of bloodshed. Use the dragon to force a surrender for the stupid bastards who'd rather die a martyr's death, screaming their faction's name. The fighting will be over and we, the survivors, can create some normality.

After ten years of darkness, it's time for us all to live.

* * *

Footsteps advance down the corridor and Buxton pushes the door wide, dressed in camouflage fatigues, though perhaps he doesn't wear anything else.

"You look rested. Are you ready?"

I blink at him. Mud and sweat streak my skin, my hair a tangled mess. My clothes are rumpled, my boots one hard scrape from falling to pieces.

"As ready as I'll ever be," I say after sorting through several responses in my head, "but I have another condition."

"Again, Anita, you are in no position to demand conditions.

When you return, you must conform to how this faction is run."

"I can conform. I'm great at conforming."

Air hisses through his nose. "What is your condition?"

"I want a say in what happens with the dragon. I want continued access and to never do any more fighting."

Who says I have to return with her to Fellhill? The People's Republic is overdue a coup. I'll leave Buxton gnashing his teeth while I clean house. He'll be the one who has to conform.

There's a plan I can get behind.

"Agreed," he says. "Now, follow me."

I hurry after his long-legged stride to his office, the setting sun bathing the room in coral light.

No Gizzy.

"I thought it'd be more comfortable for you to eat here," Buxton says, gesturing for me to sit. "We need to discuss tonight."

I select the same chair, the carpet scrubbed clean. Spread on the desk is a steaming bowl of vegetable soup, a plate of chicken and brown rice, and a bowl of apple pie and custard. Next to it sits a mug and a glass pot.

"Real coffee?"

"Of course. Do you take milk and sugar?"

"You have sugar?" The show off. I nod yes to both. "How do you have the resources to make sugar, rice and coffee? And keep lights on at night?"

"Our power generation is extremely efficient."

I sip the coffee, the mug cupped in my hands. I want to bathe in the steam.

"Fine, you have a wonderful power source. But how do you replicate the growing conditions?"

"In specially built greenhouses. It took us years to perfect but the effort was worth it. Small luxuries boost morale. We even have chocolate."

I splash coffee on his desk. "You do not."

"It's not as good but I've forgotten what the real stuff tastes like. My soldiers enjoy it."

I shake my head and tuck into the meal, not a vitamin pill to be seen. Buxton clears the dishes. I pour a third cup.

"What?" I say to his quirked eyebrow. "Some of us haven't tasted this in a long time."

No more, though. I don't want to get jittery, or need to pee every five seconds. No man's land is not the place to be caught with my pants down.

I don't want to go out there.

Darkness creeps into the office and Buxton switches on the overhead lights. He pulls a map from one of the filing cabinets lining the wall and spreads it on the desk.

"I've plotted the best route. I can drop you here, on the edge of Revolutionary Front." His finger taps the old map over a place called Linlithgow. "They seem to have no idea what goes on in their territory. My scouts pass through all the time. Nationless is a different story. The vultures aren't finished picking over its carcass and any moving vehicle is a target but a single person on foot should go unnoticed. From there, it'll take you no more than three hours to Calders at a brisk pace."

Jesus, what if I bump into Nationless survivors? If they learn who I am, they'll rip me apart. Or they'll do it anyway, for fun.

"Take care around this river—there's a den of wolf-like creatures in its vicinity. Once across, it's not too far south to your main gate." He glances up. "I hope you'll be allowed entry."

And not get fried to a crisp or shot on sight. I hope so, too.

I open my mouth and Buxton's gaze sharpens to cut me off. "I can't send anyone with you or drop you closer. That is non-negotiable. It's imperative Calders are not alerted to your double agent status. I cannot provoke Marshall."

"But if I fail, he may attack."

"Perhaps. Perhaps not. If he believes you returned purely for revenge, he may not react. Our subsequent assault would be unexpected."

How nice for him. I'll still be dead.

"Why don't you attack? They're not anticipating it and you'd get the dragon."

"For many reasons, one of which I've already explained—I do not want to risk my soldiers. Two, Calders may already be on alert. Marshall cannot be certain of your death. Once any faction has knowledge of the dragon's existence, they are going to want it. Marshall must have considered this when he sent you to us."

"He didn't consider much bar sending me to die."

Buxton shakes his head. "He has compromised his faction by delivering you to us. Tactically, it made more sense to kill you in Calders if he wanted you dead so desperately."

"Obviously, I'm glad he chose to be stupid. Like you said yesterday, I want to return and show him just how much his plan back-fired."

"Indeed. Anyway, I appreciate your concerns but I cannot change my position. I believe you will succeed. You appear to be a strong, resilient and effective soldier."

Now he decides to shower me with compliments? Right before he shoves me into no man's land. The flattery is likely a ploy. He needs me amenable to being batted between Calders and Fellhill like a ping-pong ball.

"I cannot predict what will happen once you're through the gate. Your ultimate objective is to retrieve the dragon." He takes a plastic packet from his trouser pocket and spills the contents into his palm. "This is a camera and earpiece, which will allow us to communicate with you and view what you face."

I stick the camera, no bigger than a screw-head, to the lapel of my jacket where it vanishes against the black material. The wireless earpiece slots into my ear.

Buxton comes around the desk to stand beside me. "Let's head to the gate."

Darkness has fallen during our chat, thick clouds blocking my view of the stars. Five different soldiers guard Fellhill's formidable entrance, Gizzy pacing near them. Shadows ring his eyes but the tension drains from his posture at our approach.

I guess I don't look too bad.

My lash wounds and toes throb dully thanks to a skin-healing wrap delivered to my room with breakfast. I ripped off a couple of pieces to loop around my tender nail beds. The wrap is a cellular growth factor matrix embedded with stem cells and natural analgesics to promote rapid wound healing.

We had one, locked in Marshall's office, too precious for subordinates. When he was badly burned in a fire during an inspection of the biofuel plant, he recovered with minimal scarring.

Being the leader has many perks.

Gizzy's gaze latches on mine and I stumble. Buxton's hand grips my elbow, guiding me forward as if he thinks

I'm quailing at the sight of the gate.

Why is Gizzy even attracted to me, a battered intruder? What does he gain? Is it my pretty face beneath the streaks of dirt? Or does he care about me?

Hell if I know. The behaviour of men turned me into a cynic long ago.

Buxton releases his hold and continues towards the shimmering of the boundary fence. A loud thud indicates the unlocking of the first bolt. Buxton produces a golden key from a chain around his neck, inserting it into the lock of the second bolt. It rasps open and one of the guards, a willowy brunette, pulls the third bolt free with shaking arms. The main gate of Fellhill rolls back on its runners, the road out stretching into darkness.

Only a few hours of skin-shrivelling fear then I can be in the dragon, removing the real traitors from The People's Republic.

Sorry Buxton.

He re-joins us and holds his hand out towards Gizzy. "Give me the chip."

Gizzy removes his soul-searching gaze from me and I breathe easier. He gives Buxton a contraption resembling a gun with a needle on the end.

"What is that?"

"Your incentive to return," Buxton says. "Take off your jacket."

"What does it do?"

His jaw bunches. "The implant will kill you if I press a button on the remote and can only be removed after I neutralise it. Once you return with the dragon. If you tamper with it, it will activate."

It's John and his damn dog collar all over again.

My life is a hideous series of repeats.

"What if I promise to bring the dragon back minus the incentive?"

Buxton's pale lips curve.

I sigh.

So much for leading The People's Republic. Maybe Soldiers of the Lost deserve the win. At least I can keep saying, "We didn't strike first," and not be a fucking liar.

Buxton dabs an alcohol wipe on my bared bicep while I squash the memory of Stig scrubbing the filth of the torture room from my neck. My pulse hammers under my skin. Buxton slides the needle into my muscle and I grit my teeth. I imagine the chip settling in my tissue like a dormant cancer cell awaiting a signal.

"Ow! What the—"

I clench my fist to keep from slapping at my arm.

"The implant deploys microfilaments to secure its position. The pain will fade in a moment," Buxton says, his mouth twisted in what looks suspiciously like a smirk. "It also has a GPS locator."

"Can you make sure you don't hit the button by accident?"

He pockets the injection device. "I would never be so careless."

"Will it hurt?"

"If you do what I've asked, no. Just don't make me press it."

Not comforting.

Gizzy steps in front of me and I fix on him instead of Buxton.

"You can do this, Anita," he says, cupping my cheek, his fingers warm on my icy skin. "I'll be here when you get back."

If he's so captivated, why isn't he coming with me?

I bite my tongue.

Asking him sounds too much like pleading.

"Gizzy," Buxton says. "You have her weapons."

"Oh, right."

He offers me the L4 and the cutting laser, a smile sparkling in his eyes. I slip the cylinder into my jacket.

"The gun doesn't have any bullets," I say, leaving it in his hand.

"You threatened me with an empty gun?"

"Yeah, my bad. Worked pretty well, though." I try not to sound smug.

Buxton frowns. "Give her your weapon. Then perhaps we should talk."

Whoops. Got him in trouble.

Gizzy removes the holster and Magnum from around his waist without meeting my gaze. I fasten it around my hips after some adjustment.

"Do you have a knife?" I say.

One can never have too many weapons.

I accept his ankle holster and five-inch blade then turn to Buxton. "What about the laser-cameras? You said you'd drop me off."

Buxton signals to the willowy brunette and she pushes a button on a key fob. A vehicle materialises, parked to one side of the gate. It perches on six terraform tyres, a wedge-shaped blade on the front. Similar in appearance to our Reavers, discounting the fancy invisibility.

"How—"

"Meet the Crocodile. Our best stealth vehicle."

"Crocodile?"

"Because you never know it's there until it bites. Courtesy

of the Scottish Army."

Buxton nods and the woman clicks the button. The vehicle vanishes. I walk towards where it was, one hand outstretched. A rippling not unlike the particle beam fence marks its position. My fingers touch it, the world shifting as my brain struggles to process what it can feel but not see.

"Christ, I hope you don't forget where you parked it."

Gizzy coughs into his hand. The Crocodile reappears and I jump.

"How does it work?"

"A flexible display covers the exterior. The onboard computer scans the surroundings, transmitting it as you would perceive it." My face must look blank. "For example, the right side of the vehicle scans the boundary fence but the image is transferred to the left side, which is what you would see if the Crocodile wasn't there. You don't need the specifics. It's unrivalled by anything in the other factions."

"What about thermal imaging? Laser-guided radar? Can they detect it?"

Buxton huffs out a breath. "At the moment but we're working on it. Consider this a prototype. When you return, I'll add you to the laser-camera database. Now, get in."

I climb into the back of the vehicle. The willowy brunette slides behind the wheel, a square-bodied man in the passenger seat.

The formidable entrance of Fellhill clangs shut, loud through the thick armour of the Crocodile.

35

The vehicle ploughs through a river and heads south-east into the hills, its engine silent. My eyes adjust to the screen depicting the landscape in shades of grey and white and black. Text scrolls to one side—information on vehicle status and data from the forward terrain scanner. A blinking red dot shows our position on the 3D overview map.

I stick my head between the seats. "What would it take for you two to drive me closer to Calders? There's no way they'd detect this thing."

The man glances at me but resumes his tapping on a softly glowing keyboard. "We are not susceptible to bribery, ma'am. Orders are orders."

I slump back.

Damn Buxton and his loyal faction.

I frown at my feet, no windows to divert my attention. The hushed interior reminds me of the Silencer and I fight the stirring panic.

It's not the same. My faction is hostile but not everyone believes Hannah's bullshit. Sure, that'll change when I steal the dragon. I'll become the traitor she accused me of being and whore myself to the enemy.

Or one particular enemy, anyway.

Oh god, I'm going to sleep with him. Terrifying and exciting but not my first choice. I want to remake The People's Republic into what it should have been.

But that option has been taken from me.

Another reason I avoid sex—too complicated and distracting. The trap of emotional involvement softens your heart *and* your brain.

But you still want someone to love you.

Shut up.

A scraping crunch drags my eyes to the screen. The Crocodile plunges through bushes, their skeletal branches clawing the sides. Willowy-woman and Square-man whisper to each other.

"Loch ahead."

"I see it. What's the projection if I swing further east?"

Tap, tap, tap. "Looks good."

Their words skip over me. I close my eyes, swaying to the movement of the vehicle. My fingers slip inside my jacket to rub the tiny lump beneath the skin. I stop in case it triggers the thing, and clench my hands in my lap.

Soon, the dragon and I will be reunited. I'll fly in her again and be free. Before imprisoning myself in Fellhill, hoping Buxton is true to his word and not another psychopath.

"Ma'am? Ma'am. We're at the drop point."

Who is this guy, GI Joe?

I open my eyes to a map on the screen. Square-man repeats Buxton's route, his thick finger showing the way. I hesitate with my hand on the door.

"Ma'am?"

"I'm going, I'm going. You two have a safe journey back, now. Wouldn't want you to keep me from blundering around in no man's land like an idiot."

I don't slam the door, though I want to. The whisper of the vehicle disappears, protected by its cloaking device. Blackness engulfs me and I swallow a whimper, waiting for my vision to adjust.

Why the hell does nobody give me a torch? I'm up to my eyeballs in fancy gizmos but nothing as simple as a light.

I guess I'm less of a target without one.

A branch snaps and I flinch, nothing between my delicate flesh and the slavering beasts. Three hours of this? I start jogging. Best cut it to two or risk insanity.

I pound down the remnants of a road, veering off to battle a tangle of elder and hawthorn. The clicking, clattering twigs grab at my clothes and hair. I break into a field and stumble on undulating grass hummocks, crashing into a hedge on the other side to land on my ass.

"Goddamn son-of-a-bitch."

I scrabble into a gap but it turns out to be a mirage. My stinging hands part the branches, stones digging into my knees.

Buxton's loud voice crackles in my ear. "Anita, do you read?"

I jump with an embarrassing and girly, "Yeep!"

"Anita, do you copy?"

"Jesus-fucking-*Christ!*" I whisper, swallowing a yell.

"Good, you're still with us."

Yanking free, I emerge on the edge of a wood, enveloped in the scent of pine, wet mud and leaf mould. I breathe it in, the promise of rain fresh and heavy in the air. Furtive scuttling and rustling stills and resumes as I pass. A tawny owl calls. A creature squeals.

I wince and run.

The trees circle the inky water of a reservoir, the ground squelching under my boots. I burst out into abandoned fields choked by weeds and grass, succeeding into scrub in places.

It's some comfort to know there are few people left in the area. Just me and the Nationless survivors, wild-eyed with revenge.

I stutter past blasted ruins and scorched stone, reaching the outskirts of Livingston after a breathless hour and a half.

Buxton whistles in my ear. "You didn't leave much to salvage, did you? Revolutionary Front made less mess of the other encampments and they despised Nationless."

I hunch and follow the posts of the boundary fence. The only part of the encampment left intact.

"Where are you going? The quickest route is straight through."

"Scavengers," I say. "Or hurt myself. In the debris. Best to avoid."

Buxton provides no comment on my chattering teeth.

I relax a little with the wreckage behind me. My boots slog over moorland and barren hills. I fall too many times to count and slither downhill, a forest signalling the north-western edge of The People's Republic territory. The burble of running water draws me to the edge of a river, clumps of mud splashing into the depths. The flow is strong, the water black and thick. I head north-east to where it widens and slows from a rush to a sluggish roll.

I don't want to go any further and risk encountering whatever Buxton meant by a wolf-like creature.

Ignorance is bliss on that one.

"Buxton, are the camera and earpiece waterproof?" I say, patting my pockets.

"Yes, why?"

"I'm going to wade through the river."

"Be careful."

I don't snap at him, though he deserves it. If he's concerned, he shouldn't have sent me out alone and on foot.

"Roger that," I say.

Maturity. Happens to us all.

I sit on the edge of the bank and dangle my boots in the river. Water seeps into my socks. I roll, pressing my abdomen into the dewy grass, my fingers and elbows controlling my descent. My feet touch the muddy bottom. Air hisses between clenched teeth. The current swirls around my waist and twines between my legs. I release my grip on the bank and shuffle over the riverbed, slipping on sludge and algae-slick stones. My gaze drops to the surface of the river but I force my eyes from the mesmerising eddy, goosebumps tightening my skin.

"You okay?" Gizzy says.

Warmth blooms in my chest. I resist the urge to slap myself, the sudden but justified rebuke likely to tip me into the water.

"Just freezing my ass off."

"The camera is smudged," Buxton says over Gizzy's laugh. "Clean the lens so we can see what's happening."

I open my mouth to describe my surroundings in vivid, sarcastic detail. A stone shifts under my foot, pitching me into the icy river. Bubbles roil past my face and I inhale. I dig my feet into the mud and stand, coughing and spluttering, water streaming into my eyes.

Well, the lens is clean.

"Anita! Are you there?" Gizzy says.

"I'm here." I cough again. "I fell. I'm wet and bloody freezing but I'm okay."

I haul myself onto the opposite bank. The rain begins with a shushing crescendo and a grumbling sky, lightning illuminating the forest in a blaze of silver. Forked afterimages stay on my retinas. I blunder into a tree.

"Fuck it," I mumble, my arms outstretched.

I cross a circular clearing, water pounding on my head. Stepping into the woods offers little shelter from the rain splashing off the leaves. I slip and grab a tree, the rough bark slick beneath my fingertips. Shivering, I hold my breath but the increased noise and reduced visibility masks the surroundings.

Anything could be creeping through the deluge.

A low growl, virtually obscured by the susurration, raises the hairs on the back of my neck.

"Was that you?" Gizzy whispers.

I peer back into the clearing through the water beaded in my eyelashes. Amorphous shapes ripple in a black sea.

A small group of creatures or one horrendous beast?

I release my cramping grip on the tree and unholster the Magnum at my waist, pointing it in the general direction of the growling thing/things.

Lightning flares.

"My god," Gizzy says.

36

The reddened eyes of five wolfish creatures glare at me. Wrinkled lips peel back from shining teeth.

I fire two rounds into the darkness following the eyeball-frying burst of lightning, the smack and yelp louder than the rain.

"Run, Anita!" Gizzy says.

The creatures crash after me. I flounder up an incline, cold mud coating the Magnum but the deluge washes it away. The ground levels and I plough through bushes with a noise like the snapping of finger bones. A blaze of lightning reveals an oak in my path. I dive around, not slowing. Paws slap the wet, claws clicking on stone. The creatures snarl and roar and howl, their sour breath heating the back of my neck.

Will Buxton and Gizzy have to listen to them feasting on my body?

I explode from the trees onto the remains of a road, now a river of sludge. I skate along, barely staying on my feet. The track curves, the forest blocking my view of Calders' main gate and the lasers that may save or condemn me to the same fate as the beasts.

Please let Marshall have been too distracted by smug self-congratulation.

I trip on a submerged rock and sprawl in the gloop, my mouth too full of mud to make a sound. I flip onto my back, my gun pointed at the dark tree line. Another flash strobes the night, turning the rain into silver slicing the black. My eyes fill with light and water.

Three creatures stalk towards me, the closest mid-pounce, its teeth bared. The other two slink in, one on each side. I shoot the first abomination in the chest, popping open its ribcage like a fortune cookie. Momentum keeps it flying towards me.

I'll never push it off if it lands. Trapped under the stinking carcass while the others begin to bite.

I sit up, grab handfuls of the dead beast's fur and roll backwards, wrenching the thing past me hard enough to crack my spine. My boots dig into its soft belly, a hip thrust propelling it away. It lands on the other side of the road in a gout of liquefied soil. The abomination on my right lunges, its jaw open wide. I swing the Magnum and smack it in the face, bowling it off its feet. The third creature leaps. My finger twitches on the trigger. The bullet smashes into a tree, spraying bark, but the beast twists its powerful body to change direction.

I thrash upright and sprint for the main gate. The creature I hit raises itself on its forelegs, shaking its head. I dart past and it snaps at me, its teeth clicking on air. Both abominations slosh in pursuit. I reach the curve in the road without slowing. The trees transition into a barren space of ragged stumps. A barred gate swims through the murk, water hissing as it contacts the particle beam fence on each side.

I wave my arms. "Don't shoot! It's Anita—*don't shoot me!*"

Three circles of white zero in, silver droplets of rain

morphing to slashes of black almost lost in the glare. I run at them, waiting for the boom of shotguns. There may be a flash if the lasers fire.

Perhaps my skin will bubble.

The soldiers gawp. I splat into the bars, rebound and press my back to the gate, barely noticing any pain from the impact. The creatures bay as they lope towards me. The lasers hum. Two bursts of searing red slam into each abomination, knocking them to the ground with a wet smack. Mud and water fountain into the air. Ignited fat sparks then sizzles.

Holstering my Magnum takes a couple of shaky attempts. The three guards continue to stare but they at least lower their shotguns. Electrified barbed wire crackles on the uppermost bar of the gate, separated from the rest by thick insulation.

"Soldier Carmichael, it *is* you!" Fiona pushes rain-beaded glasses up her long nose with a trembling finger. Dark hair curls from the hood of her windbreaker and sticks to her cheeks.

"Open the gate. Let me in."

We don't have fancy scanners and sparkly golden keys. Marshall wouldn't allow himself to be hauled to the gate every time a subordinate wanted access.

Buxton is a control freak, but it suits him and his faction.

Fiona pulls the bolts, assisted by the other two guards. The entrance swings open and I drag my weary body back inside Calders.

37

An awkward pause follows my inglorious entrance while the guards glance at each other. The rain drums on their windbreakers and my waxed military jacket, which should have kept me moderately dry had I avoided dunking myself in the river.

"I thought you were dead," Fiona says into the uncomfortable silence, her figure huddled against the dampness of the night. "We all did."

"Comes as no surprise."

"I better take you to Marshall."

I nod but she's turned her back, apparently eager for an excuse to interrupt the monotony.

The guards on the gate aren't allowed to use the comms systems, which are for soldiers. In an emergency, a button triggers the alarm. There's also the cameras.

I hope whoever is monitoring us in the control centres doesn't go scuttling to Marshall. The soldiers may be easily swayed by Hannah and Marshall but the ordinary people love me. They'll help me take back the faction if I ask.

I wish I could ask.

Fiona and I slog through the mud amidst the slackening shower, reduced from a downpour to a torrent. Her torch cuts a dim circle in the gloom, highlighting the churned and water-slick road.

"Did you complete your mission? Marshall said you volunteered to prove you weren't a traitor." She peeks from behind blurred glasses. "That was pretty brave."

Volunteered isn't the right word. Coerced, tricked, manipulated. Pick one.

"I've got valuable intel to discuss with him. He'll be pleased."

She ducks her head, hiding a shy smile.

"You're a better bullshitter than Carrie-Anne," Gizzy whispers in my ear.

I struggle not to twitch. Fiona may think I'm having a seizure.

"Listen, Soldier, um, Anita, I don't believe what they say about you. You wouldn't betray your sister's memory by turning traitor. Everything you do is for this faction, like during the armament battles." She drops her eyes, her cheeks flushed. "Marshall is a fool."

The armament battles were a bloody race for weapons to become the strongest faction. We looted police stations, airports, shooting estates and army barracks prior to claiming our territories and imprisoning ourselves behind boundaries. We traded with Russians and Africans before the outside world went quiet.

I sniff and pretend it's rain I swipe from my face. "It's nice to know I have one friend here."

A flash of guilt eclipses the happiness. I hope I'm long gone before she hears about the dragon. I don't want to watch her admiration turn to disappointment and anger.

"You have more than one. You treat us as friends instead of servants. You risk yourself to protect us. We haven't forgotten it was you who secured the first major weapons cache."

The implant burns a hole in my skin. I stop myself from rubbing my arm.

Traitor. Traitor, traitor, *traitor*.

I have no choice.

Damn you, Buxton.

"It was the first time you'd ever killed anyone, wasn't it?"

First time and not the last. I've lost count, the faces blurring into one. My number of kills has taken a significant leap after Livingston. From three digits to five, six? More?

How the fuck am I better than Wick?

"Yes," I whisper, stumbling in the mud, "they were the first."

When the signal went out, I zoomed to the coast from our temporary camp, with a high calibre air rifle and a katana. The rest of my team lagged behind, reluctant to scrabble in the dirt and blood for foreign weapons of questionable efficiency, despite Soldiers of the Lost and Nationless's monopoly of the Scottish Army.

Fight or die.

A makeshift pier anchored a rusting tanker, ten wild-eyed people concluding their trade. The dealers clutched containers of fresh water and food.

Scotland was still a wet and fertile land compared to theirs.

A huge, camouflage-painted truck rose from the sand, multi-barrelled guns bristling in every direction.

I stepped from the safety of the rocks and raised my rifle. "The vehicle is mine. Leave now and I won't kill you."

Pale faces gaped, bleached hands clutching knives and bats. They edged away.

One man narrowed his eyes and gestured with his blade. "That's a goddamn air rifle, you dozy cow. Single shot. Won't even kill us."

Fear turned to glee and they advanced. I squeezed the trigger. The pellet popped the man's eye and he crumpled. I tossed the rifle and raised the katana, adrenaline cleansing me of emotion. Three fled, kicking flurries of sand. The rest died, victim to the reach of my sword, though one woman managed to break my arm with her bat.

I roared away in the giant machine—a Bogatyr—and returned to the astonished expressions of my comrades. The rear compartment contained particle beam fencing and laser-cameras, boxes of Glocks, ammunition and assorted grenades.

It's why 'Russia' is stamped on most of our Glocks. A reminder of how I practically saved us from annihilation.

"It gets easier, doesn't it?" Fiona says. "Killing."

"It does. That may be the problem." I halt her outside the church with a hand on her arm. "I'll take it from here. You should get back to the gate. I'm not sure if anyone followed me."

I force a smile and she beams.

"Good luck. We're having problems with the cameras on account of the weather so Marshall won't be expecting you."

Oh god, tell her why you're here. Beg her forgiveness.

I press my lips together.

If I confess, Buxton will activate the implant, assuming I've gone rogue.

"I see how he looks at you," she continues. "The fact you don't spread your legs like the others makes me like you more."

I pause with one boot on the bottom step. "The others?"

"He calls them his Elite Guard—Kate and Lisa, mostly." She names another handful of female soldiers who never seem to do much fighting.

Spooky coincidence.

"Did Hannah know?"

Fiona shakes her head. "He was careful. Not so much around us but then some people treat servants as invisible. Unless they're pretty."

"Tell me he didn't force…"

"Not me. Too plain for his taste, thank goodness."

The bastard. How blind have I been?

"You won't have to suffer him much longer."

"Are you going to lead us?"

I turn my face towards the heavy oak door. "Probably not."

"You should. We'd follow you anywhere."

My fingertips rub an ache on my chest. "I want to but I can't."

I claim a couple of steps, the rain slicking my hot cheeks and stinging my eyes.

"Anita?"

I stop with my hand on the door.

"You're not staying, are you?"

"No," I whisper to the damp wood, "but I'll still win this thing for Ailsa. That will never change."

"Will we see you again?"

I meet her gaze, her brow furrowed.

"I'll come back when I can. I promise."

Buxton stays silent but I feel the heat of his disapproval worming into my ear.

Tough shit. The People's Republic is my faction. He can swallow his grudge and accept us as allies.

We started the war. Now we'll end it.

I slip through the door and into the church.

38

The building continues its damp decay, water puddled on the floor of the nave. Birds rustle in the rafters, dreaming pigeon dreams as the rain pours on.

"I advise against this course of action," Buxton says. "Confronting Marshall puts you at greater risk."

"Duly noted."

The voice in my head shouts *kill the motherfucking bastard. Put a bullet in his face.*

"Be careful, Anita," Gizzy says, as if I've never experienced active duty.

Shadows leap from a distant flash of lightning. I draw my gun and jerk the ringed door handle. Marshall scowls and looks up, his mouth twisted, no doubt ready to bark at the subordinate who dares to waltz into his office without announcing themselves in a deferential manner.

"Anita!"

Pleasure shivers through my gut at his wide-eyed astonishment.

"Hello, Marshall." I point my gun at his face. "Keep your hands on the fucking desk."

Palms thump on wood, a map of Revolutionary Front territory spread beneath them.

Anger boils like a pan of milk, overflowing with a sweet burning stink.

Everything is his fault. My sister, the war, my torture. If not for him, I'd be a normal woman instead of a battle-scarred soldier.

I *hate* him.

He stares at the Magnum, his face pale, skin tight over sharp cheekbones.

"I had to send you to Fellhill. Act the megalomaniac. It was a test. Of your loyalty." His tongue flicks over his lips. "One you passed admirably."

Does he believe his own bullshit?

"Shame then, since I killed Weir."

Marshall's eyes flinch but the rest of his face stays impassive. "An unfortunate accident. He knew the risks."

"That was your second mistake—sending him to drop me off. Your first and best mistake was not executing me. Do you want to know what I learned in Soldiers of the Lost?"

His fingers tense where he presses them to the desktop and his nails gouge the map. He clenches his jaw, his gaze flicking to my weapon and back.

"Whatever they said was a lie. You're family. They're trying to turn you against me."

"You did that yourself when you *murdered. My. Fucking. Sister.*"

His lips lift in a snarl. "I should have killed you both."

He lunges for the Glock at his waist. I shoot him in the head and he slumps across the desk, obliterating Lowkirk in a wave of gore. I brace my hands on my knees and blink at the floorboards, my pulse attempting to shimmy out of my throat.

Rest in peace, Ailsa.

"Get out of there," Buxton says, interrupting my moment of semi-euphoric horror.

I holster the Magnum and take Marshall's Glock, the weight and shape comforting in my hand. I jog out of the church, loping past storage units, dripping trees and the stinking rubbish pile awaiting incineration.

The rain has cleansed the streets of people.

Maybe this mission will be one of the few where I don't get hurt.

Dim lights pock the vehicle depot, shadows pooled between. Water ripples in broad streams on the sloping monolith of the neighbouring genetics lab, empty now.

I told Marshall to shut it down, helped by escaped abominations eating several of Calders' finest. Other factions continued their bioengineering programmes to produce nightmare crossbreeds with glistening carapaces and slavering teeth. The snorm was our success story—a gentle-sounding splice between a snake and an earthworm, designed to burrow into encampments. They tended to slither off once they emptied their poison sacs, leaving a trail of twitching bodies behind them.

The damn things pop up everywhere. It's why I inserted a metal slab between my tent and the ground.

I glance at the churned soil and hop into a jeep, driving closer to the garden centre, the tyres slithering on slick roads. I park in a clump of bushes far enough away to muffle the engine.

"Welcome home, Anita."

Kate and Lisa range across the path behind me, their faces in shadow, hoods up.

I don't need extra light to see the shine of bared teeth.

"Friends of yours?" Gizzy says.

Not anymore.

I raise my gun. Kate flicks her hand, the movement too fast to follow in the dark and rain. Something cracks into my wrist in a burst of pain. My Glock spins, lost to the night.

The weather must have hampered her throw for the handle to hit me. Kate's blades rarely miss.

She goes for another and I dodge, reaching the garden centre at a sprint and skidding to a halt before I clang into the massive door.

No guards, only a padlock bathed in light from a dim bulb under the eaves.

I grab the Magnum. Sparks shower like pieces of a broken star. I heave the door open and dive into the darkness, crouching on the hard floor, waiting for my vision to adjust. My hair sticks to me in cold strands, water puddling at my feet. Rain patters in, drumming on the corrugated roof. The light above the doorway illuminates a rectangle of floor. I tear my eyes away and squint into the blackness. I creep deeper into the building towards a large shape floating in the murk, my Magnum pointed at the door.

Kate can throw all the knives she wants when I'm in the dragon. She and Lisa will soon be smudges on the concrete.

A cylindrical object flies across the threshold. I shut my eyes and clamp both hands over my ears, the butt of the gun digging into my face. The stun grenade detonates. Light brightens the inside of my eyelids, my tiny blood vessels a delicate tracery etched in black.

Fluorescent strips ping on. I find myself on my back, my fists pressed to my head to keep my brain from leaking out.

38

Has the stun grenade disabled the earpiece and camera? I can't tell past the ringing.

Kate and Lisa rip the gun from my hand. I blink at their snarling mouths and narrowed eyes. More savage than any abomination stalking no man's land.

Kate bunches her hands in my jacket and pulls me to my feet. She screams in my face, her spittle misting my cheeks. A vein throbs in the centre of her forehead and I wait for it to wriggle off, burrowing deeper into her skull. Her face reddens through the spots shimmering in my eyes, the ringing in my ears becoming a roar. She removes one hand from my collar and turns her body into a right hook. The impact cuts the inside of my mouth on my teeth. She releases me and I sprawl on my stomach, struggling to gather my senses while dribbling blood on the dusty floor.

The roaring fades.

Kate continues to snarl at me, "—get what you deserve for murdering Hannah, you bitch!"

Gizzy's loud voice aggravates my fragile head. "Sir, please, send help! They're going to kill her."

"I will not send my men on some foolhardy rescue without more information. Sit your ass down, soldier, or I'll issue an official reprimand." A heavy thud. "Anita, can you hear me? You have to get out of there."

Well, no shit, you master of understatement.

Kate raises her boot. I roll to my feet, the ache in my face chasing the last of the disorientation away.

"*Anita!* Are you okay?" Gizzy says.

Lisa grabs me from behind, pinning my arms to my sides, her pillowy breasts against my back. Kate smiles as she strides over and punches me in the stomach. My breath whooshes out but Lisa's grip holds me upright.

"You shouldn't have come back here," Kate says. "Which enemy are you whoring yourself to this time? Soldiers of the Lost?"

"At least I'm not whoring myself to Marshall," I wheeze.

Anger flashes in eyes insane and bright. My ribs creak under Lisa's arms.

"We are his Elite Guard," Kate says.

"For what, guarding his dick?"

She slaps me, the movement crinkling her jacket and swinging my wet hair across my face. I jerk my hips to the side and slam my hand into Lisa's crotch. She gasps and twitches backwards. I trap her clasped hands and twist my body, ducking under her arms. The action forces her to bend and my knee crunches into her face. She collapses to the floor.

Kate's pixie features distort into a mask beneath her hood. I dodge a wild hook and kick her in the side. Bone cracks and she drops to her knees. The heel of my boot flattens her nose.

She lies still.

I pivot towards the dragon. Lisa grins, blood dripping from her chin, her Glock pointed at me.

My heart stops.

She squeezes the trigger.

"Anita!" Gizzy yells.

39

The bullet smacks into my left shoulder in a stunning burst of pain. I crumple to my knees, my hand pressed to the wound, my limb useless.

"Anita, get up!" Gizzy shouts, intensifying the flash-bang headache pounding between my temples.

I groan and reach for the knife in my ankle holster. My slick fingers brush the handle but Lisa grabs my wrists. Kate binds them with rope and uses it like a leash. I manage to get on my feet rather than be dragged on my face. Kate tugs me to the dragon, Lisa shoving to assist, and loops the rope over the dragon's neck, forcing my arms above my head. My shoulder shrieks, my nail beds unhappy with balancing on tip-toes despite the analgesia of the skin-healing wrap. Kate ties the line to a steel pipe running up the side of the building.

Wick's sneering face swells in my mind and clenches my stomach.

Gizzy returns to pleading with Buxton.

He's wasting his breath but I appreciate the effort.

"You look a little rough, Anita," Kate says, her voice choked courtesy of her mashed nose. "Such a shame. You've had a hard time recently, poor thing."

I spit blood on the floor. "Why did you do it?"

"We liked to placate Hannah. Anything to keep her happy and oblivious. And Marshall's obsession was becoming a little tedious for us, too."

"Not that, you goddamn bitch. The party leaders. You let Marshall kill Ailsa."

"Oh dear, our secret is out," Lisa says, shoving her hood down and smoothing a hand over her short hair.

Kate snickers, wiping rain and blood from her face. "She was more effective as a martyr than a leader."

"You call this shit effective?"

Kate bares her red-smeared teeth. "It will be, when we win."

God, I'm tired of swimming against the current of everyone else's bullshit.

"You might have to adjust your plans a little since I shot the motherfucker," I say.

Their faces pale.

"*You lie*," Kate hisses, her eyes so narrow it's a wonder she can see.

I smile. "Hurts when someone you love is assassinated, doesn't it?"

She howls and they attack, whirling around me, landing blows wherever they can. My booted feet lash out. Lisa slams a fist into my kidney, rocking me on my toes. Each movement rips at my shoulder, red flowing faster, mixing with rain and river water. My ribs crack under Kate's knuckles. Lisa wrenches my shoes off, my kicks suddenly less powerful. I weaken under the barrage, their fists slapping into flesh.

Smack, smack.

A hysterical giggle bubbles in my throat.

Gizzy asks Buxton once more to send help and once more is denied. Acceptance dulls his voice.

His leader has spoken.

Kate steps away, clutching her side. "Let the bitch hang. I need to bind my ribs."

I slump against the rope, my arms and wrists taking my weight, stretching my aching joints. My abdomen throbs, hot and distended. I stare at the smeared concrete. My right hand twitches, my fingers brushing a cold, slicing edge. I hunch at the fresh pain.

A voice shouts something in my ear but understanding escapes me.

I blink fluid from puffy eyes. My bound hands rest against the dragon's curled digits. Red smears her talons, bright against the silver.

I can't survive another beating. My body balances on a precipice. One punch will propel me into the abyss.

Kate and Lisa stand a little distance from me, their jackets in a crumpled pile. Lisa winds a bandage around Kate's chest. Both of them are laughing but they ignore me and I'm fine with that.

The jumbled shouting resolves into words. "*Anita!* Wake up! You said you'd come back!"

"Come on," Buxton says. "There's nothing we can do. When we take the encampment, we'll find her body and give her a proper burial."

"Not—dead," I manage to whisper on a tiny exhalation.

I hook one of the dragon's talons between my wrists and rock, keeping my movements small. The rope parts but my legs collapse. I slump to the ground, dazed by a wave of pain.

"How the hell…"

Lisa's head whips around. "Looks like she's ready for more."

I fumble for the closest weapon and pray it works despite

immersion and a serious pummelling. I focus on Kate's hate-contorted face.

"Laugh at this, bitch," I croak.

I press the button of the cutting laser and aim at a glowering blue eye. It pops like a bubble bursting. Kate shrieks, falling to writhe on her back, her cries ricocheting in the open space.

Lisa throws an arm over her face and charges. Wisps of smoke rise from her sleeve to curl in her wake. Her boot connects with my arm and the laser clangs into the dragon's side, tinkling to the concrete. Lisa reaches for her Glock in its shoulder holster. I grab the handle of the knife at my ankle.

A knife in a gun fight. I don't like my odds.

Lisa's Glock catches on the material of her top. She rips it loose. The weapon swings. I stab my blade where thigh meets groin and blood fountains into my face. Her screams join Kate's in a hideous chorus.

"Why—did it have to—come to this?" I gasp between chattering teeth. "We could've—had everything. Why..."

I sway over her. Her wide, hazel eyes lock on mine, glazing as her struggles weaken. Kate rocks from side to side despite her broken ribs, her hand clutching her face, thick fluid leaking from beneath her fingers. A keening shivers from her throat. I crawl to her on my knees and one hand, my left arm dangling, the knife scraping the concrete. Her remaining sapphire eye whirls to me.

"For Ailsa," I say, and drag the blade across her throat.

Warm liquid soaks the knees of my combats. My hair clings to my face and tangles in my eyelashes.

"Anita?" Gizzy says in a soft voice.

I don't answer. Can't.

"Anita, you need to move."

39

I cough and taste copper, crying out as my chest burns.

"What's your status?" Buxton says.

My breath rattles in my throat. *"Bad.* Very—bad."

"Stand up now," Gizzy says. "You can make it."

"Ailsa wouldn't want you to die here," Buxton says.

Oh, fuck you.

I struggle to my feet and sway but stay upright. My vision blurs, hazy spots blotting out huge patches of reality.

Get your ass in the dragon, you weakling.

I shuffle towards her, my stained socks daubing red along the concrete. I rest my head on her cool flank and leave a bloody smudge. Heaving my heavy body inside pulls small, hurt sounds from my throat.

"Hurry, Anita," Gizzy whispers.

Moving faster means losing consciousness.

I become the dragon but her strength fails to lessen my pain. I leap through the roof with a tremendous crash and scraping of metal. Sheeting rains like guillotine blades. The building screams and topples in a cloud of dust. I fly in the direction of Fellhill, the rain striking my silver skin. I focus on the musical sound instead of the throbbing, the nausea, the dizziness. The cables of the dragon cradle a broken shell. The ground flickers beneath me.

Shit. Was I always this low?

I flash over the hills, swooping into the remains of Nationless, and beyond. The landscape jitters past, chunks lost as I battle with the darkness. If I crash out here, I'll never be found in time.

"Not far now," Gizzy says, his voice filled with false cheer.

I mean to reply—maybe I do—but branches scrape my belly, another slice of the journey gone, and I can't tell how long it is since he spoke. I flap harder, so very glad the dragon moves for me.

Lowkirk glows in strips of white, its blackout screens tattered and peeling. The other encampments of Revolutionary Front are shuttered tight. Fellhill comes into view and I struggle to stay awake. A group of soldiers gathers near the main gate, Buxton and Gizzy at the head.

"Anita, pull up!" Buxton barks. "You're going to hit—"

I open my eyes to a hail of bricks, stopping short of demolishing a second row of houses. Rolling onto my side sways me in the cables in a breath-taking wave of pain. I flop out of the controls, collapsing onto the floor—flank—in a gasping, aching, shivering heap. I leave a bloody handprint on the hatch and tumble into the rain and night. Water splatters my beaten face and collects undisturbed in my mouth.

Buxton and Gizzy reach me, shadowed at a discreet distance by the crowd. Buxton's lips move. His earring twinkles like a captured star. Gizzy seems to be calling my name. He drops to his knees and cradles my head in his lap. I want to tell him to stop because it hurts, but then I realise it doesn't.

I feel nothing apart from cold.

It's too late.

The last of my strength drips from my body and pools with the rain.

40

Wick sneers, yellow teeth distorting his mouth even further. I don't recognise the dank room or the smooth rock walls. Chains rattle at wrist and ankle. Four slashes ooze blood across my chest and belly. Wick licks the wounds, his drool glistening on my stomach. His black eyes swim, lightening to Daniel then back to Wick.

"I've always liked you, Anita," Daniel says, his voice deeper than I remember it.

His claws scrape my skin. I squirm and he barks a laugh.

"But I'll enjoy killing you more than fucking you, girlie."

I can't speak. He ripped out my tongue and ate it.

His hand lingers on my stomach in an intimate caress. He digs his talons in, scooping out the steaming mass of my intestines. They slop to the ground with a hot metallic stink and he bends to them, gathering the slippery cords. Wet slurping fills the windowless room. My mouth opens and shuts but there is no air to scream.

Daniel/Wick presses his body to mine, pieces of me dribbling down his chin.

"Lights out, bitch," he says.

* * *

My eyes snap open and I scream. A figure topples out of a chair in a thrashing heap. Gizzy scrambles to the bed and grabs my right hand.

"Ssh, you're all right. You're okay."

I stop shrieking somehow. "I'm alive?"

"You're alive. You're safe."

Miracles do happen.

"Horrible dream," I murmur, relaxing under the cool fingers stroking my hand, "about Daniel Wick."

"He can't hurt you anymore."

My heart flutters. I pull in a deep breath and pain flares in my chest. My body throbs, muffled by whatever medication pumps into my veins through a drip in my arm.

"What day is it?"

"It's the sixteenth of May. You've been out for fourteen days."

Two weeks!

At least I woke up.

Gizzy rests his large hand on my unbandaged right arm, dark smudges ringing his eyes. "The doctor put you in a coma to protect brain function. She reduced the dose three days ago."

He kisses my forehead and a weird sensation shivers in my gut. It's only us in the room, nine empty cots with pristine sheets filling the rest of the space.

I need to be alone. I don't think Gizzy will harm me but I don't trust him, not yet. My fragile body wants to disappear back into unconsciousness and the thought of Gizzy hovering over me makes me uncomfortable. Which is stupid, since he's probably been guarding my vegetative state for the last fourteen days.

But I hate being unarmed and vulnerable and perfectly aware of it.

"You should get some rest," I say.

"I'm fine. I'll stay here, now you're awake."

"I'll just sleep. Whatever medication this is, keep it coming."

He quirks his mouth. "You sleep. I'll watch."

For the love of god…

"Go home and rest."

"But—"

"Go, before you collapse," I say, the forcefulness reduced by my words slurring together.

"Okay, but I'll be back in a few hours. And I'm telling the doctor so she can check on you."

I manage a smile. "Stubborn."

"Like you." His fingers brush my cheek. "Goodnight."

Is it night? Where is the dragon? Where am *I?*

Gizzy leaves, glancing over his shoulder. His broad figure dwindles beyond the frosted glass of the double door. The large white room seems empty with him gone and I scold my softness.

I've barely known him all of ten minutes.

Not that it matters. Men can still be dicks when you've known them for years.

I learned they only care about one thing when I finally capitulated to see what all the fuss was about over sex. The guy filmed me and posted it online.

The one good thing about the loss of the internet—it's harder to share virgin porn with thousands of people.

Ailsa kicked his ass. Metaphorically. Then she mothered me into her group of friends. When she got involved in politics and independence, I supported her.

If only the path was different from there. No blood, no death, no war.

Maybe war was inevitable. Ours or the rest of the world's. But I might still have my sister.

I squint against the glare of the fluorescents. A tube stings my nose and I bar myself from fiddling with it. A humming biomonitor arcs over the bed in a band of blinking green lights.

Gizzy's right—I'm safe.

The dragon is back with me, where she belongs. As far as I know. This is the end of my captivity and the start of a new journey. A road to a better life.

I settle into the mattress, downy pillows cradling my head. My eyelids droop.

I have no more dreams.

41

Buxton, Gizzy and a female doctor cluster around my bed. The sun filters through small, high windows, affording tantalising glimpses of sky. The doctor removes her thin hands from the pockets of her lab coat and tucks a stray red hair back into her bun.

"Anita, this is Doctor Sharp, she saved your life," Buxton says with his usual lack of preamble.

Sharp, like her features.

She nods, her cool blue eyes regarding me down a long nose. "You were lucky. You lost a lot of blood. I operated to remove your spleen and a portion of liver. Your heart stopped twice. You suffered a collapsed lung and I inserted a drain. I extracted the bullet from your shoulder and repaired the damage. There was bruising on the right kidney but it required no surgery. You received a transfusion of three pints of A positive. The feeding tube and catheter can be removed today."

My chest squeezes tight.

That is one extensive list of injuries and treatments.

The doctor consults a chunky watch, huge on her bony wrist, the purple tracery of vessels highlighted beneath her skin. "I'll continue the analgesics. You should heal with no impairment and will be discharged in four weeks, *minimum.*"

She spins on her heel and strides from the room.

"Four weeks minimum!" I wheeze, clinging to the sole thing that doesn't make me hyperventilate. "Get me out sooner."

"Unfortunately, it's doctor's orders and for your own good," Buxton says.

"I can't go four weeks without a proper shower."

My spleen and part of my liver. *Gone.*

The biomonitor beeps in alarm.

I'm alive, the damage reversible. I can still lead the resemblance of a life, despite having fewer organs.

The machine quiets.

Buxton and Gizzy share a glance at my expense.

"I'm sure Doctor Sharp will be happy to give you a sponge bath if it distresses you," Buxton says.

"Great," I mutter, loath to disclose the real reason for my anxiety.

"Well, if you're done whining—welcome back."

"I don't whine and scarcely made it back. Didn't you hear? I'm missing pieces."

"Not vital ones," Gizzy says, his eyes soft.

Easy for him to say. It's not his liver or spleen on the chopping block.

My hand soothes my stomach over a square-patterned hospital gown, a ridge of scar tissue palpable beneath the thin material. The machine beeps again.

Think of something else.

"The doctor seems distant."

"She lost her family," Gizzy says, his voice hushed, as though afraid the good doctor might be listening. "Her husband caught a virus from a bioweapon. Her son was impaled by

Rebel State."

God, we're savages. Just because someone is an enemy doesn't make it acceptable. I kill to protect myself but try not to be cruel. It doesn't always work if I'm desperate to escape and badly hurt.

Or they fucking deserve it.

"Was anyone injured when I crash-landed?" I say into the quiet.

Buxton shakes his head. "The occupants of the houses you demolished were watching your graceful entry."

"I blacked out or would've landed fine." I go to cross my arms, forgetting my left is in a sling strapped to my chest. "Like to see you try under those circumstances."

"You are right, of course. Your strength and will to survive surprised everyone."

High praise, indeed.

"I've moved the dragon into my main munitions factory. It is as amazing as you described. When you've recovered, as promised, you'll be in charge of it. I want the machine's capabilities documented."

A pressure in my chest eases.

Buxton's word seems to mean something.

I settle more comfortably in the bed. "What else did I miss?"

Buxton and Gizzy look at each other, storm-grey eyes to chocolate-brown. I open my mouth to tell them to get on with it but Buxton answers.

"The People's Republic attacked us two days after you stole the dragon."

Who rallied the troops in Marshall and Weir's stead— Brian and James? Were they involved in the debating room slaughter? I should've watched the whole video.

Reece still has a lot to answer for.

When this is over, we can sentence them like civilised people. Judge and jury.

Then executioner.

"Their objective was to capture the dragon, and you. I believe they wanted to punish you for being a traitor," Buxton says with a bland smile.

I've been punished enough in my humble opinion.

"They injured thirty of my soldiers." He pauses but his eyes—as direct and unreadable as ever—never leave mine. "We destroyed the whole of Calders in our counter-offensive."

The unexpected brutality smacks me in the gut.

"What the fuck is wrong with you! Most of them were good people. *My* people."

Gizzy flinches, his gaze flying to Buxton. The muscles in Buxton's jaw flex.

"Your people were the most self-righteous of all and you started this war in the first place."

"Yet you made damn sure it continued."

"Chaos, Anita. It makes us great."

"So you massacred my faction because you bore a grudge?"

"They attacked us. We retaliated." He brushes lint off the sleeve of his impeccable olive fatigues. "How is it any different to what you did to Livingston?"

Because I cared about the people in Calders. The thought of it as dust and rubble aches in my emptier abdominal cavity.

Oh, god—Fiona. I promised her I'd come back.

Buxton better not have used my dragon.

"Fifty or so survivors escaped through an ancillary gate we were unaware of," he says.

Well, whoop-de-fucking-do.

"The woman you spoke to fled unharmed."

Wonderful. She can die a slow, horrible death—or maybe a very quick death—in no man's land.

People rarely survive the annihilation of their faction because there's nowhere else to go. I doubt any Nationless soldiers are still alive, as nice as it is to believe Stig found his absolution.

Happy endings are for fairy tales.

I frown at my pale hand where it rests on the hospital gown. "We need to search for her. And the others. Bring them in."

A slight pucker knits Gizzy's brow.

"Anita," Buxton says on a sigh, "I will forgive your amnesia on our conversation prior to the mission but this is the part where you follow *my* orders. I don't know what you're used to in The People's Republic. Here, you must earn the right to advise me."

"Delivering the dragon should earn me that right."

"Perhaps, had you not been under duress."

My fingertips rub the tiny scar across my left bicep, where the implant must have been removed during my coma.

"Can you at least watch out for them?"

I choose not to add 'your Highness'.

"That, I can do," he says.

Doctor Sharp marches in clasping a syringe.

"This will make you drowsy," she says, attaching the syringe to a portal on the drip bag and depressing the plunger.

A wash of coolness blooms in my arm.

Probably my imagination.

"I'm going to remove her feeding tube and catheter. I'm sure she will not want you present." Doctor Sharp makes shooing motions at Buxton and Gizzy. "Out, both of you."

I fall asleep as soon as they leave, unconscious for the indignity of having my various tubes removed.

42

Bones mend, incisions heal, bruises fade. Doctor Sharp monitors my progress and, yes, gives me sponge baths. She never passes my care to the rest of her medical team, despite how busy she seems. I grow fond of her and her aloofness thaws after some perseverance. She lets me address her by her first name—Emily.

Gizzy visits as often as his duties allow and I appreciate the daily break from monotony, as short as it is. He probes delicately about my experiences as a prisoner. I evade. He frowns but doesn't press.

I like him. Confessing that I soiled myself and prayed for death is very unappealing.

We talk about the usual things and it makes the world feel normal—faction philosophies, epic battles, what we do in our downtime.

We don't talk about the future.

Desire builds at each meeting, a pleasant throbbing replacing the ache of my healing wounds. The strength of it confuses me, though it's probably my own fault. Abstinence will do that. Other people have sex all the time, and not necessarily with those they trust. I trust Gizzy not to be a sneering, gloating bastard like the rest.

That's enough, for now.

My restlessness increases as the days pass. Gizzy catches me doing a series of self-defence moves one evening. He folds his arms and leans against the wall, a black hooded jumper hugging his broad shoulders.

"This doesn't look like resting."

I quit my less-than-fluid actions and pace in front of him. "I've rested enough! I'm going insane in this room. If I never see these walls again, it'll be too soon."

"Are you going to complain every time I visit?" He captures my hand and forces me to stop. "Doctor Sharp says a couple more days."

Little electric shivers run up my arm from the brush of his skin.

"A couple more days won't make much difference." I peek at him from under my lashes. "Besides, the quicker I'm out of here…"

He closes the space between us. "God, Anita, you're not the only one who's struggled these past few weeks."

Without waiting for a reply—as if I could've given him one— he kisses me. I open to the slide of his tongue, moulding my body to his. He tastes smoky, like log fires and malt whisky. The hospital gown rises and his hands slide downward, his fingers cupping my ass over the thin material, pulling me closer. His arousal presses against my belly.

Approaching footsteps force us apart. I dive into bed, my flushed cheeks likely to give me away. Emily strides in, her sensible heels clicking on the polished floor. She wears black trousers and a cornflower-blue top the colour of her eyes underneath her ever-present lab coat.

Does she feel naked without it, as I do minus at least one

gun?

"Gizzy. I'm afraid you must go. Anita needs her sleep before she leaves."

Although her face stays blank, there's a tiny twitch of her lips. I smile despite being interrupted from the enjoyable activity of exploring Gizzy's mouth.

"Yes, Doctor Sharp," he says, hiding a grin.

Emily checks me over once he's gone. I beam at her and she throws me an amused glance, her cold stethoscope pressed to my chest.

* * *

The glorious day arrives when I'm released from the makeshift prison Fellhill calls a hospital.

Buxton hands me a large canvas bag. "I gathered some clothes and necessaries from our supplies. Hopefully, everything is your size."

In the bathroom, I peel off the hospital gown and dress in a white t-shirt, faded blue jeans and a serviceable pair of trainers. My trusty boots were lost while I was getting battered half to death in my now extinct faction.

Extinct. It continues to wound me. I never imagined a situation where The People's Republic were annihilated. We were well-trained, our defences superior. We fought to right the atrocity committed by savages in the other factions.

Shows what I knew.

I join Buxton and Gizzy in the hallway, the black bag of clothes slung over my right shoulder. My left isn't back to normal, the scar shiny and pink, my muscles liable to twinge.

"Do you want me to take that?" Gizzy says.

"It's fine. I can manage." I force myself not to glance at him. "Where will I stay?"

"Gizzy's offered for you to live with him if that's acceptable?" Buxton says, shepherding us through the corridors.

Emotions swirl—fear, excitement, arousal, irritation at his apparent presumption. They drain, leaving only heat. Gizzy watches me, his eyes dark.

Is he picturing me naked? For once, it doesn't make me shy away with revulsion.

"Fine," I gulp, my mouth dry.

Do I even remember how to do it? I'm practically a nun.

At least I don't have to worry about contraception. Female soldiers received mandatory injections in The People's Republic. The workers could volunteer, though a few chose to raise a family, their children assisting in the war effort.

Some factions train them.

I shiver. Child soldiers—ancient eyes in innocent little faces. I kill anything coming at me with a weapon but kids leave a mark.

Even if they are intent on gutting you like a fish and flailing around in your entrails.

We step outside, the sunlight warm on my face. Situated atop a wooded rise, the hospital offers a view of part of Fellhill sprawled in the sunshine.

A woman throws a ball and a Labrador pants after it. A crowd engages in a noisy game of football, covered in dirt and sweat. Rows of bustling industrial buildings. The black bulk of a Raider-3 patrols on squealing tracks. Fatigue-clad soldiers exercise with weapons, the crack of blanks splitting the air, a background chorus of explosions softened by distance.

42

Saorsa? Or Revolutionary Front?

Buxton and Gizzy wait for me to finish my appraisal. I flash an embarrassed smile and follow them to an open-topped jeep for the drive to Gizzy's house.

Is the Venus-DR back in his garage? Maybe we can take it out for a nostalgic trip.

"I hope you settle in well here, Anita," Buxton says. "I know it's been hard and will take some adjustment."

Yup. Particularly as I've not forgiven him for what he did to The People's Republic.

He leaves the vehicle parked at the kerb and strides down the street towards his office. Gizzy leads me up the slabbed border to his house. The door closes and I push him against the wall, one hand on his firm chest. His jaw drops.

"Where's your shower?" I say.

"Upstairs, turn left, it's the door at the end."

I salute, plant a kiss on his mouth and march up the stairs. His laughter chases me to the bathroom.

Transparent gold curtains frame a frosted glass window, the surrounding tiles a cheery yellow. I drop the holdall on a multi-coloured splodge of a rug and cross to the mirror above the sink.

Pale, dull skin tight over sharp cheekbones, huge eyes. My hair hangs limp despite the sponge baths, steeped in the clinical smell of the hospital. I look terrible but at least I have all my teeth, if not my original organs.

Oh, wait—all my teeth bar the ones buried in the rubble of Livingston.

I shudder.

I need to stop conjuring that period of my life or risk the return of the nightmares tormenting me during the only time

I lower my guard.

I stick my tongue out at my reflection and dive into the shower. Scalding water prickles my skin. Yelping, I dance out and adjust the dial.

Hot running water! Not a tepid splutter with macerated bits of leaf.

I could get used to this.

The spicy soap smells like Gizzy. I scrub every inch, my fingers lingering over the new scars. The welts on my back crisscross in rough, raised bands from shoulder blade to lumbar spine. The pale-pink abdominal scar starts under my sternum and runs past my bellybutton. Thin and neat, owing to Emily's skill despite the emergency nature of the surgery. The mark from the bullet wound is an elevated, irregular circle bisected by a line where she extended the injury to remove the bullet. A tiny scar nestles between my ribs from the chest drain.

Will Gizzy be attracted once he sees me naked? Will he recoil at the missing toenails, the exposed beds thickening into something resembling a nail?

Don't be stupid. He's not going to know what hit him.

I step onto the rainbow-vomit rug and pat myself dry, flushed and dewy from the heat. Wrapping the yellow towel around me, I go in search of Gizzy. He sits on a wooden chair in his bedroom, sharpening a knife, his head bent, the scrape of metal loud in the quiet. He glances up.

The towel pools at my feet.

43

Gizzy stalks towards me and I back up until my spine hits the wall. My hand tightens into a fist, half-raised, but he cups my face and his mouth steals what little breath I have left. My fingers relax and tangle in his hair. I arch my back, my hips pushed hard into him. He moans, his hands skating over my sides to brush my breasts.

It's been so long since I was touched like this. I hope I don't embarrass myself.

I pull his t-shirt off, breaking the kiss. His body is perfect—broadly masculine and muscled, his dog-tags settled between the solid planes of his chest. A neat trail of hair runs from his pecs, past his impressive abs to disappear into his trousers.

No scars.

He didn't react to mine but then he knows about the shoulder and belly, though seeing them is a whole different thing. Does he care I have scars? Am I the only one who does?

I curl my toes into the carpet.

He pins my hands to the wall. My brain screams at me to struggle, *fight!* Gizzy distracts me by trailing kisses down my neck to my nipple, drawing it into his mouth. A rush of pleasure unfurls in my belly and smothers my alarm.

He's not trying to hurt me.

He sucks my breast hard enough to feel the scrape of teeth. I slump against the wall and he grins, apparently delighted by my response to his sweetly erotic torture.

Two can play that game.

I pop the button on his trousers and lower the zipper. No underwear. My fingers wrap around him and squeeze, his pulse thudding and thick under my hands. His eyes flutter shut. I move upwards to the bead of moisture at his tip and massage him in lazy circles.

"Jesus, Anita."

He opens his eyes and my heart stutters, my skin swollen and slick and aching. He kicks out of his trousers, his legs as hairy as mine, which is strangely comforting.

The rest of him is so perfectly groomed.

I brace myself, the hunger on his face hinting he may forget and slam me against the wall.

I'm almost certain I won't punch him.

He stays out of reach. Before I can protest—or, god forbid, beg—his fingers slide inside me. I moan and writhe against the wall. He strokes me, stretching and teasing, in and out.

"God, you're so wet."

"Please," I breathe.

Dammit. There goes my no begging rule.

Pleading for sex is an acceptable exclusion.

Gizzy growls low and grips my hips, lifting me without effort. My legs wrap around his waist, my body desperate to be closer and filled with something other than loneliness and regret. I flinch when his hand glides up my back, his fingers on the lowest ridge of scars. He thrusts himself inside me and I cry out at the forgotten sensation. His mouth swallows the sound.

It's hard and fast and everything I want.

The orgasm explodes between one thrust and the next. We end in a sweaty pile on the floor, my damp hair knotted around us.

"Worth the wait," he pants.

It takes me a few seconds—hell, minutes—to say, "Mmm-hmm."

It's the best I can do.

Abstinence was easy. No one in Calders made awareness quiver through my body. It was harder to ignore the craving for simple, affectionate human contact—a gentle touch, a hug—but I almost managed.

We crawl, laughing and wobbly, to Gizzy's king-size bed. He spoons against my back, one arm over my hip. I wriggle my butt in close to his groin.

"Oh god, don't do that," he says. "Not yet."

"Rest first. But then I don't plan on getting out of this bed. And not because I'll be sleeping."

He nibbles my ear. "You read my mind."

I enjoy the warmth, cradled in his arms. My eyelids droop.

"Gizzy?" I say, drifting and half-asleep.

"Hmm?"

"Promise you won't hurt me."

"I promise," he murmurs.

* * *

The setting sun touches the horizon in a blaze of orange and gold when we're forced to stop having sex long enough to eat. Gizzy climbs out of bed to leave me alone and naked, apart from a thin blue sheet draping my chest. He kisses me, his hand travelling under the cover to caress over thigh and hip.

"If I didn't need food…"

I wiggle my eyebrows. "Well, the night is young."

"Wait here." He pulls on his black combat trousers and pads away on bare feet.

I flop into the scattered pillows on a sigh that expands from my toes. I stretch with a moan, aching in neglected places, my muscles tired and sore from the glorious abuse. My injuries nothing but the wisps of a nightmare.

One hell of a way to end my abstinence.

I slither from the covers and wrap the sheet around me, shuffling to the window. Dusk bathes the streets in bronze and softens the landscape, the sky darkening to a strip of pale blue. Stars glitter, though fewer than usual given the light pollution.

The world really is a wonderful place.

Christ, one marathon sex session and I get sentimental.

Crockery rattles. Saliva floods my mouth at the scent of cooked meat. Arms circle me and Gizzy kisses my bare shoulder. I lean into him.

It's nice to finally have someone to cuddle.

We stand in silence and enjoy the night, gilded by the glow of a streetlight.

He presses his cheek to my temple. "Let's get you back to bed."

His lips start below my ear and work upwards. He unwraps me from the sheet, his palms skimming my breasts.

My knees weaken. "Yes, please."

He scoops me, naked and laughing, into his arms and plops me on the bed beside a tray of steaming plates. My stomach grumbles, the sex forgotten.

I've certainly worked up an appetite. I also need to put on weight—my arms and legs are way too thin after my hospital stay.

Gizzy pours me a glass of red wine to accompany the steaks.

No doubt Buxton grows special grapes in his fancy-pants greenhouse.

I sip. "Are you trying to get me drunk and take advantage?"

"Most definitely," Gizzy growls.

My glass clinks on the bedside cabinet seconds before his heavy body presses me to the mattress, his kiss barely letting me breathe.

It's hot and all but, man, I really want that steak.

44

I wake curled towards the window, naked and chilled, Gizzy wrapped in a cocoon of the sheets, only his head visible. I wriggle closer to kiss his cheek. He stirs. I trail my lips along his jaw and push higher on my elbow. He watches me with limpid brown eyes and a sleepy smile, his hair mussed.

I straddle him. "Morning."

"God, you're voracious."

"That's a good thing, right?"

I rock my hips and he groans. I lift my weight and he fights free of the sheets. He shudders as I mount him, my hands pressed to his broad chest.

The desire in his eyes confirms I'm more than a soldier, a captive. A victim.

My body arches above him and he thrusts to meet me. A warm heaviness builds, bursting when he plunges himself deep, so powerful it's almost painful. My head falls back on a cry, my eyes closed, the pleasure overwhelming any unpleasant ache. He rolls me unresisting and pounds into me. I writhe underneath him, my nails digging into his shoulders. He jerks inside me and collapses on top.

"Can you die from too much sex?" I gasp, my ribs struggling to expand beneath his weight.

He pants in my ear.

He isn't dead yet but talking seems beyond him.

A smug little glow warms my chest.

We pull our clothes on, Gizzy dressing in another pair of black combats and a t-shirt. He looks damn good in black. I rummage in my bag and find dark-green trousers and a short-sleeved top.

In the kitchen, he spoils me with a breakfast of bacon, eggs, sausages, fried tomato and toast, plus limitless cups of coffee.

It's the first time I've eaten properly in years.

Soldiers of the Lost keep their own staples and feed themselves. We had it dished out to us like schoolchildren, not responsible or trusted enough to avoid frittering resources. Gizzy even grows vegetables in his garden.

"Am I to work on the dragon today?" I say around a mouthful of my third piece of toast, scattering crumbs on the table.

"Not today. Buxton wants you to settle in. Tonight there's an initiation ceremony to officially welcome you as one of us."

I stop in the act of taking another bite. "What does that mean?"

"It'll be a nice surprise."

"Yeah, not a huge fan of surprises."

Gizzy shakes his head, gathering his empty plate and cup into a pile. "You don't have to sound suspicious. It's nothing bad."

"It's not some hazing thing?"

"It's to *welcome* you."

"Most factions are distinctly *unwelcoming*."

His fond smile says I'm being cute. "We're not like most

factions."

I finish my toast and coffee.

"Anyway, I have to go out," he says, accepting my plate and adding it to the pile. "You'll be alone for most of the day."

"Can I explore your house?"

"It's your house, too."

He clasps my hand across the table, his fingers twice as wide as mine. I flash back to the muscle-bound guard who pressed me into the chair to be electrocuted. Hands large enough to palm my face. I internalise a shudder, not wanting Gizzy to ask what's wrong and force me to lie. He isn't quite the goliath size of the guard, his eyes warm and caring rather than cold and empty.

No comparison.

Gizzy stands and clears the dishes into the sink. I jump to help, welcoming the distraction.

I send him off with a kiss and he walks down the street in the sunshine, waving before he turns out of sight. I lean on the door.

What the hell am I doing, living with him already? Depending on him. I should've insisted on my own space. Everything is happening too fast.

Sighing, I push away from the door.

Don't ruin it, for god's sake. Enjoy it instead of wondering how it might end in disaster. Trust him. He's kind and sexy and he wants me. And he promised.

He promised.

* * *

I'm lounging in the sun when Gizzy returns from whatever he

does in Fellhill. He presents me with a pile of folded clothes, a pair of black boots balanced on top.

"For your initiation ceremony."

I pull on the olive trousers, shirt and military jacket in his bedroom, smoothing my hands over the material and the row of metal buttons. I tie my long hair into a ponytail, the black beret perched on my head. The boots fit perfectly, polished to a shine.

I look smart and tough. Like a soldier.

But am I a soldier anymore?

I thread the dog-tags from under my shirt and trail my thumb over the embossed letters. A pang of loss hollows my stomach.

Calders is a part of me. A reminder of how the people supposed to protect you can turn out to be the ones who hurt you most.

With that depressing analysis, I take a deep breath and jog downstairs. Gizzy stands in the hall, straightening his uniform in the mirror.

"I do like a woman in uniform," he says.

I slap his wandering hands from my butt. "No time. I have a very important ceremony to attend."

"Later then. I will peel this sexy uniform from your body and you will beg me to fuck you."

His lips curl in an arrogant smile. I close the distance and stroke him through his trousers.

He really does like the outfit.

"We'll see who begs," I say.

He shudders and I release him, slipping out of the house into the growing dusk. Catching up, he captures my hand and we walk the streets. I snort as we reach the sports centre. Light bathes the big hall and the folding metal chairs occupied by soldiers. A hush falls at our entrance. I linger in the doorway, Gizzy tugged to a stop on the end of my arm.

Will they accept me? I want to be respected, like Calders in the early years, not drooled over by some and hated by others. I may be a reluctant addition but none of us has much choice.

And at least I have a home.

It could always be worse.

I raise my chin and let go of Gizzy's hand. His fingers tighten for an instant before he releases me and I march down the aisle of packed chairs.

I want to be judged for my contributions not who I'm with. Sleeping my way up the hierarchy isn't what I'll be remembered for.

I am not an Elite Guard.

Buxton surveys our approach, the nine soldiers behind him dressed in crisp uniforms identical to mine. I hop up three steps to the stage and he raises his hands.

"Soldiers of the Lost, tonight we welcome another into our ranks."

Standing at his side, I aim for calm and confident instead of squirming and uncomfortable. I avoid staring into the sea of faces, their collective gaze prickling along my skin. Gizzy joins the nine, highlighting his position of power to the people amassed in the hall.

"Many of you will recognise Anita, some as the sister of Ailsa Carmichael, others as our invader of more than a month ago. For this achievement alone, she deserves our admiration. More significantly, however, she delivered the machine that will win us the war!"

The crowd erupts into wild cheers and applause. Buxton

raises his hands again. Silence descends, broken by muffled coughing and the shuffle of bodies.

"I ask for you to accept her into the Lost, as we have accepted all others who came to know the truth. She has earned our respect. We must give her nothing less." He holds his hand out to me. "Welcome, Anita Carmichael, to Fellhill. Your home."

Home.

Is it home?

I clasp his outstretched hand to sedate applause, hoping he can't feel me shaking. Gizzy presents a pair of dog-tags stamped with my name, faction and encampment.

"But I'm not a soldier anymore," I whisper.

Buxton hesitates at the beaded chain already disappearing beneath my shirt before slipping the new pair over my head.

"We all fight for the Lost," he says. "We do not worship our soldiers above the rest."

He doesn't need to speak for me to hear him sneer, "Unlike some factions."

Man, he really hates The People's Republic, and we didn't even murder his leader.

A Magnum and a box of bullets follow, the polished chromium flashing under the lights. I buckle the holster around my hips, my fingers stroking the wooden handle of the gun.

"No chance of a Glock?" I say out the corner of my mouth.

Buxton's face twitches then smooths. He sweeps his arm towards a seat in the front row.

Over the next half-hour, I listen to a brief overview of my new faction: history, standard protocols, hierarchy and important individuals. Personnel I'll communicate with on a daily basis introduce themselves, though the whole encampment can't fit into the hall. A buffet of drinks and snacks ends the ceremony, people clustered in groups, chatting and laughing. Buxton joins Gizzy and me where we talk to Carrie-Anne of the excellent bullshitting.

Turns out she's hilariously droll and not irritating at all.

Could she become another friend, alongside Emily? Someone I can be close to and—maybe—confide in.

In a few years, when I forgive myself.

"You will start on the dragon tomorrow," Buxton says, our conversation reaching a natural lull. "Report to the main munitions factory at 0800, I'll meet you there. Gizzy will tell you where it is."

The crowd takes his exit as their cue to disperse. More soldiers shake my hand, offering personal words of welcome, their faces and names blurring into one. My jaw aches from smiling, a facial expression I've not had much use for this last decade.

Back at the house, Gizzy keeps his promise. I have no idea who begs first.

Probably me.

The main munitions factory soars over the other buildings in the industrial area, a ridge of belching smokestacks crowning the armoured structure. An elevated air-train line curves around, its white floatway bright in the overcast day.

Buxton leads me through a massive pair of double rolling doors into a cavernous room where the dragon crouches, as glorious as ever.

My blood has been cleaned off her.

People mill around a long conveyor belt, forklift trucks zipping by carrying pallets of rattling boxes. The ring of striking metal comes from one corner, blocked by machinery. A large extractor fan in the far wall stirs air reeking of vegetable oil and fireworks.

Buxton slides a hand along the dragon's silver flank. "I want you to create me an exhaustive file: weapons, reloading, functionality. Is it as indestructible as claimed? What material is it made from?"

I don't tell him what Wick already said—graphene and carbon nanotubes. It may mean something to Buxton's people but the longer I work on the dragon, unravelling her mysteries, the happier I'll be.

"Imagine our army if we constructed other unbreakable

vehicles. Nothing could stop us."

The light in his eyes unsettles me. The last thing our conflict needs is another zealot viewing people as less significant than cockroaches.

"I'll assemble a team to assist you: scientists, engineers, weapons experts. Anything to complete this research quickly. Perhaps I'm being too cautious but I want to be familiar with the machine. Having other indestructible support would make the task of stopping the war easier, and less risky than pinning our hopes on one weapon." Buxton faces me, his eyes intent. "Do you understand what I want you to do? This assignment is critical and I'm entrusting it to you."

Talk about pressure.

"I understand. And, thank you for letting me do this. I'll do my best to get you the information you need… sir."

See, conforming.

His lips twitch.

I clear my throat. "It'll speed my research to be re-familiarised with her controls by taking her out—by completing a test flight. I could find somewhere remote. Use her weapons to their full capacity."

I stop talking instead of babbling about how much I ache to fly in her again.

For research purposes, purely for research purposes.

Buxton pins me with his probing gaze.

Is he wondering if I'll steal her? He said he trusted me but leaders lie.

"I understand where you're coming from…"

There's a 'but' in there somewhere. If he refuses, I'll argue until he concedes or threatens me with his little gun again.

I need her power and the taste of freedom, especially as I

almost died to reclaim her.

Good point. Tell him he owes me one.

"I won't object as long as you're careful and bring it back in one piece. Don't rely on the apparent indestructibility. And come find me in my office on your return."

I open my mouth to tell him he can't stop me and realise he agreed. Excitement tingles to the tips of my nail-less toes.

"Yes, sir!" I fist my hand to keep from tossing him a goofy salute.

Probably a bit much.

"Try not to alert too many people to the machine's existence. Stay away from populated areas and don't get out of it, not for any reason."

"I won't. I'll be careful," I say, grinning like an idiot.

"Okay, I'll see you when you return."

I lower the hatch in the dragon's belly and wriggle inside the welcoming dark to stroke the cables, helmet and goggles. My last piece clicks into place with the seamless booting of the brain-computer interface.

I stretch my wings, the tips touching the walls on either side of the room. Everyone in the building halts in a scrum of gaping mouths. A spanner rings on concrete. My steps chime in the stacked crates of bullets. I stalk outside in a roll of liquid grace, the dull light unable to dampen the silver glory of the dragon.

She is magnificent.

I bunch my legs, head to the sky, and propel upwards in a whoosh of air. I circle the expanse of Fellhill twice, twisting and diving, untouchable and safe.

This is my element in the heavens—me, the dragon and limitless wonder.

Better than sex. Sorry, Gizzy.

Spiralling above the elevation of any plane or bird, I open my mouth, a burst of flame dissipating in the oxygen-deficient air. I hover for a second then tuck my wings and plunge. Wind roars over my body, the ground rushing in a blur of green and brown. The blood thrums in my veins.

I am unstoppable.

Instead of obliterating most of Fellhill, I flash over the encampment, trees bending in my wake. Soldiers of the Lost nestles in the western mountains, the natural barrier another reason why few people bother them. I follow the valleys of old roads and fly south down Loch Lomond, now more swamp than loch.

Rebel State drained it to foil any poison plot. Rumour has them using the excess in an elaborate fountain in their central square, and for bathing.

I can't recall the last time I had a bath.

I skirt Glasgow, probably little more than a speck in the clouds to any savage perusing the sky. My elevated position protects me from viewing their welcome mat of corpses on poles.

Ayrshire passes in a blur of green, the fields gone fallow. The purple bloom of heather marks the hillier regions. Staying high, I enter the barrenness of Dumfries and Galloway, land of mountains and pine forests.

Thousands fled to England ahead of the fence being weaponised, including those with political affiliations for unionism rather than independence. Those who didn't make it gathered in the south in what became the Borderlands— an area with no faction, just tribes of feral people pissed at everybody. Life expectancy is low due to a combination of in-fighting, abominations, exposure and cannibalism.

It's the least populated area I can think of.

My recce confirms I'm the only thing with a heartbeat for at least a couple of miles.

I dive into the remnants of a village in a bowl of land, crumbling a building with one clawed foot. Bullets, lasers and missiles pelt another, dust drifting in billows of white. For a few pleasant hours, I test the weapons, a grin stretching my face and laughter bubbling in my chest.

This is freedom.

I launch into the air when I run out of structures to destroy and leave the village resembling the aftermath of a nuclear apocalypse.

Or Livingston.

My stomach clenches but I shake it off.

No more guilt. The truth sucks but I'm a different person—no more killing; no more fighting for a lie. Or to prove my faction is the most righteous. The dragon is my life. I'll use my knowledge of her to direct Buxton into forcing surrender with the minimum of casualties.

There will be no repeat of The People's Republic. He can take his inevitable losses without slaughtering everyone.

I head east over the rough landscape previously known as the Scottish Borders, now part of the Borderlands. If I fly a little further, I might spot the fence and see if England still exists.

I swallow and bank away. What would be worse—people living happy lives ignoring us, or a scorched landscape and scattered bodies? If they're at war, the rest of the world must suffer the same chaos.

Meaning there is no sanctuary. No escape.

I don't want to know, don't *need* to know. Fellhill is my home and we're going to stop our war.

I'll make my own peace.

46

"I assumed the small earthquake heralded your return," Buxton says, glancing up at my knock on the door frame.

"I do like to announce myself."

"Indeed." He clicks the cap on a red pen he was using to annotate a map spread over his desk. "What did you learn on your test flight?"

I describe it in detail, throwing in some extra information on heavy smoke over Embra.

Turns out that cornflower-blue-eyed bastard was right all along—I was a fool to be so sure of my faction.

Buxton opens his magical desk drawer and hands me a datapad. "Compile notes on this. My team will meet you at the dragon at 0800 tomorrow."

I jog back to Gizzy's—our—house to find it empty, inhale some food and return to the dragon to sit on her splayed foot, my stylus tapping the datapad screen, scribbling a rough diagram of her exterior and interior. I list her weapons and make a note about her reloading requirements. Yawning, I glance at the clock.

Ten pm! I must have been too absorbed to notice the darkening light and the silence from the factory as sensible people went home.

I leave the datapad in the dragon's belly and close the hatch, though it doesn't lock from the outside.

There's little risk of sabotage. No one in Fellhill would dare risk Buxton's displeasure.

The roads are deserted, the walk skirting a mixture of barracks and normal-looking residential areas on the way to Gizzy's house. *Our* house.

Must remember that.

Footfalls clack on concrete, keeping pace. I wait and my inept stalker enters the bronzed glow of a streetlight.

"Who the fuck do you think you are?" she hisses, one polished fingernail jabbing at me.

Shiny blonde hair curls over the shoulders of her fitted jacket, the vest top beneath revealing an excess of cleavage.

I stick out my hand and plaster on a smile. "I'm Anita. I don't believe we've met."

The woman recoils, tottering on strappy sandals. Her aquamarine gaze sweeps me from head to toe. She doesn't seem impressed by my baggy combats and long sleeves, in comparison to the skirt barely covering her ass.

"You think you can muscle in and steal what's mine?" She staggers but catches herself, her legs pale in the darkness.

Is she drunk?

How unprofessional.

No wonder The People's Republic banned the stuff. I suspect Marshall kept it for himself and his buddies. It was easy to identify when Reece panted his moist, yeasty breath in my face.

"I haven't stolen anything from you," I say.

We're alone on the street. I slide back a step.

I could outrun her in those ridiculous shoes, though I'm not averse to knocking her on her pert little derrière.

She sucks in a breath, straining her top. "Gizzy is *mine*."

Hello, jealousy, long time no see. What has it been—like five fucking minutes?

Dread unfurls in my stomach, clawing upwards to slice my throat. Will this be another awful repeat? From Hannah and Marshall to this half-sloshed beauty and Gizzy? It only takes one person to twist the hearts and minds of others.

Wars start over less.

"Gizzy doesn't belong to anyone," I say in a mild tone.

"He belongs to me." She slaps her chest, nearly bowling herself over. "You don't deserve him and you don't deserve to be here."

"I deserve to be here as much as you. I almost died to deliver the dragon."

Okay, I was coerced. But she doesn't need to know that.

"You'll wish you hadn't come here."

I roll my eyes. "I'm not going to stand and argue with someone who's drunk or high or… Whatever you are. Go sleep it off and leave me the hell alone."

I walk away to a stream of obscenities centred on my promiscuous sex life.

The clack of her heels doesn't follow.

47

The audacity of the bitch. From the sight of her, she hasn't suffered one day of hard battle, pampered and safe in Fellhill.

I stomp into the lounge. Gizzy comes out of his kitchen, drying his hands on a dish towel.

"Hey, long day for you! What—" He frowns and cups my cheek, placing a soft kiss on my mouth. "What's wrong, what happened?"

"Do you know a woman—tall, blonde and extremely pissed at me?"

His hand falls from my face and his gaze slides away. He slumps on the leather couch, elbows on his knees, his bare toes disappearing into the plush rug.

"Lianda," he sighs, finally looking at me, his normally expressive eyes guarded. "What did she say?"

"She said you belonged to her and I don't deserve you. She threatened me."

He stands suddenly. "What else did she say to you?"

I wave my hand. "Something about making me regret coming here. Who the hell is this woman and why does she hate me?"

"She and I were together—kind of—for a few months." He reclaims his seat, running his fingers through his hair. "We

254

were together that night, ah, the night you and I met."

My skin prickles. He refuses to meet my eyes.

"The night you and I met. The night I infiltrated Fellhill and you nearly kissed me. You were in a relationship with someone else?"

Should I be angry, disgusted, hurt or indifferent? He was no saint, unlike me. But he was willing to cheat. To betray someone. It shocks me, especially as I'm the one trying to trust him.

I don't know a damn thing about him.

"No! It wasn't a relationship—we were having sex, having fun. As soon as Buxton dismissed me, I went to her and ended it. I'd considered breaking it off, anyway. The sex was great but she got possessive and needy and—"

His mouth snaps shut.

I do not want to hear about his fantastic sex with some other woman. A woman he instantly dumped for me, the newcomer.

His warm arms wrap around me. "Anita, please believe me. I was going to finish it with her. You were so beautiful and wounded. I felt more for you in that second than I ever did for Lianda. I should have told you about her."

"No wonder she hates me. Now I feel sorry for her." I raise my chin. "Will you hurt me, too?"

He brushes a strand of hair behind my ear, his fingers trailing down my cheek. "I will never hurt you. You have to trust me."

"It's hard to trust anyone."

Sadness fills his face. And disappointment. They're not something I thought I'd see when he looked at me.

"You don't believe me," he says.

"Not yet, but I want to."

"You have to trust me," he says with more force, clasping my shoulders as if he might try to shake some sense into me.

He'll earn himself a punch if he tries.

"You can't keep holding back. I've been patient but it hurts that you won't share the full story of what happened when you were taken prisoner."

I flinch in his grip. "Why the hell is that relevant? I don't want to remember it so I don't want to talk about it. I might never talk about it."

"You have to if you want to move on. Heal."

"Who are you—my therapist? I have moved on. Rehashing it isn't going to make me feel better."

I happily forget about how good it was to share a portion of myself with him in the alleyway.

Totally different.

"But I want to know everything about you."

"Believe me, you don't want to know this," I say, quietly, then a little louder, "and do you tell me all your secrets? No. You've been holding back, too, as I've recently discovered."

"That's not fair." He steps away, his face stiff.

I sigh. "Look, I don't want to fight. It's just… You have to give me some time."

"I don't want to fight, either." He holds out his hand. "Let's go to bed."

But we don't have sex.

* * *

Sunlight dapples my closed eyelids. Soft kisses tickle my cheek. Gizzy props himself on one arm.

"I'm sorry," he says. "Take all the time you need."

A pressure eases in my chest.

We're going to be okay. Lianda is an adult. She'll recover from her unceremonious dumping and move on, find someone more deserving of her attention. I accept Gizzy's apology for not telling me.

I need to trust him because if I don't trust him, how can I ever love him?

He leans over and crushes his lips to mine. I open my mouth to avoid cutting myself on my teeth.

Sex I understand.

We roll across the bed. T-shirts flutter to the floor. I wrap my legs around his waist and twist, sending us to the carpet. He laughs as I trail kisses down his chest, groans when I lick where he lies flat against his stomach and suck him into my mouth.

"God, Anita."

I sit on my heels and smile at his dazed expression. He lunges for my wrist, dragging me on top of him and flipping us over. His hands skate down my sides but avoid where I desperately want him to touch me. A sharp tug and my underwear disappears.

I suppose I can practise my sewing skills from Revolutionary Front.

Gizzy pushes himself inside me.

For fuck's sake. I like a quickie as much as the next girl but teasing is nice, building sweet anticipation. The first few times were amazing but the pounding is getting a little tiresome.

I start to say something but he collapses on top, suffocating me against his chest. He hammers into me and cries out, driving himself deep.

"God—god," he gasps.
At least one of us is having fun.

Five people wait for me at the munitions factory, petting the dragon and talking in hushed voices. I saunter over, glancing around for Lianda, though I have no idea if she works here. It probably won't help but I need to tell her I understand, even empathise with, her furious jealousy. Gizzy treated her horribly.

So why does she want him back?

The group stop their chatter and introduce themselves. A scientist duo envelope me in fleshy hugs, their crimson hair tickling my nose. The engineer grunts. The final members are weapons specialists and a couple, tribal tattoos encircling muscular arms.

They're bulkier than Gizzy.

We move the dragon to waste ground in the far north of the encampment, nothing beyond the fence but hills. We spend an enjoyable day testing the weapons at our disposal, trying to damage her perfect form—missiles, rays and bullets, grenades and bombs. We blast her with lasers and flamethrowers, toss acid and other corrosive chemicals. An EMP has no effect on her controls.

We exhaust the arsenal we can unleash on her safely and she stands smudged black and lightly scratched but unharmed and unbreached. Her armour may weaken from weapons fired at the same spot over and over. But no one will ever get close enough. She is, essentially, indestructible.

My team—*my* team, I lead a team—marvel such a weapon was created, and by Nationless. A faction they disregarded due to the psychosis of its leader. Even the engineer grins at the full power of her weapons.

We return her to the factory and my team disperse. I scribble on the datapad, making a note to ask Buxton for another member to complete the Super Squad—a computer geek to decipher the interface and internal circuitry.

To me, it's magic and fairy dust.

I spy Lianda a couple of times, wearing a jumpsuit and combat boots instead of a skirt and ridiculous heels. She scuttles away, a snarl twisting her face.

Perhaps she's a lost cause.

Back at the house, I grill a plate of sausages with mashed potato, having forgotten to eat anything since breakfast.

I'm still not used to three huge meals a day.

Gizzy enters the kitchen as I scrape my dish clean.

"Hey, you want me to make you dinner?"

He kisses me on the head. "Nah, I'll grab some toast. Got a strategy meeting Buxton's called at the last minute."

"On what?"

He jams bread in the toaster, his muscles sliding under his black t-shirt. "On the dragon and how it can be used effectively. He's keen to proceed after your tests proved how indestructible it is."

News travels fast to Buxton's ears.

The toaster pops. Gizzy slathers the slices in butter and turns to me, munching, his black combat-swathed hip against the counter top.

"Shouldn't I be there?"

"I, ah, don't think you've been invited. It's for his closest advisers."

Gizzy finishes his toast and opens the fridge, gulping carrot juice straight from the bottle.

"He said I'd be involved in all aspects of the dragon and how she's used. I'm coming with you."

"You can't just show up."

"Why not?"

"Because… he hasn't asked you to be there. If Buxton wanted your input, he'd tell you."

"Well, I'm going. Where is it? His office?"

Gizzy scowls, slamming the fridge and mopping juice from his upper lip.

I guess my stubbornness isn't so adorable now.

"Yes, but—"

"Look, let's not argue. Buxton should have asked me, so I'm going."

His worship of Buxton is disconcerting, and a little frightening, or maybe that's just me. I'm not exactly an unbiased voice on the suitability of leaders. Marshall tricked me for years and Wick represented a whole new level of insanity. John isn't a leader but he can still go to hell.

Buxton and I will clash over the dragon. Where will Gizzy's loyalties lie?

An awful, sinking feeling suspects it won't be with me.

Gizzy huffs and stalks out of the kitchen. "Fine. Do whatever you want."

I roll my eyes at his stiff back. Tonight will be fun but I'm not staying home to soothe his ruffled sensibilities. Planning the dragon's deployment damn well requires my presence.

A small, feminine part of me—freshly awoken and batting her eyelashes—urges me to do what he says. To placate him by remaining behind like an obedient little woman.

Screw that.

We leave the house, stomping the short distance to Buxton's office. Gizzy marches ahead, his legs devouring the pavement.

I guess it'll be another night of no sex. Being alone is soul-crushing at times but sure as shit simpler.

Gizzy joins his leader and the nine soldiers gathered in the office. More chairs have been brought into the room and the other people occupy them in a loose semi-circle opposite a large map on the wall. Gizzy claims the last seat without looking at me. His rigid face points towards Buxton, who fails to notice me hovering in the doorway. I snap the door shut. Whispers swell like wind rustling through grass. I straighten my shoulders.

The dragon is mine. Buxton has no right to hold the meeting in my absence.

Bet Gizzy wishes he kept his mouth shut, patted me on the head and skipped self-importantly out the door.

"Anita, what are you doing here?" Buxton says. "This is for close advisers only."

I force myself not to squirm under the weight of his disapproval.

I'm a soldier, *dammit*, and risked my life for the dragon. It means something.

"You told me I'd be involved in what you did with the dragon. That is why I'm here. Because *you* said I could be." My voice is reasonable but the undertone implies he can go fuck himself.

His jaw twitches, his diamond earring flashing in the

overhead lights. Heat pools in the small of my back.

"Fine. *Stay*." He strides to the map on the wall.

I release a breath and walk behind the seated soldiers to perch on the window ledge. Several people twist in their seats to watch me. Gizzy's eyes remain steadfast on Buxton and his map.

If he's going to be a child, I'll snub him, too. Though it hurts my chest a little.

And he wants me to trust him. Definitely no sex. I'll generously consider it in the morning but only if he doesn't treat my body as a warm hole for him to pound into. I want to be worshipped. I want him to tease, to drive me to the delicious edge again and again and again. Delaying the gratification until I'm flushed and trembling and desperate.

Now *that* would be good make-up sex.

Buxton snaps out a metal pointer and whips it against the map. He pivots to regard his advisers, his elite guards. His *conformers*. Me, he ignores.

"This meeting is to inform you of my strategy for the dragon machine, now the claims of its indestructibility have been supported."

Yes, by me. You're welcome.

"I want your input. I need your backing and loyalty. I need you to be one hundred percent behind me because how we proceed may end the war in weeks."

The soldiers murmur to each other, falling silent as he continues.

"We need to hit hard and fast to show it is surrender, or die. Our first targets will be the biggest strongholds: Glasgow, Stirling, Inverness and Dundee." He smacks each place marked in red on the map. "Destroy them and the meek will follow. We cannot be half-hearted. We must raze these encampments to the ground. If their factions refuse to yield, we pick them off until they comply." He collapses the pointer between his palms. "Make no mistake—this war is ours if we use the machine to its full capabilities. We must prove we cannot be defeated. Their one option is to bow before us and submit."

The soldiers cheer.

"Are you insane?" I say, my words dropping into noise and spreading outward in silence.

Buxton's face stiffens. "You *do not* speak—"

"If you show the other factions the truth of what happened in the debating chamber, they have no reason to keep fighting. The dragon won't be needed at all."

"Do not be naive, Anita. You were blind to the truth in your own faction. Self-righteousness blinded you, as it did with every other faction that blamed us. We finally have the means to avenge those wrongs. You understand that, given your thirst for vengeance so recently sated."

Gizzy slides lower in his chair. It stings more than Buxton's snide remarks. One of the lackeys sniggers, his bulbous head shining under the fluorescent lights. I glare at him and turn my attention to Buxton, the smug son-of-a-bitch.

"We need to bring the country back together not burn everything to ash because you still hold a grudge."

"This is the chaos that brings great change. The Lost will be the phoenix rising from the ashes of Scotland."

"Fuck your chaos."

Someone honest-to-god gasps. Colour flares in Buxton's cheeks.

"You don't care about stopping the war or saving lives," I

say, "you just care about winning."

"How many precious lives did you spare in Livingston?" he says, his sneer cutting deep. "This is a war, Anita. Sacrifices must be made. We will have our peace but it will be paid for."

I take a deep breath. Another. The air burns all the way down to the fury swirling in my chest.

"And what about the rest of the world? It could've taken this long for them to recover. What if they're watching, deciding their approach? They could panic and declare war on us. Sanctions, punishments. We could all be tried for war crimes."

His eyebrows elevate. "Who gives a shit about the rest of the world, or what's left of it? If they respond with violence, we'll retaliate with the machine. We'll show them we are a ruling faction to be feared. We will not be dismissed again."

Heads bob.

"I know quite well your attitude regarding the machine but it is not your plaything. It is a weapon. The machine belongs to Soldiers of the Lost and, ultimately, to me. The final say is mine, *not yours*." He flicks his fingers. "Thank you for your input, Anita. You can go."

His advisers stare, except for Gizzy, who'd struggle to sink any lower in his seat and not slide to the floor like a spineless blob.

I gape at Buxton, too stunned to argue.

Why did he bother to wait? He could've assigned one of his special few to gather his data, leaving me oblivious in the hospital.

Another useless leader corrupted by power.

"You are a *fool*," I say, my face flushing, "and will be the death of us."

The bulgy-headed lackey levers himself to his feet and

cracks his knuckles.

Great. A fucking goon.

I swallow the words 'bloodthirsty' and 'savage'—and maybe some expletives—and stride out, the slamming of the door ending the shocked silence. I stomp into the gathering dusk, rain clouds massing, and am almost back to the house when tears scald my cheeks. I swipe at them.

Don't you dare cry because of Buxton and his drones.

I slump onto Gizzy's bed fully clothed and yank the sheets smelling of him over my head.

Where else can I go?

Gizzy said we won't work if I don't trust him. The same applies if he treats me as secondary to Buxton. If he refuses to stand for me and fight. Is everything he said a lie? Will I be another Lianda—used for sex and discarded when I annoy him?

It upsets me to imagine being kicked out of his house to live alone, pitied and ignored. Worthless and useless. Banished from the dragon and never allowed to fly in her.

Lianda will be deliriously happy.

I sob a little as the fantasy of a normal life in Fellhill shatters at my feet, each shard an unreachable dream.

I am the fool.

49

A commotion jerks me from a restless doze. I sit up and rub swollen eyes.

No more tears. If Buxton refuses to tell the truth about the lie we've been fighting for, I'll do it myself. I'll steal the dragon from the third goddamn faction and fly to each stronghold. If they don't believe me, I'll take my chances with the rest of the world and leave the idiots to die in the dirt and blood of Buxton's vengeance.

Even without the dragon, Soldiers of the Lost are formidable.

Footsteps slap the pavement below Gizzy's bedroom window. People call to each other in high voices. The thud of their passage swells and fades.

I swing my legs out of bed, my boots on.

It might be an attack, though no warning siren. Maybe there's an impromptu party to celebrate the dragon dominance plan, soldiers flocking to Buxton's office to pat their magnificent leader on the back. Congratulating themselves for harbouring the victory machine. A weapon they didn't lose one drop of blood to claim.

But I did. Three pints of it, and some organs.

Night cloaks Fellhill in a dome of blackness held at bay by

the streetlights. I head towards the faint shouts to discover what calamity has befallen my comrades. Or blessing. It doesn't necessarily mean something bad.

Based on life experience, I expect bloodshed rather than presents and cake.

Voices bounce off buildings, coming from everywhere and nowhere. Similar to the evening Gizzy herded me into the alleyway, using the acoustics to confuse. He manipulated me exactly where he wanted me.

Trapped and vulnerable.

Is his initial kindness—and the end of my self-imposed abstinence—blinding me to his true nature, my instincts attempting to warn me with doubt?

I force the question away. It doesn't matter. Now is as good a time as any to take my dragon and get out of here.

I find myself pulled in the direction of the hospital.

Perhaps there are casualties in the unfolding disaster, or someone has returned injured from a mission. I haven't seen Emily since leaving her care. She was absent during my initiation ceremony, tending to a group of ill soldiers.

Spots of rain hit my face, the muted glow of windows shining between interlocking trunks. My boots shuffle up the incline, the wind ruffling my hair. I pause after a couple of strides.

The damn yelling is coming from the opposite direction.

Sighing, I retrace my steps.

It'd be nicer to sit and talk to Emily rather than find out what's riling people. The hospital seems more sanctuary than prison now that I'm no longer bedridden inside it.

I pass Gizzy's house, the windows dark, and follow the path to Buxton's office, roots from the trees on either side distorting the concrete. The commotion drifts from somewhere beyond, the exact location shielded by residential streets. I lose several minutes stomping through avenues and cul-de-sacs, cursing under my breath. A tang of smoke wafts on the swirling wind.

It explains the fuss. Something—or someone—is on fire, or has been on fire. A lack of flickering light suggests the object/building/person no longer burns.

I hop over the uneven border of waste ground, following the floatway above me, and cross between two hulking structures in the first row to reach the source of the ruckus. A crowd swarms about the main munitions factory and spills through the doorway. It appears most of Fellhill are in attendance, kitted in a variety of jumpsuits, uniforms and camouflage-patterned gear. I tap the arm of a guy on the outskirts. He turns, mouth open.

"What's going on?" I shout, glancing from him to the munitions factory, the crammed bodies obscuring my view.

He blinks protruding eyes.

Helpful.

I push into the crowd, trying not to use my elbows or kick people in the shins. After several frustrating minutes of bouncing off a fleshy wall, or being jostled away, I abandon politeness and jab at soft spots. People twitch out of my path. I move from spitting rain to noisy barrage, the air heavy and hot with sweat and exhaled breath.

Everyone is somehow taller than me. And broader.

Does Buxton add growth hormones to the filtered water to form an army of super-soldiers? I wouldn't put it past him, the controlling, dismissive bastard.

Conversations echo and slap at my ears. Smoke purls in

grey clouds. A tickle starts in the back of my throat, each breath increasing the urge to cough. The acrid tang of burnt electrics stings my nose.

Is the dragon okay?

Genuine anxiety curls in my belly with the swallowed smoke.

"Excuse me, pardon me, coming through."

The bubbling uproar smothers my voice. I glimpse one of my team in a flash of maroon but am too intent to delay my momentum. Panting and dishevelled, I pop free of the tight edge of people. The horde ranges in a heaving, multi-limbed circle, cloth whispering as bodies shimmy against each other. I scrub the tangled hair out of my eyes and squint at the object of everyone's attention.

My kneecaps strike the concrete like two hammer blows.

"No," I wheeze.

This can't be happening.

The dragon—*my dragon*—stands shining and silver and beautiful, her defiant head above the crowd.

But her days of flying are over.

50

Odorous smoke puffs from the dragon's mouth as though she lives, breathing fire deep in her belly. I wait for her to roar and turn her head, one burst of brilliant flame reducing us to ash. She stares at the doorway through shattered obsidian eyes. More smoke curls out the open hatch, a patina of soot dulling her skin. The marmalade light of the blaze flickers within her interior.

She'll never fly again.

Sobs build in my throat, my chest threatening to explode and paint the ground with lung and bone. Tears drip to the grimy concrete floor, forming circles of brown paste.

She was my prize for surviving Wick's torture, my acceptance into the Lost. She held infinite possibilities in her clawed hands if I was brave enough to take them—freedom, sanctuary, peace. Now there is nothing. Nothing but a cold, bloody cavity where my heart used to beat.

She was the only thing I loved in the whole damn war.

Who did this? No one from Fellhill is stupid enough to destroy their victory weapon. Another intruder? Perhaps the Lost's strength is a mirror, its perfect reflection masking the rot beneath.

The world narrows, framing the ruin of my dragon in

271

shimmering white. The fidgeting people fade. My bruised knees go numb. I shut my eyes and bow my head to mourn.

A voice among the crowd pierces my bubble of grief.

"It was her! *She* did this!"

<h1 style="text-align:center">51</h1>

The declaration slices the noise.

The confident voice sounds like Lianda, though I'm no expert on her dulcet tones.

I raise a heavy head. The dragon swims in my vision, shining and smoking, and I hunch against the ache in my chest. People shift, their eyes as hard as polished stones, lips curled into sneers.

What does that mean? Who did what?

"She's a traitor," the helpful woman continues.

Who's a traitor?

Why is everyone looking at me?

Horror slithers through my frozen limbs and replaces the loss in my stomach. The jostling at my back increases, a rumble vibrating through the crowd.

I can't watch their welcome turn to loathing and become the pariah a second time—the *traitor*. Where is Lianda? She destroyed the dragon—*my dragon!*—to reclaim Gizzy, as if, with me gone, he'll realise he loves her, my company nothing but an amusing distraction.

She'll fucking *die* for this.

I plant my foot, my eyes scanning the crowd for her blonde hair and whatever ridiculous tit-showcasing outfit she's wearing. A blow knocks me to the concrete, grit shifting under my splayed palms. A kick thumps into my ribs and I curl into a ball. The thud of boots on flesh replaces the snarl of the mob.

Smack, smack.

Wick's hateful face expands in my skull. I whimper and press my fists to my forehead.

Get up, you cowering fool, or the bitch wins.

Bodies surge above me, their humanity stripped to bared teeth and glittering eyes. I struggle to my hands and knees, striking at the boots whirling around me.

They aim for my exposed stomach.

The bastards. I sacrificed my spleen and part of my liver for them, what more do they want from me?

I growl low in my throat and tense to lurch to my feet. A boot connects with my temple. Rainbow stars explode.

I'm going to die.

Rough hands yank and the crowd withdraws. Fingers bunch in the dusty collar of my shirt, dragging me upright to stand on quivering legs. Muscles throb beneath scraped and oozing skin. My vision steadies to meet frosty eyes the colour of a winter sky.

"Buxton," I say, my voice strangled, "I didn't do this. I almost died to bring her here."

His teeth flash in the lights. "Is this your way of saving us, Anita? Is this you teaching me a lesson?"

He pulls me close and I tug at his fingers. The mob watches, their collective breath loud in the enclosed space.

No sign of Lianda or Gizzy.

"Why would I destroy something I loved?"

"Some people enjoy hurting what they love. You betrayed

The People's Republic when you stole the dragon. I should have realised—once a traitor, always a traitor."

The word shivers through the crowd.

"You sanctimonious bastard," I breathe. "*You*—"

He slaps me. I rock in his grip, blinded by my hair. My head swivels back, slow and painful enough to creak through my spine. Buxton drops his hand from my shirt.

"Where are your witnesses, where is your proof?" I say, my cheek stinging. "Are you so quick to believe the accusation because I disagreed with your plan?"

I falter. The dragon is gone, ruined. There is no plan. There is nothing.

I renew my glare. "You don't like opposition, do you, Buxton? You like your soldiers mute and obedient. Fucking nodding puppets."

Storm clouds roil in the depths of his grey eyes.

This is not helping, you idiot.

I scan the sea of hostile faces again.

Where is Gizzy? He won't believe I destroyed the dragon. He understands how hard I fought for her.

And he promised.

Siding with Buxton will do more than hurt me.

Where is he?

"I saw her do it."

My head snaps around. Lianda glides forward in a froth of white skirt. Red heels clack as loud as rifle shots. She shines like a diamond among the darker clothes of her comrades.

"I saw Anita running from the dragon with petrol cans. I was too late to save the machine." Her eyes flick from Buxton to me, and they sparkle.

Sparkle.

The balls on this bitch.

"*You* did this!"

She smiles, not a hair out of place when mine clings to my sweaty, dirt-smeared face. Her skin glows. Blood dries and crusts in patches on my own.

"The lies of a traitor," she says.

Scathing words clog my throat and choke me. "You goddamn stupid bitch! Don't you know what you've done?"

I step towards her, my fists clenched.

She'll resemble Wick in the end—a pink, glistening concavity where her face used to be.

Some people deserve to die.

Her serene expression shimmers to uncertainty. Buxton's hand fastens around my arm and jerks me to a halt. I strain against his hold.

"Don't blame one of my people for what you've done."

I meet his thundery eyes without flinching. "I'm one of your people."

"Not anymore."

What more do I need to do to prove myself? Half-broken and battle-scarred, my mind a trap of awful memories. What else can I give without fracturing into pieces?

"Well, Anita, here's my witness."

I open my mouth to inform him of the reliability of said witness but he raises his voice.

"The punishment for destroying the machine and betraying your faction is death, by firing squad. Effective immediately."

He graces me with a pitying smile but I'm too distracted by his message to deliver the punch he deserves. Sweat liquefies the dried blood on my skin and I bleed anew.

Where the *fuck* is Gizzy? Perhaps he'll watch, his expressive eyes guarded. Or he may try to stop the madness, imploring Buxton until he's told to shut up and get out of the way. Which he will. Or he'll arrive too late and cradle my body in his strong arms, globs of lung dribbling from my lips.

I glimpse him in the crowd and my heart leaps.

"Gizzy!" My high-pitched voice echoes from the roof of the building. "Gizzy, tell him I didn't do it. You know me better than that. Tell him, *please.*"

He muscles through the crowd, his comrades watching his progress with eager eyes. The dragon rears behind him, broken shards of obsidian winking in the light. The smoke purling from her mouth lessens, winding between her sharp teeth and caressing her snout.

Lianda's gaze fastens on Gizzy. She cocks a slender hip and arches her back. He ignores her.

My hope sparks like a struck match flickering in a cupped hand.

Gizzy's eyes flit from Buxton to me. "Sir, I don't think Anita would—"

"Are you questioning my judgement, soldier?" Buxton's soft words blast through the room.

Gizzy's throat bobs, a drop of sweat trickling past his temple. He avoids looking at me and my heart plummets into my stomach.

"No, sir," he says.

"Gizzy, you know I wouldn't do this. You know me—"

"I don't know you," he says, staring at the floor. "I don't know you at all."

My knees threaten to buckle but a wave of prickling heat keeps me upright.

His leader—his *god*—judged me guilty and it's enough. Did

they plan this as a way to get rid of me once I brought them what they wanted? Did they laugh at how easily they caught me in their deception?

How stupid to imagine I could be loved.

Gizzy finally looks at me, his eyes dark, almost black, but unreadable. He scans the crowd, a flush rising in his cheeks, and settles on his leader still attached to my arm.

"How can you believe I'd do this?"

Gizzy's gaze fastens on mine, the certainty growing on his face and slicing my insides.

"If Buxton says you're a traitor"—he raises his chin—"then you're a traitor."

Buxton shoves me through the crowd. Warm bodies dance behind like rats following the pied piper. Victorious light suffuses Lianda's face. I jerk towards her but she melts away. Buxton hauls me into the rain, steering me between a rusted signpost and a glowing streetlight.

"Wait!"

The footsteps of the mob smother my cry. Shadows hide their faces, their eyes the only thing that glitters. Rope binds my wrists and stretches my arms wide. I open my mouth but no sound comes out. Buxton barks and soldiers scurry. Three men cradle shotguns and position themselves in a line. Buxton holds another out to Gizzy.

Gizzy shakes his head. "Sir, I—"

"She betrayed us, but you most of all. We welcomed her into our faction, trusted her, and she threw it back in our faces. She made fools of us both."

Gizzy licks his lips. "She did, sir. She has, but I still can't—"

"Take the shotgun. That's an order."

I strain against the ropes, his name trapped in my throat.

He won't do it. He can't. There's following orders then there's doing the right thing.

I need him to do what's right.

Gizzy takes the shotgun.

52

How did I not see this monster in my bed, deceiving me with a handsome face?

I tug against the bonds, the ropes biting deeper into my wrists.

There's no escape from this. What's the point? No dragon, no home. No life. I wish Stig had left me to be raped and chopped into pieces.

It would've hurt less.

And poor Emily. Her hard work, the resources squandered to heal me. I'm about to be reduced to a red, quivering mess beyond even her surgical skills.

I swallow a giggle threatening to end in a vomiting fit and suck on damp air. Buxton folds his arms, his face betraying nothing, the rain leaving dark circles on his fatigues.

"Ready!" he shouts.

I jump. Four shotguns cock with a harsh *chuck-chuck*. The crowd presses closer in a mass of steaming bodies. Lianda's smirking features aren't visible but her triumph burns along my skin.

"Aim!" Buxton raises his arm, straight and true, his finger pointed to the sky.

Four shotguns lift, the butts snug into shoulders. Rain

slices bronze streaks in the streetlight. Beyond the crowd, my dragon stands abandoned, the current events more riveting than her glorious carcass.

I blink water from my eyelashes and glare at Gizzy, though it pains me to look at him. His aim wobbles but steadies.

The callous bastard. How dare he claim my body as a trophy one minute and prepare to blast it to ruins the next? I'll shove his blind conviction down his throat until he chokes on it.

Buxton opens his mouth. I whip my head towards him, my wet hair slapping my face.

"Wait!" I yelp. "Just fucking wait!"

The shotguns waver, several pairs of eyes flicking to Buxton. I force my hunched body upright.

"You're so certain I did it with what—the testimony of one scorned woman? I thought you were fair, Buxton. Rational. Where is your proof?" Each word settles my quavering voice and unfurls over the crowd. "Where are the supposed petrol cans? Why don't my clothes stink of fuel? And where the hell would I get fuel? I've been in this cursed faction all of ten minutes."

"She stashed them and changed her clothes," Lianda yells from somewhere in the throng. "And the fuel is stored here, as always. She walked past it when she worked on the machine, planning her attack."

The multitude parts to reveal Lianda, her hands on her hips. The hair plastered to her face makes her eyes huge. Beguiling.

She and Hannah would've been great friends.

"Have the decency to humour me before you murder me, Buxton. Search my—" I wince, the pain a punch to the gut. "Search *Gizzy's* house and Lianda's house. If nothing is found in either place, shoot me and be done with it."

I sag in the ropes. Heat drains from my body, taking the last of my strength.

I can't fight anymore. I tried so hard.

"No!" Lianda squeaks, her throat bobbing. "Don't listen to her. She's desperate, blaming me to spare her worthless life."

Her eyes narrow at my snort.

Payback's a bitch, bitch.

Buxton taps his finger against his chin, watching us both with mild interest. He shakes his head and water droplets scatter from the tips of his shorn hair. I jerk, almost overbalancing, and hurl my final card.

"Unless you're afraid I'll prove you wrong."

I raise my chin, the effect somewhat ruined by my chattering teeth. Maybe no one will notice.

The horde gasps—again with the gasping—and Buxton's face darkens. He swivels to the firing squad and I brace myself.

Lianda has won.

"Search both houses and report back here."

Two men snap forward, one the muscled beast who sniggered at me in Buxton's office. They salute, place their shotguns on the wet ground and jog into the gloom.

My breath trembles out.

I may actually live through this.

But it doesn't seem like much of a victory.

"No!" Lianda shrieks. "She's playing you, making you look a fool."

Gizzy and the last man in the firing line lower their weapons. Gizzy frowns, glancing between Lianda and me. Fear etches lines into her stricken face and what does she need to be afraid of, unless she's guilty? Doubt floods his handsome features. His gaze rests on me but I refuse to meet it.

His epiphany comes too fucking late.

Lianda lunges for a discarded shotgun. I thrash against my bonds, the fibres of the rope stiff with water. While Gizzy gawps, the older man beside him stomps on her hand where it curls around the barrel of the closest gun. She howls, yanking her arm back and falling on her butt. Cradling her hand to her chest, she bursts into tears. Buxton cocks an eyebrow but makes no move to interfere.

Gizzy's shotgun droops further, horror and guilt ugly on his face. An icy flame of satisfaction flickers in my chest. It holds no warmth but my pain huddles around it.

Lianda sobs into the silence, guarded by my defender. Twenty minutes pass while we await a signal to resume. Bodies shift, coughs muffled in fists. The tension of the rope burns my wrists and screams through my joints.

The two soldiers return, preceded by the sloshing of petrol cans. They carry one apiece and place them at Buxton's feet with a clang. He looks at the containers then back to his men.

"Stashed at Lianda's house, sir, plus a pile of singed clothes."

Saved by stupidity.

"Bring her here," Buxton says.

Lianda weeps, her face blemished by tears. My guardian dumps her on her hands and knees at Buxton's feet.

Hesitant fingers touch his boots. "Buxton, I'm sorry! Don't hurt me. *Please!*"

Gizzy crosses to me, splashing in water flowing through the gutter. He unties the ropes. I shy away from the heat of his body, bile searing my throat. His eyes shimmer, wide and pleading. I struggle not to vomit, shrugging off his clinging hands instead of punching him.

The cobalt flame in my heart leaps higher. I am ice and steel and fury.

I stomp to where Lianda begs for her life. My boot connects with her bowed face in a crunch of delicate bone. She wails and flops into the road.

The voice in my head says *hurt, punish*. Kill.

"You were going to watch me die!" I growl, kicking her in the ribs. "Because of jealousy! You destroyed everything because you were fucking *jealous!*"

I stamp on her head and raise my boot again. Arms hoist me into the air.

Gizzy pants against my cheek. "Enough, Anita. She's had enough."

"Don't fucking touch me!"

My boots thump on concrete. I whirl and he recoils.

"Touch me again, I'll rip off your hand and feed it to you."

I march back to Lianda and yank her hair. Dazed, red-rimmed eyes meet mine.

"Congratulations. In a single day, you've betrayed your faction and sentenced yourself to death. For one man who doesn't want you. And you know what?" I bend low to whisper in her ear. "The sex wasn't even that good."

She hisses but my fist catches her jaw and tumbles her into the filthy road. A clump of hair ripples in my clenched hand.

"There's your traitor," I say, stalking towards Buxton. "One of your people after all. Bet you feel pretty fucking stupid."

For god's sake, don't taunt him.

He sucks in a breath and eases it out.

"I believe we all let anger rule our judgement tonight."

Typical leader. Power over everyone but responsible for nothing.

Clenched teeth stop me from spitting.

52

Buxton's gaze slides from mine, his face settling into rigid lines. "Lianda, you are guilty of destroying the machine. Punishment is death by firing squad. Effective immediately."

The words slither through my body.

Not me. Not me this time.

"No! Please, Buxton! Don't do this!"

Two men haul her to her feet. She flaps at them but they ignore her, tying her between the posts. I edge behind Buxton on shaking legs. The heat of the crowd pushes at my back, the whisper of my name weaving through.

I want to sit, hold on to something and catch my breath. I lock my knees, my face stiff with the effort of keeping it blank.

I should never have relaxed my guard and let someone in.

I'll not make that mistake again.

Lianda keens and thrashes against the rope. Her skirt clings to her thighs, red underwear obvious through the wet material.

She fastens wild eyes on me and grinds her teeth. "Bitch! Ugly whore! You'll die alone with no one to save you."

"I don't need anyone to save me." I mean for it to be loud and confident but it comes out more of a whisper.

I hug myself, trembling and brittle and cold.

"Ready!" Buxton shouts.

My breath hitches.

I don't have to watch this. I can leave.

"Aim!"

My feet freeze to the ground. Lianda stares at the shotguns.

"Please, Gizzy, I did it for you," she says. "I love you."

His shotgun doesn't waver.

A tear scalds my cheek and merges with the rain, dripping from my chin to be lost in the dark.

Do I cry for her or me?

Buxton raises his arm. Lianda gasps. My stomach clenches but I can't look away.

"Fire!" he says, sweeping down.

The guns boom and I stagger. A shot pulverises half of Lianda's face, leaving one eye to glare at me. The other shots cluster over her chest, liquefying flesh and shattering bone. She coughs a plume of pink mist and slumps in the ropes.

Did Gizzy aim for her face?

The ground tilts under my feet. I lurch a few steps, my hands on my knees. The air tastes metallic. I stumble off the road and vomit in the bushes. The crowd disperses, their voices too loud, too bright.

Perhaps they've seen it all.

They are Soldiers of the Lost. Blasting a body to jelly is what they do.

Gizzy slings the shotgun across his shoulder and joins Buxton. The other men in the firing line untie Lianda's corpse and drag it away. She leaves chunks of tissue like a twisted trail of breadcrumbs, leading to her grave instead of home.

"Anita."

I crawl from the bile-stained mulch, flinching at Buxton's voice. Turning my head takes an hour. His mouth moves but a buzzing in my ears drowns out the words.

A hand settles on my shoulder and I find the strength to run.

53

The squeak of my boots echoes in the empty corridor. I careen down the steps to the basement, sprawling on my face at the bottom. Moaning, I shove to my feet and hammer on the door carved with an intricate border of tangled flowers.

Emily pulls it open in a wash of golden light. "Anita? What's the matter? Are you hurt?"

I stumble into her arms and she staggers under my weight. My tears dampen the collar of her lilac shirt. She coaxes me, panting and shivering, into the living room. Candles flicker, the space softened by shadows, helped by the gunmetal-grey walls. A glass of wine sits on a table next to a book. She tries to lower me onto the couch but I pace on the rug, round and around.

"I need to get out of here." My teeth chatter in the cosy warmth. "I want to go home."

"This is your home."

I shake my head so hard it hurts my neck.

"Calders? There's nothing there anymore. Anita, please sit. Take a deep breath."

"I can't. Can't stay here." My chest tightens. "I'll die in no man's land but it'll be better than staying with them."

The struggle to breathe forces me to stop. I sway and Emily

steers me onto the settee. She presses my head between my legs, her cool hand rubbing my back.

"I want to go home," I sob.

Jesus, how pathetic do I sound?

"I know, honey. I know."

The soothing touch disappears. My tears drip on the laminate. The floor swims, a pulse pounding in my swollen head.

"Here, take this." Emily eases a pale blue pill into my mouth, guiding a glass of water to my lips. The rim clinks against my teeth. "Let's get you to bed. We'll talk in the morning."

She leads me into a room off a short hallway, the walls the same colour as the tablet dissolving in my stomach. A four-poster bed of dark wood and gossamer canopy occupies the centre. She floats around, her murmuring voice vibrating through my tired muscles. She peels me out of my damp clothes and dresses me in a cotton nightie, tucking me into bed. Small and safe. I sink into the mattress.

Her fingers brush my cheek in a waft of lavender. "Sleep, now. Tomorrow, I'll help you."

I blink and she's gone. Blackness cloaks the room and soaks into my skin. What the hell has she given me? My limbs are heavy, my breathing like the rush of waves on a beach. The events of the evening blur.

Why does she have whatever this glorious drug is so close to hand?

Perhaps she uses it herself when the pain gets too much.

* * *

The diazepam, as it turns out, clears hysteria but does nothing for pain in the cold light of morning. My heart sits in my chest like shattered glass.

How could the kind-eyed soldier who treated me with compassion when I was an intruder, behave so cruelly when I became his comrade?

More than his comrade.

How could Gizzy have known me, touched me, and been prepared to execute me on nothing but the word of his leader? Do I mean so little that his loyalty is worth more than my life?

I shudder. Emily comes out of the kitchen and hands me a cup of coffee. I curl around the warmth.

"Are you sure you won't stay? You can help me in the hospital. There's more than enough space for you here." She perches on the arm of the couch, one graceful leg crossed over the other.

"Thank you, but this damn war has had enough of my blood. It'll be harder to escape without the dragon but all I need is a vehicle to get me to the coast." My voice shakes, the scalding coffee not enough to distract from my loss. "I'll swim if I have to. Or whittle a boat out of a tree. The chaos of a foreign country has to be better than this."

"What about England? I realise Ireland is out since the west coast is too dangerous." She sips from her cup, her other hand smoothing her navy skirt.

"Maybe, if I can get around the fence."

She cocks her head, her cool blue eyes steady on mine. I raise my mug to my mouth and inhale fragrant steam.

"The world is not as chaotic as we believe. People in England may be alive."

I choke, coffee burning my nose. "How the hell do you know that?"

"Quite by accident, really."

She smiles a tiny smile and hands me a napkin. I dab my face. She watches me with her usual calm expression.

"Emily, for the love of god, tell me."

"I unearthed a radio while trying to find something else," she says, her eyes sparkling. "Lovely little relic. After some effort, and a little rewiring, I tuned it. I heard a broadcast. From England."

I jerk forward and almost spill my cup in my lap. "When? What did it say? Are you sure it wasn't a trick?"

"Not a hundred percent, no, but it sounded legitimate. It was, oh, two years ago now."

"Two years ago! But—"

She raises her hand. "I'll get to that. The message repeated, like an emergency broadcast, but it wasn't a recording. It asked for the border fence to be disabled and called for a response on the channel. It also said survivors should go to New London."

"New London?" I slam the mug on the table, sloshing liquid onto the polished surface. "What happened to the old London?"

"It didn't say."

"Did you communicate with them? Is the radio here? What are they saying now?"

"I gave it to Buxton."

"Why?"

She smiles again. "Well, he and I were close at the time."

I almost topple onto the carpet. Emily and Buxton, an item? Not important.

"What did he say? Why hasn't he done anything?"

"He was worried at first, suspected it was a trick, like you.

I believe he wanted to respond but he says the broadcast stopped after a couple of days and never came back."

So he says. But Buxton's word means sweet fuck-all.

"Well, that seals it then," I say. "Someone's out there. I want to know who."

54

I brace my hands against the wall, taking deep, even breaths, then straighten my spine and stride into Buxton's office. He sits at his desk, his head towards Gizzy, who's perched on the window ledge while massaging his temple. I force my numb legs forward instead of running away.

Soon, I'll never have to see them again.

Gizzy shoves to his feet, his hand extended. "Anita, thank god—"

"Shut. The fuck. Up."

He makes a strangled sound, his hand curling to his chest. I focus on Buxton, too sick and angry to spare Gizzy more than a glance.

If I look at him, I'll attack him. Bitterness clenches my throat tight. I want him to hurt, want the shame and guilt to hollow him out until he's a broken husk, shuffling miserably through life.

As I'm trying desperately not to be.

I raise my chin. "I want out of the gate."

"Why?"

"I need out temporarily. I want to go to Calders."

The pack on my back smoulders beneath my clothes.

Emily gave me a billowy waterproof jacket to conceal the

292

small lump. The bag contains the essentials: paraframe knife, matches, snare wire, first aid kit, water purifier. Anything more and it would be obvious.

"You can't go out there!" Gizzy blurts. "It's too dangerous. You almost died last time."

I narrow my eyes. His face flushes and he drops his gaze to his feet.

How did I miss this weakness? He's a sheep. I'm a wolf. A lone wolf.

"He's right," Buxton says. "It's dangerous. No man's land is no place to go for a stroll, and there's nothing left of Calders to return to."

Because of *you*, you unbelievable bastard.

I swallow my pulse and keep my breathing slow.

Emily told me to stay calm. Buxton has a strong sense of obligation. He'll give me a vehicle, but only if he thinks I'm coming back.

"It is dangerous out there and I nearly died but I was on foot. Loan me the Crocodile. Let me go for a few hours." I don't fake the next part. *"You owe me."*

Gizzy cringes. The muscles in Buxton's jaw clench.

Emily agreed with my plan—the shimmering invisibility of the Crocodile will provide transport to the coast and a safe place to sleep. She embraced me before I left, her fragile bones and delicate skin like hugging a sparrow.

"Fine, if it will help you move on," Buxton says. "But then I expect you here to plan how we proceed without the machine. You are the one who is so confident the simple truth will get people to lay down their weapons."

Oh, now he wants my input?

He sighs, running his hands over his shaved head. "Gizzy,

get the Crocodile and meet us outside."

Gizzy opens his mouth but does what he always does—he shuts his face and completes his orders. After he leaves, Buxton slides open a drawer in his desk and pulls out a remote.

I frown. "What are you—"

He points it at me and presses the button. My hand flies to my arm. To the small scar where the implant was removed. Or so I assumed.

What a trusting moron.

"You goddamn bastard," I whisper, my cheeks blazing. "Did you cut me to make me think—"

"No. Gizzy did, while you were unconscious."

Another betrayal. He tricked me from the start. Somehow, it hurts more.

"I'm glad he had the foresight. Your emotions are clouding your judgement—demanding to go out there alone in broad daylight. The Crocodile is not impenetrable."

My shoulders stiffen.

Did he just imply I'm being a hysterical woman?

"This will at least give you clarity when you find yourself overcome with suicidal thoughts of running away."

Yup. Maybe now I should punch him.

* * *

The Crocodile hulks at the kerb, silent and menacing. Buxton climbs in the passenger side and I slide into the back. He explains the controls. Gizzy drives, sneaking glances at me. I clench my hands in my lap to keep from plucking out his eyeballs.

Buxton clears the screen. "Having one driver reduces the

functionality but I take it you don't—"

"No. I want to go alone."

We reach the gate, five unfamiliar soldiers snapping to attention. Gizzy slips out, clicking the fob. He holds the driver's side door open and I blink to process the floating darkness of the interior. In daylight, the shape of the Crocodile is more obvious, like peering through distorted glass. I settle into the seat, warm from Gizzy's body, and refuse to meet his gaze.

"Anita, I am so, *so*—"

I shut the door in his face.

Nothing he says can ever repair what he's done.

"Tamper with the implant and it'll kill you," Buxton says, shadows transforming his eyes into pits. "Come to my office when you return."

I nod, my lips pressed hard together. He leaves and I track his progress via the on-screen cameras as he crosses to the gate to complete the laborious unlocking procedure. Gizzy huddles around himself, the desolation on his face highlighted in sharp detail.

The main gate of Fellhill rolls on its runners. I power through without hesitating, glad the Crocodile has no windows, rear or otherwise.

There's no one back there I want to see.

55

Buxton was right.

Tentative shoots of green peek through the wreckage of Calders, bright shards of life amidst the grey. The posts of the boundary fence cant in all directions, like dislocated fingers. Plump rats dart between tunnels formed by scorched brick and scarred stone. Dogs, their ribs visible through matted fur, sniff at the detritus.

They don't appear abnormal but hunger can turn any animal into a ravening beast.

I stop the Crocodile on a rise overlooking the ruin of my home. My boots crunch on desiccated branches and the wildlife scatters. The clunk of the door echoes around the wasteland, my feet carrying me further from the vehicle without a command from my brain.

How were we defeated so easily? I understand an attack leaving us wounded but not this devastation.

Buxton must have used the dragon. The weapon I delivered to him brought the end to my people.

I trip and land on my knees, the dust of my comrades powdering my combats.

Ignorance allowed me to imagine Calders continuing on. My home, my faction. There to return to and lead, when I got the chance. We could have allied with Soldiers of the Lost and shown the other factions the possibility of peace.

"Fiona?" I call over the soughing of the wind.

Sometimes, I delude myself. Calders is gone—Fiona putrefying somewhere in no man's land—and Fellhill may as well be another obliterated pile of debris for all the comfort it offers.

I have no home.

You don't need one here. Get off your damn knees.

I shove to my feet and lurch deeper into the rubble, hunched inside my jacket. My boots slip on tilted slabs and dodge water-filled craters. A skull watches me through bottomless sockets, its decayed flesh clinging to its cheekbones, shrivelled lips drawn back.

I've no idea who it was.

Shivering, I climb onto a flattened plane of unmarred concrete and dangle my legs off the edge. The horror of the previous night, and so many nights before, threatens to swamp me. A single, harsh sob escapes. I suck in a breath sweetened by rot.

Enough. This is my chance to be free. I'm done with fighting, done with killing. What was it all for anyway? A cause buried beneath a mountain of bodies and a faction based on a lie. Screw it all. I just want a life.

And I kept my promise to my sister.

There's no reason to stay. I can flee to join the rest of the world if I struggle a little longer.

Maybe I'll find sanctuary there.

As soon as the implant is out of my arm, I'll find another way. I refuse to be held captive in Fellhill, even if I have to pry the gate key from Buxton's stiffening fingers.

Time to fight or die a little longer.

Returning gives me the chance to steal more supplies. I need tools, *weapons*. The single Magnum strapped to my waist offers little protection, especially if I can't sneak a vehicle out.

Back to emulating Rambo.

I hop off the concrete and march towards the broken boundary fence, bone ash swirling despite the lightness of my steps.

Where the hell did I park the Crocodile?

"Well, isn't this lovely," a familiar voice says. "So nice *you're* still alive, Anita, when everyone you know is dead."

I bow my head and sigh.

Fucking typical.

56

My fingers twitch towards my gun.

"Keep your hands raised and turn around, there's a good girl."

I grit my teeth. "My prayers for your untimely death have been ignored, John. How disappointing."

He grins, his blue eyes cold. An ancient Ruger 10/22 rifle points at my face, the walnut stock gouged and stained. Gayle stands to his right, aiming her own rifle, a smirk on her thin lips.

"It'll take more than Nationless to destroy me," John says. "Though, I'm sure you can imagine my distress when I found you gone. I had such plans."

Both wear camouflage fatigues and small packs on their backs.

Livingston's attack must have hit hard to risk a harvest of no man's land, as plentiful as the meat supply may be.

"Well, ain't this a great big reunion?" John laughs, his hearty voice grating on my ears.

Why couldn't he have died?

"But we won't take you back to Lowkirk. We'll throw a private party."

Gayle tracks the sight of her rifle down my body. "You're

bad fecking luck. Wherever you've been, it gets destroyed: we were attacked, Nationless annihilated and Calders—your own blissful home—ruined. You're Patient Zero."

"Where have you been?" John shifts closer, his pet knife riding his hip. "We heard Wick caught you. I hope you enjoyed spending time with him. Being his prisoner was a fate worse than anything I could imagine."

I struggle to keep my face blank. "I killed him and obliterated Livingston. How's that for enjoyable?"

John roars and tosses his head. Gayle peeks at him, her angular face softening into something almost human.

"You mean we have you to thank for weakening Nationless and ensuring our victory? Oh, Anita. So pious, so pure. But it doesn't stop you from slaughtering the fuck out of thousands of people."

His guffaw bounces between the mounds of pulverised stone. I fist my hands instead of throwing myself at him.

"I believe Carol and Roysten also experienced your tender ministrations." The merry light dies and his expression hardens. "You will be sorry, you irritating bitch. Now, where the hell have you been? Don't make me ask again."

His rifle focuses on the region of my kneecap.

"Fellhill," I mutter. "I've been in Fellhill."

"You've joined Soldiers of the Lost?"

"Yes."

"Then what you doing out here?"

"Going for a walk."

"You'll wish you hadn't."

Gayle titters. Sweat prickles my skin.

"Toss the Magnum over here," John says. "Try anything, I'll cripple you."

The Magnum thumps at his feet. Gayle bends without taking her gaze off me, one hand scrabbling in the dirt and snatching the gun, tucking it into her waistband.

I raise my eyebrow, aiming for defiant. "Come on, John, I expected something more theatrical. You afraid I'll win if you attack with your knife?"

"I have nothing to fear from you. If you want to bleed in the mud, that's your choice."

"How many times have I escaped you? Christ, it's easy. Even when you stabbed me, your blade work was sloppy. You should practise more."

His fingers blanch on the rifle. I try not to pant, air whistling through my nose.

Careful, *careful*. Too much and he'll shoot me.

"Let's see if you bleed me faster than I tear you apart." I wiggle my fingers and bare my teeth. "Come at me, you fucking psychopath."

Gayle opens her mouth. "John—"

"Quiet."

He thrusts his rifle at her. She takes it after a pause, throwing the strap over one bony shoulder. Her gaze flicks from me to John but he doesn't meet it. His steely focus is all for me. I widen my stance, my hands loose.

Oh god, this could hurt.

John strokes his knife and inches towards me, his boots sliding through rubble. I move to keep his body between Gayle's rifle.

"How do you want to go?" I say. "Same as Carol?"

John grips the ivory handle and pulls his knife free with a flourish. The polished blade glints silver in the grey of clouds and stone.

"You seem awfully confident for someone who's about to be gutted, Anita."

"Maybe, but answer me this." I tilt my head, hoping he doesn't notice the pulse bounding in my throat. "Do you want to stab me because it's the only way you'll get inside me? Can't get it up anymore, John? I'm sure it's no great loss. Right, Gayle?"

John lunges on a growl. I smother a yelp and step into him. The blade gleams, stabbing for my stomach. I sweep my arm into his, grip his wrist and tug, twirling him around as though we're dancing. I mould myself to his back and guide the knife to his neck, both hands clamped over his, one arm throttling him.

Gayle gapes, her rifle drooping in the eddying dust. My heart thuds against John's spine.

"You fuck—"

"One more word and I'll slit your throat." My high-pitched voice ruins the threat somewhat. "Drop the weapons, Gayle, or I'll kill him."

Her pale face pales further, panic flashing in her eyes like sunlight on glass. Two rifles and a Magnum thump to the ground.

"Don't do what she says!"

John pushes into the knife and I press the blade harder into his throat. A trickle of red slithers down his skin. Gayle whimpers.

She loves him. And it weakens her.

"You have rope in your pack?"

The rapid bob of her head flutters her hair around her face.

"Toss it over here and lie on your belly, hands behind your back." I jerk my chin towards an area a decent distance from the weapons pile. She pulls out a braided rope and does as I ask. "Same for you, John. On your stomach."

He lowers himself, grumbling obscenities. I follow with the blade. Sharp, white pain sizzles up my left arm. The sleeve of my jacket yawns at the forearm but hides the extent of the wound.

The bastard has cut me after all.

I grimace but ignore it, prying the knife from John's grip. He crosses his wrists in the small of his back. Gayle watches, grit peppering her cheek.

"I'll wear your goddamn spleen as a hat, you bitch!" John snarls, each hot word puffing into the dirt.

"It's been claimed already. Pick another organ."

I tie the rope around his wrists but the fingers of my left hand don't quite work. Smothering my alarm, I section the cord to bind his feet. He thrashes, his face turning red.

"I'll hurt you, Anita. I'll cut pieces off you."

Just like Wick. Maybe I should kill him.

I secure Gayle's hands and feet. She stays stiff, her lips pressed tight together. Blood oozes from under my cuff. I cradle my left arm and climb into the wreckage, balancing the knife on a pillar of stone.

"When you tire of fantasising about ways to kill me, wriggle up there and cut yourself free." I jump down and collect the weapons. "Don't wait too long, though. The worst abominations come out at night."

John's howl of fury chases me to the shimmering shape of the Crocodile.

Her face floats to me from a distance. I herd my lips into a smile.

"Emily. How long was I out?"

"No more than an hour," she says, standing over me. "The cut was deep, involving some muscle laceration."

"How bad?"

"You'll heal. I've sutured the wound with a combined core and perimeter stitch involving the epi—" She waves her hand at my no doubt blank expression. "Never mind. The sutures are subcutaneous and absorbable so you won't have to take them out. I've placed a strip of skin-healing wrap over the wound to speed incisional healing. It can take a month to regain tensile strength in the muscle."

"What does that mean?"

A dressing covers my left forearm where it lies on the pristine sheets of the hospital bed. I fist my hand and wince at the crackling pain. Emily places her cool fingers over mine, pressing gently until I relax.

"It means you need to rest it as much as possible. There will be some weakness in the arm during recovery but I have exercises to help."

Left arm. I can still fire a gun. Everything is fine.

She drops a plastic bag in my lap. "You'll need to change the bandages once a day for the first five days, more if they become wet or dirty. I gave you an injection of antibiotic. You've had a painkiller today so take the ibuprofen from tomorrow, as and when you need it."

"I can't stay another month. What am I going to do? Buxton won't open the gate a second time. I have to get out of here, Emily."

I stare at my lap, twisting the sheet in my good hand. The walls bulge inward, crushing the air.

I'm still in a cage. The damn war is a prison.

"Tell Buxton *I* want him to let you out the gate," Emily says, the steel in her voice dragging my gaze to her. "And to give you a survival pack with extra weapons."

"He won't."

"He will or I'll form my own splinter group, demanding we spread the truth to the rest of the factions and contact the outside world."

"He'll punish you. I can't let you risk it."

"Oh, I wouldn't worry. Our hard-nosed leader has one soft spot and it's me. Plus, I'm a doctor—I'm untouchable."

"You're too good to me," I manage, my voice choked.

She shrugs. "He won't give you a vehicle, even under the threat of rebellion. He's too stubborn and my influence only extends so far."

"It's enough. What you've done is more than enough. I'll be less conspicuous on foot as he definitely won't give me the Crocodile."

"True." She laughs and pats my arm. "Stay here tonight, rest, no rushing out. Doctor's orders. I'll make sure you're safe."

She bustles around, showing me the exercises to assist

muscle recovery.

"I hope we'll meet again," I say.

She pauses with one hand on the door, her eyes glistening. "I hope so, too, Anita."

The door shushes closed and I settle into the pillows. I fall asleep and dream of Gizzy saying, "I don't know you at all," while he shoots me, again and again.

* * *

Gizzy slumps at my bedside, dimming the golden light streaming through the high windows and ruining a perfect blue sky with his muscled carcass.

How did he sneak past Emily?

He raises bloodshot eyes. Stale sweat wafts from crumpled clothes. His face is still handsome but I've glimpsed the ugliness those features hide.

"Anita, I am so sorry. I don't deserve it but please give me another chance." He smiles, softly. "I love you."

Lianda said the same and he shot off her face.

"You don't love me."

"Of course I do!"

"If you loved me, you wouldn't have called me a traitor and pointed a fucking shotgun at me."

His gaze darts away. "Buxton's my leader. His word is law."

"And you were willing to believe him without a scrap of evidence. That's exactly why I can't stay here."

"You believed that mince about The People's Republic being the only ones who didn't strike first. What evidence did you have?"

Shit. He has me there.

I shake my head. "What if Buxton orders you to shoot me again because he's having a bad day?"

"I don't think—"

"That's just it. You don't think. Buxton does your thinking for you."

Gizzy frowns, his shoulders hunched. "That's hardly fair."

"Isn't it? How could I ever trust you when you'd rather kill me than defy him?"

"After the way you acted in the meeting, his suspicions seemed valid," Gizzy says, sitting forward in his seat, his large hands clasped on his knees. "He admitted he was wrong when new evidence came to light."

"Christ, you're so quick to defend him. Shame you didn't have the balls to defend me."

Spots of red flare in his cheeks. "You're the one who antagonised him. If you had just listened to me, to him, everything would've been fine."

Oh, sure, *fine*. Slaughtering everyone as a, 'ha ha, fuck you, this is what you get for blaming us,' is way beyond fine.

"Sorry for not blindly obeying your rules," I say.

"It's called loyalty."

"Loyalty has to be earned."

Gizzy throws his hands up. "Buxton was right—you always have to be coerced. Everything is a battle. You have no one to blame but yourself and your stubbornness."

My hands curl into fists and pain lances my forearm. "Get the fuck out."

He hesitates as if he may refuse, and perhaps I'd respect him more if he did, but he seems incapable of resisting the urge to follow orders.

Even mine.

The chair screeches on the polished floor and Gizzy spins on his heel, stomping away through the swish of the double doors.

What did I ever see in him?

<h1 style="text-align:center">58</h1>

I leave the hospital after another hug from Emily and a scan to confirm the duplicitous duo haven't slipped a second implant into my flesh during my unconsciousness.

Yesterday, I drove straight to Buxton's office on my return from Calders, blood dripping from my lacerated forearm despite my field dressing. He pressed the button on the remote while I stood rigid, expecting him to kill me. I cut the chip out myself and slammed it on his desk, a black pebble in a splotch of red.

Today, I'll be the one with the power. This is my choice. Risking my life on a treacherous journey through no man's land for the promise of normality is better than risking my life for a lost cause. Buxton may be right about the other factions not accepting the truth. Or maybe they won't even care. It could take years for a ceasefire.

I'd rather beg asylum with England than spend another second in Fellhill.

I pause to steady myself outside Buxton's office, stroking the dog-tags through my t-shirt. The People's Republic next to Soldiers of the Lost. Symbols of what I survived.

And a reminder of how very hard you have to fight sometimes, just to live.

I hitch the holdall higher on my shoulder and enter the room. Buxton sits at his desk, Gizzy behind him—a bulky, ever-faithful shadow. Gizzy probably scuttled straight over from the hospital and briefed Buxton on my plans.

"Gizzy tells me you want to desert," Buxton says, his hands clasped on polished wood.

Nailed it.

I inhale and ease it out, counting to five. "Yes. I'm sure you understand why."

A scowl twists Gizzy's face, redness flaring in his cheeks.

"If I let you leave for good, you will most likely be killed," Buxton says.

"While I appreciate your concern, let's not kid ourselves that you'll be too cut up about it. We've disagreed on almost everything since I got here. I go, and you get your little land of yes-men back."

His fingers twitch and relax. "Perhaps you should learn how to speak to those in authority."

"Turns out I'm not great at conforming."

"Indeed. Do you have any other demands?"

"Yes—you're going to kit me out so I don't die."

"I'm afraid that's not poss—"

"Emily wants you to let me out the gate with a survival pack and extra weapons," I say.

Gizzy frowns, glancing between us. Buxton leans back in his chair and tents his fingers under his chin.

"She does, does she? And what else has the good Doctor Sharp been saying?"

"She told me about the radio. If you don't do what she says, she'll form a splinter group to demand contact with the outside world. If I have to stay here, I'll run the fucking thing."

Gizzy frowns harder.

Buxton huffs. "It appears I have no choice."

"Yeah, doesn't feel so great, does it?"

His grey eyes spark.

For god's sake, Anita, shut up.

"Gizzy, go collect what the doctor has requested."

"But, sir, you can't give her one of our packs." He stabs his finger in my direction. "If she's so desperate to leave, let her fend for herself. She'll soon regret it."

The despicable little bastard.

"Gizzy." The word snaps through the air.

"I'm sorry, sir. I'm on it."

Gizzy marches out of the room. The ache in my chest eases at his fading footsteps.

"Where will you go?" Buxton says in the silence.

"England, if I can find a way around the fence. You weaponised it. Can you switch it off?"

"Only Simmons could."

"You didn't bother to ask how before you executed him?"

Buxton levels me a cool stare. "You have considered how dangerous it will be to get there? How dangerous it may be once you get there?"

"I have to try. It's got to be better than this."

He shrugs one shoulder. "This life is what you make it. I've built a community here. A family. We all want the same thing."

And what is that—domination, victory? Where's the joy in reigning over the dead?

Are my team working on the shell of the dragon, struggling to reawaken dreams of glory? Recreating her external armour could salvage their situation. A platoon of indestructible vehicles would still win Buxton his war.

Gizzy trudges in carrying a forest-green rucksack covered in matte-black zippers, and a padded gun bag. He dumps both at my feet, returning to stand beside Buxton, his eyes fixed on a point over my shoulder.

"A survival pack, as ordered." Buxton walks around his desk, crouching to pull weapons from the gun bag. He hands me a Glock in a holster, and a knife. "The Magnum belongs to the Lost but I know you like Glocks."

I humour him with a tiny smile and fasten the gun around my waist, my left hand clumsy from trying not to move my forearm. The knife I tuck into my boot. Buxton produces another gun, his lips twisted.

The same model he used to threaten me our first night.

It almost disappears in my hand, small but hefty.

"What is it?"

"We call it an SL2. Our own design—9mm, eight hollow-point bullet capacity. It may look dainty but it's powerful enough to blow a fist-sized hole in anything."

It joins the knife in my boot.

"This is an electrigun you secure to your—" Buxton glances at my bandage. "It usually goes on the non-dominant arm."

"I'll manage."

I strap the long, grey weapon to my left arm and adjust the position to avoid pressing on my wound.

"It's solar-powered. Three settings: stun, maim and kill. Useful for hunting, or if you run out of bullets."

I turn the setting to two. The trigger is a bulb able to slide into my hand at one flick of the wrist. Since flicking my wrist will tear my stitches, I pry the trigger out to dangle between my fingers and lock it in place.

I drop the holdall to the carpet, removing Emily's bag of

dressing material. "Can I keep the clothes you gave me?"

"There are clothes in the rucksack, they should be your size." Buxton cocks an eyebrow at Gizzy, who nods.

I swing the heavy rucksack onto my back and slide my injured arm gingerly through the strap.

Gizzy stays, issuing no heartfelt goodbye.

What an unforgivable lapse in judgement.

Buxton drives to the main gate in an open-topped jeep. A hint of summer thickens the air. I enjoy the warmth as he unlocks the gate, his five minions looking on.

He holds out his hand. "I hope I won't see you again."

"The feeling's mutual."

You domineering fuckwit.

I walk out of Fellhill for the third and final time but stop myself from skipping.

Must be professional.

The road stretches ahead, arrowing through miles of hostile landscape populated by soldiers, abominations and Border-landers. Days of battle and toil before I reach the coast, with no idea how to navigate the watery barrier. Numerous means of dying but the only way to live.

The road stretches ahead, and it has one name.

Salvation.

Let Me Know What You Think!

Thank you for reading my book! Did you love the stubborn and mouthy Anita? Wince at everything she went through? Leave me a review and let me know. I enjoy hearing from my readers. Reviews also help me find other people, like you, who'll love my books.

Can't wait to hear from you! And if you can't wait for Anita to finally get something good in her life, check out book 2.

Buy the Sequel: *Salvation Road*
Will Anita find the freedom she craves? Or will her journey test her more than the prison she's escaping from?

For a free prequel to *The Faction War Chronicles,* you can also join my mailing list at nadinelittle.com/free-prequel by scanning the QR code below:

Also By Nadine Little

About the Author

Nadine Little lives in Scotland and is an ecologist with an interest in botany. She writes science fiction and fantasy in her spare time when she's not reading or playing *Fortnite* on her PlayStation.

The year 2020 seemed the perfect time to publish her debut trilogy *The Faction War Chronicles* since it all went to hell. Sometimes she worries that people will look at her differently.

But not really.

You can connect with me on:

- https://nadinelittle.com
- https://twitter.com/Nadine_Little_
- https://www.facebook.com/nadinelittleauthor

Subscribe to my newsletter:

- https://nadinelittle.com/free-prequel